I0702426

Night of the Trickster

Night of the Trickster

NATHALIE L'H GOLDSTON

LitPrime Solutions
21250 Hawthorne Blvd
Suite 500, Torrance, CA 90503
www.litprime.com
Phone: 1-800-981-9893

© 2023 Nathalie L'H Goldston. All rights reserved.

No part of this book may be reproduced, stored in a retrieval system, or transmitted by any means without the written permission of the author.

Published by LitPrime Solutions   05/15/2023

ISBN: 979-8-88703-246-7(sc)
ISBN: 979-8-88703-247-4(hc)
ISBN: 979-8-88703-248-1(e)

Library of Congress Control Number: 2023908472

Any people depicted in stock imagery provided by iStock are models, and such images are being used for illustrative purposes only.

Certain stock imagery © iStock.

Because of the dynamic nature of the Internet, any web addresses or links contained in this book may have changed since publication and may no longer be valid. The views expressed in this work are solely those of the author and do not necessarily reflect the views of the publisher, and the publisher hereby disclaims any responsibility for them.

Contents

Fall 1965

Sunlight peeked through the tangled canopy of tree limbs over the Vermont forest. Bright orange leaves of Fall belied the hidden danger within. Intent upon finding their quarry, the two hunters ignored the beauty as they navigated the steep descent into the ravine below. Age old Maples and Birches crowded the trail forcing the two men to walk one behind the other. Recent heavy rains exposed knotted tree roots crisscrossing the path. Rocks now slippery and wet, added to the treachery. A simple misstep could result in a broken limb or worse.

Riley Bristol followed his friend in silence. Since their arrival in the Temple Falls Reservation dread had permeated his soul. He was being watched. This feeling intensified with every step downward. It was a good thing John was walking in front of him. His constant need to look behind would have provoked snide comments. It would have only added to his misery.

Once they reached the bottom, the two men prepared for the hunt.

"Wow, this is really beautiful." John turned in a full circle. An outcrop of enormous grey boulders sat in the center of a large clearing. Their location forced a rapid stream to take a sharp detour before it continued on into the forest.

"Listen. Do you hear that?" Riley put his arm out and stopped John from moving forward.

"Hear what?"

"Exactly. I don't hear anything. Except that water." He pointed at the stream.

John frowned. "Yeah, I noticed."

He didn't like the look on his friend's face. He could tell Riley was frightened.

"Seriously? You believe all those stories?" John shook his head. "Come on, Riley. A forest can't be dead."

Riley raised his arms and let them flop against his sides. "Do you hear anything? Anything at all?"

John shook his head again. "Don't you get it? It's just a bunch of crap the Godfrey family invented to keep people out of certain parts of the Reservation. It's all about control."

"I'm not so sure." Riley couldn't meet his friend's eyes.

"Man, you really believe this place is a dead zone, don't you?" John rolled his eyes. "Come on, let's find some deer before the boogie man gets you." He didn't let on that the utter silence of the place was beginning to bother him as well.

John walked towards the huge, grey boulders. "I think we should follow the creek that way." He pointed upstream. "Might catch a buck taking a drink." He laughed in an attempt to lighten his friend's mood. Riley nodded in tacit agreement refusing to look him in the eye.

John threw his rifle over his shoulder and sighed. There was nothing he could say now that would ease his friend's fear. He followed the edge of the stream towards the trees. It was as he was passing the rocks that something odd at the bottom the creek caught his attention. He stopped and knelt down.

"What the hell?" John felt his stomach roil.

"What? What's up." Riley peered over his shoulder.

"Look." He pointed downwards. His hand was shaking.

Riley dropped to his knees. Several inches below the clear, rushing water was a forearm partially covered in the remains of a camouflage jacket similar to the one he was wearing. White hand bones protruding from the material appeared to be grasping a rock.

"Shit. I knew we shouldn't have come here." Riley stood up quickly. "This place gives me the creeps. I'm done. Let's get outta here."

His friend cast a wary look into the dense trees. "Yeah, maybe you're right." He looked back at the severed arm. "I think we need to tell the sheriff about this".

"No way! We're not telling the sheriff. Dad warned me about this place. Said it was evil. Been that way since the Abenaki lived here." Riley's voice quivered. "He said when people come here and they never come back. Look, let's go. It was a dumb idea to hunt out of season anyway. You can tell the Sheriff if you want, but don't include my name. I'm outta here." Riley slung his rifle over his shoulder. He nodded towards the narrow dirt trail leading upwards. He turned, then froze. "What the hell?"

His friend whipped around. "What?"

"Did you see him?" Riley was transfixed. The color drained from his face.

"See who? Are you trying to scare me?" John nudged his buddy.

"No...John...look," Riley's voice rose. He pointed where the creek took a sharp turn before disappearing into the trees.

"I don't see nothing. Quit trying to scare me, Riley," John was now annoyed.

"Holy shit, look at his face," Riley was horrified.

"What face? Come on, man, give me a break," John gave Riley's shoulder a shove.

"Go, man, go!" Riley grabbed John's jacket and pulled him towards the dirt path.

His terror was infectious. John didn't argue. The two hunters scrambled up the side of the ravine one behind the other. Riley, in his hurry, dropped his rifle. It slid back down the muddy trail.

"Leave it, Riley. It isn't worth it." John yelled as Riley went after it.

Riley didn't answer. He waved the other man on. "I'll catch up."

John scrambled forward. When he reached the top of the ravine, he looked back into the trees.

"Riley," John called.

There was no answer.

"Riley," he called again. A shot rang out, then another.

"Riley?" John hesitated. The back of his neck tingled in fear. He wanted nothing more than to get in his truck and leave, but out of loyalty to his friend, he waited. When Riley still didn't appear after several minutes, the hunter went back into the Reservation. He wouldn't leave his friend behind. John retraced his steps all the while listening for any approaching danger. He stopped before the trail's final plunge. From this vantage point, he could see the creek and the familiar outcrop of boulders. There was no sign of Riley. No sign of anyone.

A breeze swirled through the trees. With it came a strange rotting smell. It was so strong, so close, it made John take a step back. He scanned the rocky ravine. He could see no animal carcasses in the vicinity, but he recognized the stench of death. Out of the corner of his eye, he saw something large and dark dart across the creek. He lifted his rifle.

Dead, my ass. Show yourself, you bastard? He gritted his teeth in determination.

The Reservation remained silent, pristine. John glanced one way then another. He inched his way down the embankment. The clearing was empty.

"Riley?" he called in a hoarse whisper.

The familiar sound of rushing water was the only response. Keeping his rifle raised, John made his way across the clearing. He retraced his route upstream until he came to the boulders. It was then he saw his friend, Riley lying face down. The back of his camouflaged hunting jacket was saturated with blood. His right hand was cupped over a rock. A thin trickle of red fell slowly in the running water.

"Shit, Riley." The hunter rushed towards his stricken friend forgetting the danger still within the woods. He ignored the rotting smell when it assailed his nose for the second time. He could only think of his friend.

"Riley?" he crouched down. Something wasn't right. The hunter's discovery came too late.

"What the...," he screamed when a man, complete in Riley's clothing, rolled over and grabbed him by the leg. John kicked his hand away. The man grabbed him again and held him fast. John grappled for his rifle. The man grabbed at it, too. A fierce struggle ensued.

The sound of a rifle shot echoed through the forest. Then the Reservation fell deadly silent once more.

Temple Falls

Caroline struggled to see through the night's opaque darkness. Relentless rain kept her imprisoned. Only a single carriage lamp at the end of the drive was visible from her living room window. A lone car speeding by sent a rooster tail of glistening rain water up over the stone wall. Time was slipping away. If her lover didn't come soon, her plan would be ruined.

Her heart leapt in anticipation as another unknown vehicle passed. It too, disappeared into the darkness. An antique Tiffany mantel clock strategically placed over the center of a lavish fireplace chimed the top of the hour.

"Why isn't he here?" she glanced with irritation at the clock. Its incessant bong grated on her nerves.

"Shut up, shut up, shut up." Caroline yanked the facing on the clock open and stopped the pendulum before it could finish its mission. The room fell silent.

Her eyes drifted upwards to a large, dour portrait of Paul's great grandfather. A shiver of fear coursed up her spine. She was traveling into dangerous territory and she knew it.

"Stop it," Caroline pushed the thought out of her head.

Every piece of furniture, every painting and every ashtray

had a designated spot. Her husband, Paul, demanded immaculate housekeeping. The room exuded wealth, perfection and arrogance. It was also completely devoid of any warmth or feeling much like their marriage. Caroline glanced back up at the portrait of Robert Paul Godfrey. She contemplated making a big X in the center as a going away gift to her husband.

"A match would be more fitting." She said with loathing. A tilted floor lamp caught her attention. Caroline paused and out of habit, straightened it.

"Stop, you don't have to be perfect anymore." She admonished herself turning the lamp slightly askew again. Years of living with Paul and his family had created habits she could not break, at least not right away. Her only regret was that she wouldn't be there to see the expression on his face when he read her note telling him she was leaving him for another man; a man younger, richer and better in bed. She made sure she emphasized the latter in great detail. Caroline placed the note in front of the mantel clock where she knew he would see it as soon as he got home. Winding the clock precisely eight times was the first step in his nighttime ritual. It was only one of his many irritating habits she had grown to despise over the years.

Caroline returned to the bay window. A gust of wind blew the trees in the front yard momentarily obscuring her view.

"Come on. Where are you?" She pleaded. Then she saw headlights coming up the driveway.

"Thank you, Lord." She exclaimed rushing towards the back of the house. Before entering the kitchen, she retrieved a large suitcase hidden in a hallway closet. Then she hurried to the back door. She congratulated herself on perpetrating the perfect ruse.

"He thought he was so smart," she said smugly. Paul had been duped into giving the servants the night off at her suggestion although it was actually against her suggestion. In a brilliant stroke of manipulation, she went behind his back telling the downstairs maids to stay late that night to do some "thorough" cleaning. Paul overheard the servants talking about the extra money Mrs. Godfrey was going to pay them. He promptly sent everyone, including the chauffer, out of the house. It was exactly what Caroline hoped for, an empty house. There were absolutely no regrets tweaking her conscience. The thought of leaving Paul had energized her for weeks. Now that it was finally here, she couldn't wait to get away.

The bright headlights from the approaching car momentarily blinded her when she stepped out into the driveway.

"I thought you would never get here, darling. What took you so long? We have to...YOU!" She exclaimed before her world went dark forever.

Chapter 3

"Madame, Mr. Paul Godfrey is on the telephone." said the butler handing the receiver to the small, elderly woman reclining on the sofa in front of him.

Anastasia Renault Godfrey, "Princess" to her friends, family and some acquaintances took the receiver off the silver tray with little enthusiasm.

"Next time you enter my room, Ronald, be sure you are not wearing any spots." She said pointing disdainfully to a single black smudge on his otherwise pristine white jacket.

"Very good, Madame," Ronald responded with a slight bow. He turned leaving the room as silently as he had arrived. It was forbidden for any of the Godfrey servants to be present when Madame was on the phone.

"Yes, Paul, what is it this time?" she asked without even trying to mask her annoyance.

"Grandmother, my office building is surrounded by reporters. The police just left moments ago. They tried to take me to the station for questioning but my attorney managed to get them to ask their questions here. They think I'm responsible for Caroline's disappearance," Paul Godfrey said with his characteristic whimper.

"Good God, Paul. You're a Godfrey. Quit sounding like some infantile imbecile. You're president of a multi-million-dollar, company, act like one. Is this why you interrupted my afternoon repose? To tell me you're surrounded?" his grandmother replied harshly.

"Grandmother, please, I need to know what to do," Paul continued.

"Is your attorney still there?" she asked.

"Yes," he answered.

"Good. Let your lawyer handle this. That's why we pay him good money," and with that she hung up the phone.

Princess then picked up a small silver bell from the mahogany table and rang it once. Ronald, the butler appeared again almost instantly. He wore a new clean, crisp, white waist length jacket free of any offending black smudges. Without a word, Princess Godfrey handed him the phone and waved him away.

Robert Paul Godfrey III, or Paul as her oldest grandchild was called, never ceased to disappoint her. Princess wearily threw the coverlet off her legs. Her grandson was a brilliant businessman, but an utter idiot when it came to women. Every time one of his affairs came to an end or his wife, Caroline upset him, Paul would turn into the whimpering sniveling child Princess detested. She never consoled him rather she would use the occasion to remind him what a fool he had been to marry unwisely.

It was the duty of the Godfrey men to marry well and produce heirs to continue the family existence. Princess knew the moment she met Caroline Westin that Paul had made a mistake. Caroline was too independent, too smart for her own good. Worst of all, she was a tall, beautiful woman and rarely discreet. If there was one quality a Godfrey woman must possess, it was the ability to be discreet. Caroline's inept socializing after a few glasses of Chardonnay made that impossible. It meant she could never be trusted when it came to the privacy of the family.

Princess raised that concern prior to the couple's nuptials. Paul was too besotted to listen. She couldn't dissuade him right up to the day of the ceremony. Caroline's fate was sealed the moment she put that wedding band on her finger.

A vision of a USO dance flitted through Princess's mind. She wished someone had raised concerns regarding her own marriage so many years ago, however, the very idea of refusing a Godfrey then was as unthinkable as it was now.

"Oh, Robert," she said softly rising from the chaise lounge. She was so in love with him in the beginning. A deep, all-consuming love that was gradually eroded by his infidelities and the fate he couldn't out run. A fate that turned her husband into the hateful man she ultimately came to despise.

Princess walked slowly to the window. Daylight was dwindling much like her strength. Tomorrow the sun would come again like it always did, yet she was never sure if this would be the last time she would see it. She looked out into the distance beyond the stone wall and massive gate that separated the Godfrey estate from the rest of the world. The dense New England forest surrounding her, known as the "Reservation" to those who lived in Temple Falls was resplendent in brilliant fall foliage. Princess noted ironically that the beautiful colors belied the evil lurking within.

"Caroline," she shook her head. "You foolish, stupid girl."

One of the gardeners raking on the front lawn caught her attention. Every now and then he would raise his head, look around then resume raking a little bit faster. The other men in his team were near an old pickup throwing bags of leaves into the back. They too kept looking around in anticipation of something or someone.

Princess watched with amusement as the gardener, called his men over. They huddled in a small group periodically pointing towards the Reservation. Princess could tell their conversation was intense, heated.

They're frightened, she surmised.

Rampant town gossip of ghostly apparitions seen in and around "Pinehurst" as well as, several unsolved mysterious murders blamed on the Godfrey family over the years had made it difficult for Princess to sustain reliable help. She continued to watch the heated conversation taking place on the lawn below her window. The idea of searching for new gardeners to keep the grounds as she liked made her even more tired. There were no landscaping companies left within a twenty-mile radius willing to work there anymore, no matter how much money she offered. A soft noise distracted her.

"I know you're there, Maria. You needn't stand in the doorway," Princess didn't turn around. "The gardener seems upset. I suspect this will be his last day working here. Did something happen?"

"Yes, Madame." The maid curtsied as required. "The gardener, Madame." The maid hesitated in her narration. She nervously fingered her apron.

Princess turned away from the window. She leveled an unemotional, cold stare at the young woman. "And?"

The maid looked down at the carpet. "He heard someone screaming in the forest."

Princess sighed. "Is that all?"

The maid was visibly trembling. "He said he's not coming back no matter how much you pay him."

Princess sighed again. Her narration was more irritating than surprising. "Hmmmm...I suspect not. Anything else?"

Maria raised her eyes briefly and met Princess' stare. "I heard a woman scream last night, Madame. Cook heard her, too."

Princess raised her hand and stopped the maid from telling the rest of her story. It was all too familiar.

"Cook already left."

"And you?" Princess voice softened.

"No, Madame. I've decided to stay. I...I need this job," Maria wiped a tear away.

Princess took a deep breath. Servants were becoming harder to come by as well.

"Thank you for telling me, Maria. I will look into your story. I am sure there is a logical explanation. I suspect Miss Elodie may have been playing one of her many pranks. If you will take over Cook's duties, I will see to it that you receive a raise in your salary." Princess smiled slightly then turned back to the window.

Relieved to be dismissed, Maria curtsied again then hurried away.

"Ronald!" Princess called sharply.

The butler appeared in an instant.

"Have you seen R. P. this morning?" Princess kept her back to the butler

"No, Madame," came his reply.

"Find him and check the cellar as well," she waved her hand in dismissal.

The front lawn was empty. The gardener and his crew were gone. Princess shook her head sadly.

"Damn you, R. P.," she whispered.

Chapter 4

Princess's bedroom door burst open abruptly disrupting her thoughts. Elodie, her youngest grandchild sauntered into the room in a waft of cigarette smoke. Tall with a stock of black curly hair and dazzling blue eyes, Elodie resembled her grandmother in her looks. She was most like her grandfather in her promiscuous and infuriating attitude. It was an effort for Princess to be in the same room with her.

"Yes, you *may* come in." Princess braced herself for the inevitable confrontation. "For God's sake, Elodie put that cigarette out. You know smoking is forbidden within my house." Princess yelled in the strongest tone she could muster.

"Oh hell, Grandmother, you're dying. What's a little smoke in your lungs?" Elodie paused between puffs. "So, did you do it or did you pay someone to do it?" She released a huge plume into the air. Then with even greater exaggeration, she inhaled deeply and released one more.

Princess gave her granddaughter a withering look. Elodie didn't respond to outright antipathy. It took a more, subtle approach to get her attention.

"Did I do what?" Princess stared with abject hostility into Elodie's eyes.

"Kill Caroline. Everyone knows how much you hated her." Elodie watched her Grandmother for some sign on discomfort. None was seen.

Princess smiled slightly. She reached for her cane on the sofa. With great difficulty, she rose and stood in front of her granddaughter. "Remember, my dear, without my signature you would be hard pressed to buy the cheapest cigarettes on the market."

Elodie looked away. A slight flicker of fear registered on her face then disappeared quickly. Money or the lack thereof, terrified her and Princess knew it. Elodie extended her arm holding the cigarette with the tips of her fingers. Slowly, with great ceremony, she flicked its ashes on the floor all the while staring into her grandmother's eyes.

"Fine, you old bitch. Have it your way… for now." Their hatred for each other was mutual.

"Elodie, apologize to Grandmother right now." Danielle Godfrey stood in the doorway witnessing the drama. "What's the matter with you?"

Danielle or "Dani" to her friends and family had black curly hair and the same blue eyes as her younger sister. The comparison stopped there. She was short, stocky and prone to obesity. The loss of her mother when she was a toddler made her an insecure and clingy adult. Her attempts to wrest even the smallest sign of affection from her grandmother only intensified the enormous emotional gulf between them.

"Shut up, Dani. You can't stand the old bat either," Elodie sneered. She turned and threw the cigarette into the flames of the fireplace.

"Sometimes Elodie, I wonder if you were spawned. Why don't you go to the west wing and have a nip? Your personality needs to be drowned in alcohol. Grandmother, a young man called while you were taking a nap. He said he was calling to confirm an appointment with you? He said he was a journalist with some magazine out of New York. Is this true?" Dani asked.

Princess nodded while she avoided meeting her granddaughter's eyes.

"Grandmother, what are you doing? Who is this man?" Dani continued.

"Well, if you must know, not that it is any of your business, he's from Columbia University. He is interviewing me for an article. An article he is writing about the family." Princess walked unsteadily towards the chaise lounge.

"An article about the family? Now? With the police at our door. Are you insane, Grandmother? You can't be serious," Dani said.

"Great, let's tell everyone what a sick twisted bunch of bastards we are," laughed Elodie maliciously.

"Enough!" Princess yelled. She walked threateningly towards Elodie. Her granddaughter immediately backed up until the closed bedroom door stopped her. Princess was seething.

"One more word out of you and I will be more than happy to show *you* the way out. I may be old, but I am no fool. You would be wise never to underestimate me, Elodie. A mistake like that would cost you dearly."

Elodie was visibly shaken by her grandmother's fury. Princess was at least a foot shorter than she and weighed fifty pounds less, however, she was a formidable presence when she was angry. Elodie said something unintelligible before she fled the room. Princess turned to address Dani.

"Any *more* questions?"

"No, Grandmother," Dani hurried past Princess on her way out of the room.

Princess straightened her dressing gown until it appeared almost smooth. She pushed an errant curl off her brow. Even the slightest movement left her feeling drained. It was becoming more difficult to hide her dwindling energy from her grandchildren. She retreated to the chaise lounge.

Dani was right. Caroline's murder had thrust the family and its sordid history into the spotlight yet again. Allowing a writer into the house was dangerous.

"Maybe I am insane," Princess mused.

"Foolish old woman," A man's voice hissed.

Princess sat upright. "Robert?" His voice was unmistakable. She felt her heart skip.

"You can't change anything," the voice continued.

She didn't believe it. Her eyes darted around the room. "Who's there?"

"It's your *beloved*, Robert," the voice's words dripped in sarcasm.

"No, you're not Robert. He's been dead for years. No, this is my mind playing tricks on me again," she shook her head.

The voice laughed.

Princess thoughts drifted to the past. Her last conversation with her mother-in-law, Louisa came into her mind. It was an encounter Princess remembered vividly. One that haunted her every thought to this day.

It was months after her son, R. P.'s birth, Princess' mother-in-law tried to prepare her for what was to come.

R. P. had a slight fever. His incessant crying had made it a difficult morning. Princess was exhausted. She had just put him down for a nap when her mother-in-law, tapped on the bedroom door. Without waiting for a response from Princess, she entered the nursery. Privacy was not a respected notion amongst the family.

"How is he doing?" she asked.

"Better. The doctor said he is cutting his first tooth. He'll be all right," Princess rubbed her son's back. "Please, sit down, Louisa."

Louisa waved the offer of a chair away. "No, let's go into your room for a moment." She pointed towards the door.

"All right," Princess wondered what Louisa wanted. They never spent much time together. The enormous mansion allowed them to live separate lives for the most part. Princess took a moment and studied her mother-in-law. Louisa was a cold, unexpressive woman. Although she exuded strength and confidence, it was a carefully crafted facade. Completely dominated by her husband, she rarely made any of her own decisions. She was "milk toast" in Princess' eyes.

Once they were in the adjoining room, Princess sat in a nearby chair while her mother-in-law remained standing. Louisa nervously twisted the handkerchief she held in her hands. She did not offer a reason for her visit.

"What's wrong?" Princess finally asked. She had never seen her so upset.

"I've tried many times to visit with you since your wedding but Bob...he told me to mind my own business." Louisa glanced at the door expecting her husband to barge in. "There is something I must tell you. Something I must prepare you for."

She glanced nervously at the door again. "I am sure you've heard rumors about the Godfrey family and its curse?"

Princess' mouth dropped open slightly. She never expected a Godfrey to come right out and confirm the notion of a family curse. She nodded her head robotically.

Louisa paced back and forth in front of her. "Yes, the stories are true. I can tell you don't believe me. I didn't believe the rumors at all until several years into my marriage. Oh, there were signs, many signs. Unfortunately, I didn't understand them until it was too late."

"Signs?" Princess' curiosity was aroused.

"Yes, signs of madness." Louisa wrenched the handkerchief a little faster. "First, it was Bob's father. He would start arguments over foolish almost nonsensical things, like the silverware not aligned properly next to his plate or a strand of hair pulled lose from my bun." She instinctively touched the back of her head. "His tirades were horrible. I can't tell you how many servants quit. Then he began taking walks into the Reservation. In the beginning, he would be gone twenty, maybe thirty minutes at a time. Nothing that aroused any suspicion in my mind until he began disappearing for long periods mostly at night. My mother-in-law would wake us up and demand that Bob go out find his father before...before..."

"Before?" Princess wasn't sure she wanted to know the answer.

Louisa dropped her voice to a whisper. "Before bad things happened."

"Bad things?"

"Yes, horrible things." Louisa stopped in front of Princess and leaned forward.

"Sometimes after my father-in-law spent the night out, there would be reports of a murder in Temple Falls."

"You don't really believe Robert's grandfather actually killed people? Do you?" Princess was aghast.

Louisa's hands twisted the handkerchief one way then another. "I never really found out for sure, but my mother-in-law knew. I know she did." Louisa's voice trailed off.

"What is it, Louisa? What are you trying to tell me?"

She leaned down and spoke directly into Princess's face. "The men in this family go mad." She pulled back sharply.

"I witnessed it in my father-in-law and I believe Bob is showing the same signs of this curse. The stupid arguments. The horrible tirades and now the same long walks at night in the Reservation." Louisa's voice trembled. "Yesterday my friend in town told me the police found a man at the edge of the forest, dead. I found Bob in the cellar this morning covered in blood. He didn't remember being gone. He didn't remember anything."

"We must call the police," Princess reached for the phone.

"No!" Louisa snatched the receiver out of her hand. "That's

forbidden. I am telling you this because it is the duty of a Godfrey wife to protect her husband, the family."

Princess looked at her in astonishment. "The duty of a Godfrey wife? You want me to protect a murderer?"

"Yes, even if you believe your husband is a murderer," she spoke softly. After a long pause, she shook her head then continued. "I spoke too soon. I don't know if Bob is a murderer. We never knew his father was one either." Louisa straightened her back regaining her composure. Her entire demeanor changed. The coldness returned. She pushed the knotted handkerchief into her pocket. "Now that you are here and you've produced an heir, my time is over. This belongs to you." Louisa shoved a tattered journal into her hands. "Keep it safe."

"What is so important about this journal?" Princess was surprised at her abruptness.

"Robert's mother gave it to me. She said it has all the answers. She said for the family's fortunes to continue, it must be protected. I confess, I tried to read it, but I wasn't successful. Maybe you will have better luck. In any event, you are responsible for its safety. It is only to be given to the oldest woman in charge of the household."

"But Louisa you are the woman in charge of running the household. Why are you giving it to me now?" Princess felt an uneasiness envelope her.

Louisa sighed. She smiled weakly. "All I can say is...you will know when to pass it on."

The next day, Louisa died. The family doctor declared it was a heart attack. Princess wasn't so sure. There was no autopsy. She was buried in the family crypt almost immediately.

"You will know when to pass it on," Princess repeated the last words Louisa ever spoke.

"You will know when to pass it on," A male voice mocked her.

"Stop it!" She covered her ears.

A hand touched her shoulder. Princess lurched forward violently in response.

"Grandmother, are you all right?" Dani grabbed Princess' hand. She was on her knees in front of her staring into her eyes. Confused, Princess met her stare for a brief moment.

"Grandmother, are you all right? I could hear you all the way down the hall."

"What? Yes, I'm fine."

"You look pale. Can I get you anything?" Dani had never seen her Grandmother look so disoriented and distraught.

"No, you go on. I'm going to rest now." Princess leaned back and closed her eyes.

Dani knew she was dismissed. She straightened her grandmother's coverlet.

"Call me if you need anything," she gave Princess a quick peck on the cheek. Princess nodded in return never opening her eyes.

Dani quickly scanned the room then left. She stood for a moment on the other side of the closed door. It had definitely been a man's voice she heard in passing. When she opened the door, she expected to find her cousin, Paul standing in front of his Grandmother receiving one of her infamous tongue lashings. It was a surprise, therefore to find Princess alone.

"Glad it wasn't me," she turned and walked away.

Chapter 5

"Let me guess, you know something about the Godfreys, right?" Detective Cody Davis waved his new, young partner, Detective Brian Smith towards him.

"How'd 'cha guess?" Smith said completely taken by surprise.

"You'll learn once you've lived in Temple Falls for a while that anytime something big happens like a murder, suicide or disappearance, the Godfrey name always comes up. Kind of like the sun rising in the morning," Davis replied sarcastically. "So, let me guess again. Paul Godfrey has an airtight alibi. He has no idea why anyone would harm his adoring wife. He's *upset* that she might be dead because there was enough blood on the driveway to assume that possibility. Am I right so far?"

Detective Smith nodded his head robotically. Davis thumped both of his elbows on his desk then rubbed his face with his hands.

"Yeah, I bet that sleaze ball of a lawyer was there, too, right?"

Again, Detective Smith nodded.

"The Godfreys are made of Teflon, Smith. Nothing bad ever sticks to them. My Dad used to say in the old days, if you bad mouthed a Godfrey, you just disappeared. People learned to keep away from them. Temple Falls very own version of the Sopranos," Davis said with a wry smirk. "Okay, I'm done. What do you have?"

Detective Smith cleared his throat. He laid a folder on Davis' desk. "Forensics found a hair, actually several hairs that they can't identify."

"What do you mean? They can't identify the person or what?" Davis asked.

"They can't identify whether it's from a dog, cat or what," Smith said.

"Or what..." Davis mused. He opened the folder. He studied the report for a moment then laid it back down with a sigh. "Nothing ever changes when it comes to the Godfreys. So, let's review what we *do* know. Caroline Godfrey, Paul Godfrey's wife was running away with another man. We know this because she left a note on the mantel. With the exception of the chauffer who was in his room over the garage, she was the only one at their home that night why...?"

"Because her husband gave the servants the night off," Smith added.

"That's right. The sum total of our evidence is the note she left on the mantel, her overnight bag left on the driveway and the large pool of blood on the asphalt."

"Looks pretty cut and dried," Smith said.

"Yeah, seems that way doesn't it?" Davis answered. "Where was the Mr., when all this was going on?"

"He was with some clients at the Manhattan Club. More than a dozen people have verified that," Smith said.

"And the rest of the family, Princess, her son, R. P., her granddaughters, Elodie and Dani Godfrey?" Davis asked.

"All at Pinehurst. All have alibis," Smith said.

"Okay, we need to interview Paul and his grandmother. Make sure you tell Mrs. Godfrey's butler that you want the entire family there or we'll get the run around for weeks. If anyone gives you a hard time, tell them we *will* bring them all down to the station, if they don't cooperate. Also, see if you can get a search warrant for Paul Godfrey's house *and* his office. "

"But they have…," Detective Smith stopped talking when Davis gave him a don't-argue-with-me look. A rebuttal was useless. Smith walked out of the room. Davis rocked back in his chair. He watched the door close behind the young detective. He had argued with the Captain about the need for an additional detective within the department. Especially one so young, inexperienced, and "hot" as Bess would say. Cody felt a twinge of jealousy. His argument did little to sway the Captain. Now a year later, he had to admit his partner was indeed a considerable asset to the team. Especially when it came to any investigation concerning the Godfrey family. Brian had the uncanny ability of stating an opinion about the family that offered a whole new perspective. One that Cody never thought of before.

"It's probably because he grew up on the West coast," Bess reasoned.

Another twinge of jealousy pecked at him.

"West Coast, my ass." Something about his insights bothered Cody, if he could only figure out why.

The detective swiveled his chair around until he was looking out the window behind his desk. The Godfrey family was always on his mind.

"Maybe this time, we'll get them, Adam," Davis said softly. "Maybe this time."

Chapter 6

Detective Cody Davis and Paul Godfrey were born in the same year. Both at the different ends of the social spectrum. Their respective paths only crossed a few times in their lives. One particular meeting was enough to make a lasting impression on the young Cody Davis. It was the first time he actually spoke more than a few words to Paul and it happened when they were both nine years old. They met quite by chance and briefly. A meeting he wished he could erase from his memory forever.

It was the first day of summer in 1976. The weather was perfect. There wasn't a more beautiful place to be then in a lush forest in the state of Vermont. The William Davis family lived at the edge of the Reservation. The house was too far for one to walk, but only a short ride in the car from town. The small Dutch colonial house was situated on the back half of an acre of land surrounded on three sides by the Temple Falls Reservation. It was the ideal location for his controlling, psychopathic father who kept his family as isolated as he possibly could. "Don't need anyone prying into our business," he would say.

Adam, his older brother by three years, resembled his mother in his thin, lanky frame, brown eyes and ash blond hair. Cody, on the other hand inherited his father's short stocky build, square jaw, blue eyes and brown hair. Cody loved playing outside, while his brother preferred to sit under a tree and read much to their father's chagrin. William Davis thought there was something unnatural about a boy who liked to read instead of hunt. In his obtuse opinion, reading was for girls and fags, not a son of William Davis. More than once he tried toughening Adam up by forcing him to hunt. It was a futile effort. The boy couldn't stand killing anything. His refusal to pull the trigger unleashed a scathing appraisal of his manhood. William even accused his wife of adultery because he truly believed he could not have sired such a "sissy". His father's low opinion of him was one of many reasons why Adam sought solace in the pages of a book. It allowed him to dream of places where his father couldn't find him.

Cody, on the other hand, was the exact opposite of his brother. He enjoyed anything involving the out-of-doors. This only spared him some of his father's critiques. It was their mother, however who was the one who took the full force of William's psychotic rages. She, like her sons, spent her days avoiding beatings from her unpredictable husband. Once a pretty woman, years of emotional and physical abuse made Sally Davis look well beyond her thirty years.

On that fateful summer day in 1976, Cody's life changed forever and it all began with a simple plan. A plan Adam devised to get the boys out of the house for the entire day. Away from the scrutiny of their father. So, he waited for one of William's rare happy moments, which arrived rather unexpectedly. After months of unemployment, William declared at the dinner table that he was going to do an odd job for a local farmer the following day. If things worked out, the farmer might take him on as a hired hand. Cody couldn't remember the last time he saw his father smile so much. He could tell Adam noticed the difference, too.

His father then gave his wife a list of things he wanted her to do while he was gone. Before he could do the same for the boys, Adam jumped in and asked if he and Cody could go fishing at Tandy's pond. William was surprised by his oldest boy's request. He knew how much Adam hated killing anything, even a small trout. Cody remembered his father sitting back in his chair studying Adam's face for any sign of deception.

"What's up?" he accused his wife. "Did you put him up to this?"

Sally shook her head and looked down at her lap fearful a blow would follow. When the blow never arrived, she cautiously looked up. William was staring at Adam intently. Adam didn't flinch. Sally was surprised when William was the first one to blink.

"All right, you can go, but you two better have all your chores done by the time I get home or else…"

Sally and the boys were stunned by William's response although they wisely hid their astonishment. They didn't want him changing his mind. What William didn't know was that inside Adam's tackle box under the usual assortment of lures and bait was a well-hidden book. What no one knew was that Adam had no intention of going to Tandy's pond. He had decided to fish in a creek a couple of miles from their home. It was an isolated, quiet creek that even the he-man, William wouldn't dare visit; Bloody Creek.

This infamous creek ran through the state reservation the Godfrey family was instrumental in creating. Its creation was one of the many times the Godfrey family interests clashed with the town of Temple Falls. The Godfrey family's wishes prevailed as always.

Cody's father enforced strict rules as to where his children could and could not go. In no uncertain terms were they *ever* to fish in the Temple Falls Reservation particularly Bloody Creek. It was strictly off limits. To reinforce his ban, their father told them horrific stories of dead hunters and bodies found floating in its deadly water. He said the place was so haunted with the souls of the dead, even animals refused to live there.

"The forest is dead. Dead like the corpses found rotting in that creek." He warned.

Adam scoffed at his stories. His little brother, Cody believed every word.

"There's no such thing as ghosts," Adam said and to prove it he told his brother they were going "fishin'." in Bloody Creek as soon as the time was right.

"Bloody Creek," Cody murmured softly. It was hard to say even after so many years.

Its ignominious name was well deserved. In the late 1700's, a French fur trapper by the name of Reynard Pillion Gillett arranged a meeting between the British troops and the Abenaki people who lived in the vicinity of present day Temple Falls.

Reynard was a trusted friend of the Abenaki. It was said the fur trapper saved the life of a young Abenaki girl and from then on, he was considered one of their own. Therefore, the Chiefs believed him when he said the British came in peace and good faith. The meeting took place at one of the Abenaki tribe's main encampments along the banks of a large creek. This creek flowed for several twisted miles until it eventually ran into Lake Champlain.

Generations of the Abenaki people had lived, loved and died next to its rippling water. The small clearing beside it was their home. It became their graveyard.

The Abenaki who survived the massacre claimed the British never intended to negotiate a treaty. They only wanted to take their land. So many innocent people died that day it was said the creek's water ran red with blood for weeks thereafter hence the name--Bloody Creek.

The survivors fled into the surrounding forest. Some went north to Canada. The British ultimately got the land they wanted, but their victory came at a huge price. Attempts by the first incoming settlers to erect a town on the site of the old Abenaki encampment met with disaster. First, disease ravaged the small colony. Then, what was once considered a bountiful forest, became barren. All the creatures fled leaving the colonists to starve--their lifeless bodies found scattered in Bloody Creek.

The settlers, who followed, proclaimed the ground where the Abenaki and the first colonists died as hallowed. The silent, abandoned forest was penance for man's evil ways. It was believed that subsequent unexplained deaths near the creek were considered a warning from the dead not to go there...ever.

A new location for the settlement was chosen several miles away and the history of the massacre became part of local lore. The ominous reputation of Bloody Creek, however, never diminished. The number of its victims continued to rise steadily over time.

Cody's father hoped his graphic stories would keep the boys away from the infamous creek. That and a stern word about the whipping they would receive if they chose to defy him. It didn't take much to convince Cody. His father wasn't as sure about Adam. No amount of whipping could change that boy's mind when he was determined to do something. William concluded he was too much like his mother. On that fateful day, their father left the house early as planned, leaving the task of supervising the boys' whereabouts to his sleeping wife.

Cody was ready the moment his father's truck disappeared out of the drive. Adam cautioned him. It would be just like William to return unannounced. So, he made his brother wait. Once he was convinced they were safe, Adam retrieved their fishing poles and a tackle box he had hidden the night before in the oft chance his father changed his mind. With a nod of his head, Adam began walking to Bloody Creek. Cody noticed the changed direction immediately.

"Hey, this isn't the way to Tandy's pond," he said.

"I know," Adam answered. "We're not going to Tandy's pond."

"Where we going?"

"Bloody Creek."

"No, Adam we can't. There's ghosts and everything there. Besides, if Dad finds out we're gonna get a whippin'," Cody cried.

"No, we won't. We'll be back before he gets home, besides there's no such thing as ghosts. Dad's just trying to scare us," Adam said.

Cody refused to go forward. "No, I don't want a whippin'."

"Come on, Cody. It'll be fun and Dad will never know. I promise. Come on, It'll be an adventure," Adam pleaded.

Cody reluctantly agreed only after Adam threatened to go alone. He loved his big brother and didn't like the idea he might have this big adventure without him.

The first mile was followed by another that took a meandering course through the Elms, Oaks and Maples of the surrounding forest. A bed of thick leaves provided a dense ground cover with an occasional rock sticking up in between. Eventually, the path led the boys to a steep, rocky ravine. Bloody creek lay at its bottom. Cody followed his big brother as best he could to the water below. The sharp descent made it hard to stay upright. More than once, he slid down on his backside to keep up all the while fretting about the punishment he was going to receive for getting his jeans dirty.

The summer sun tried making an appearance through the trees. Long, ghostly shadows danced over the rushing water. It would have been a setting worthy of a Kodak moment, if a deer or raccoon wandered by. But the woods were quiet, eerily quiet. The quietness was one of the first things Adam noticed. He wondered if his father's stories might be true although he kept his observations from his younger brother. *No such things as ghosts,* he told himself repeatedly. It was the only way he could calm his apprehension.

Once the boys reached the bottom, they climbed up on top of several large boulders situated on the far side of the creek. Cody immediately threw his line into the moving water. Adam pulled his book out of the tackle box. While Cody waited in hopes of a bite, Adam began to read. Cody scanned the trees surrounding them.

"How come I don't see no birds?" he asked uneasily.

"We probably scared them off *talking,*" Adam said pointedly.

"It sure is quiet, Adam. Do you think Dad was right?"

"Right about what? Ghosts, dead forests, murderers?" Adam said with a forced calmness. The last thing he wanted was to agree with his brother, particularly when the silence was bothering him, too.

"You know Ben Simons says a man named Riley Bristol and his friend were found dead in this creek. Right near some big boulders. Said his arms and legs were torn off," Cody went on.

"Oh, what does Ben know," Adam scoffed.

"Do you think it happened here? Maybe we should go home, Adam. I'm scared," Cody whimpered.

"Are you a scaredy cat?" Adam sneered. "Gonna run home to Mama."

Cody didn't answer. His big brother's opinion of him matter more than his fears. Besides he was afraid to walk home alone.

"You sound mean like Dad."

"I'm sorry, Cody. I shouldn't have called you a scaredy cat." Adam immediately regretted his harsh tone and his brother's comparison.

"That's okay," Cody said with a slight smile. The boys fell into an uneasy silence. A ray of sunshine pierced the leafy trees overhead. It briefly lightened the boys' mood. Cody began needling his brother about his crush on Amanda Meyers. Since Adam's twelfth birthday, girls began encroaching on the time the two brothers spent together. Although Cody was still blissfully unaware of nature's calling, he could see his brother slipping away from him. He hated it.

"Did you kiss her?"

Adam blushed revealing his transgression.

"Eeeww," Cody scrunched up his face at the image. "Adam and Amanda sitting in a tree K*I*S*S*I*N*G..." he recited.

"Shut up," Adam demanded.

"First comes love..." Cody stopped mid-taunt. "Hey, what's that smell?"

"No, I mean it, shut up," Adam said with a look of fear on his face. He stood up and turned towards a path that went up the other side of the ravine to their right.

"Did you hear that?"

"Hear what?" Cody said grabbing his brother for comfort.

"I dunno but I think I heard someone calling my name. Let's get outta here," Adam yelled throwing his beloved book down on the rock. Cody needed little convincing to do the same. If his brother was willing to sacrifice his precious book, it had to be serious.

Cody began sliding down the opposite side of the rock, when Adam suddenly pushed him off. He landed on a small sand bar at the side of the creek. He looked back in time to see his brother jump. He fell sideways grabbing his leg, while shrieking in pain. Cody rushed to him. A streak of blood floated away from Adam's ankle. Cody pulled him out of the rushing water and dragged him to safety. A bit of white bone could be seen sticking out of Adam's skin. His ankle was horribly broken.

"What do I do?" Cody felt helpless.

Adam was crying uncontrollably. "Get Mom," he said between agonizing sobs. "And hurry."

Cody didn't balk at Adam's request. He charged up the ravine towards home. The steep incline made it difficult. He fought to stay upright. For every step upwards, he slipped two backwards towards the water and his crying brother. It was taking forever to reach the top. Finally, he saw the edge of the pavement in the distance. He ran towards the road. In retrospect, Cody would often wonder if the adrenaline that accelerated him through the woods that day was due to his brother's plight or the frightening sensation he felt of being pursued. A sensation he hoped he would never experience again.

When his feet touched the paved road, a boy appeared out of nowhere. It was Paul Godfrey. Cody was too upset to notice the incongruity of Paul's sudden appearance in front of him. The Godfrey estate was on the other side of the Reservation. Many miles from this particular spot. He ran past Paul telling him that Adam was hurt down in the ravine. Again, when he revisited his memory of that moment, he failed to notice the look of horror on Paul's face. He assumed the boy was showing concern for Adam's broken ankle.

"Where is he?" he remembered Paul asking.

"Down by Bloody Creek. Next to the big boulders." Cody yelled over his shoulder while continuing his run for home.

The police never really would say what or who killed Adam. They said he died from loss of blood. The townspeople however, held an entirely different view. One that no one said outright. It was more an undercurrent of hushed whispers and furtive glances which belied their true beliefs. To speak outright would have invited the same calamity to visit you or your family. The town of Temple Falls went collectively silent.

The Davis family was devastated. Cody's father drowned his sorrows in Southern Comfort. He died a year later of acute alcohol poisoning. Sally suffered a complete breakdown after identifying her son. Cody's grandfather stepped in when it became apparent she could no longer take care of her remaining son. His mother was eventually committed to Resthaven Psychiatric Hospital, where she maintained a silent vigil for her oldest boy until her death.

The full impact of his brother's untimely death didn't really hit home with Cody until that night. It was the first time he had the bedroom to himself. He cried until he couldn't cry anymore. Sleep eluded him. The morning's events kept replaying in his mind no matter how hard he tried to stop the images. Something was in the woods that day that truly frightened his brother. It wasn't a bear or a mountain lion. In fact, the more he thought about it, Cody became convinced he saw something too, but Adam pushed him off the rock before he could get a good look.

The police officially closed the investigation several weeks after Adam's remains were found over the objections of his younger brother.

"Son, your brother is gone. You must move on," the detective told Cody after the boy pleaded with him not to stop looking for the killer.

Cody couldn't talk to his parents. They were too consumed by their own grief. His father was so angry the boys defied him, he banished Cody to his bedroom after a sound thrashing with his belt.

"Stay in there until I say you can leave." He snarled pushing his son into his room. For once, Cody didn't object to his father's harsh treatment. His beating was nothing compared to the one he was giving himself for leaving his brother alone in the woods.

That night on the first night of his banishment, Cody's life experienced an unexpected change. He had finally fallen into a fitful sleep. He was in the midst of horrible nightmare, when he felt a tug on his foot. Startled, he awoke. At first, he thought his mother was making one of her forbidden trips into his room. He rubbed his eyes and noticed a faint glow towards the bottom of his bed. It was Adam.

His brother's appearance scared him so completely, he screamed. The vision disappeared when his mother came running into the bedroom. The next morning a small smooth rock lay on Cody's bedside table.

The following night Cody fought to stay awake hoping Adam would appear again. Sleep overtook him within the first hour. The next morning another smooth rock lay next to the one placed there the night before. On the third night, he heard a soft voice whisper.

"Cody, are you awake?"

Cody sat straight up in bed. He stared towards his feet.

"Adam?" he called softly. The faint glow appeared like before. Cody's eyes opened wide in wonder. He watched the light grow brighter until Adam was standing on the other side of the footboard.

"Adam?"

The vision nodded. It stood for several moments staring at him.

"Adam, you're really here," Cody gasped.

Again the vision nodded. Cody pushed the sheet covering his legs off and sat up on his knees.

"Are you a ghost?" he asked.

Adam shrugged sadly. Cody put his hand out. He crawled towards the apparition.

"Can I touch you?" he asked.

A frown crossed Adam's face. He put his hand up stopping his brother from coming any closer. Cody pulled his hand back.

"I'm so glad you're here," Cody said. Tears welled up in his eyes. "I miss you."

Adam smiled.

"What happened to you?" Cody asked.

Again, a look of anger appeared on Adam's face. He opened his mouth only to disappear before speaking.

"Cody, who 'ya talking to?" His father stumbled into his young son's room.

Cody instinctively put his hand up to protect his face against the expected blow.

"Nobody," he said.

The smell of alcohol surrounded him. William was drunk.

"I heard ya talking to someone. Who was it?" he demanded leaning unsteadily over his cowering son.

"Adam, I was talking to Adam," Cody cowered.

"Adam? You were talking to Adam?" his father screamed raising his fist. A noise on the opposite side of the bed stopped the blow from being delivered. The room became bitterly cold. The sharp change in temperature was not lost on William.

"What the…" shocked, he stumbled backward. An unseen force pushed him up against the far wall. Then he heard someone speak in a strong forceful voice, it was Adam.

"NO!"

Cody knew his father heard Adam. He inhaled sharply. His eyes went wild with fear. He spun around on his heels and fled the room.

"Adam?" Cody called out softly.

The dim glow reappeared next to his bed. Soon his brother was standing next to him.

"Thanks, Adam," Cody said.

"Anytime little brother."

"How come you can talk now?" Cody asked.

Adam shrugged. "Don't know."

"Are you a ghost?" Cody asked.

Again Adam shrugged. "Don't know."

Cody thought carefully before he asked another question.

"Are you in heaven?" he asked.

Adam shrugged once more.

"Maybe," he said.

Cody fell silent. He sat back against the headboard. He studied his brother for a moment. Nothing seemed different about him. Same curly hair, same striped t-shirt although it was much dirtier than he remembered. All in all, he looked just like he did the last time he saw him the day they went fishing with one notable exception; he was standing upright. Cody moved to the edge of his bed and looked at Adam's feet.

"How come your ankle's not broken no more?"

Adam looked down, too. He pulled up the leg of his pant. His sock and shoe were soaked in blood. The bone in his ankle stuck out like it did before.

"Don't it hurt?" Cody gasped.

"No," said Adam. "It quit hurting when…" his voice trailed off.

"When you died?" Cody finished his sentence. Adam nodded in agreement. Cody wanted to ask him what happened that day, but he remembered Adam's reaction the last time he asked that question. So he brought up a different subject instead.

"Adam, did you see Paul?" he asked.

At the mention of the boy's name, Adam put his hands over his ears. It was as if he was blocking out the most horrific sound. His eyes rolled upwards. He began shaking his head.

"What's wrong? What I do? Please don't leave me." Cody cried frightened at the sight of his brother, yet unwilling to let him go.

Adam dropped his hands. He reached out and grabbed his brother's arm. Instead of the warm touch of his hand, Cody felt a bitter coldness.

"It was the Trickster," Adam said.

"What's a Trickster?" Cody whispered.

In a flash, Adam was gone.

Cody didn't understand what his brother meant no matter how many times he replayed his message in his mind. It was a memory he tucked away into the far recesses of his brain should he learn the answer one day.

As for Paul Godfrey, he denied ever being on the road that morning. Cody challenged his story. Princess Godfrey, his Grandmother provided the boy with an unshakeable alibi. It wouldn't be the last time Robert Paul Godfrey III evaded the law with an airtight alibi.

"Like Teflon," Cody whispered turning his chair back to face his desk.

Chapter 7

The soft click of the bedroom door told Princess Dani was gone. She opened her eyes slowly. It was an effort to do so. Her energy was spent.

"Robert?" she whispered softly. The room remained silent. A tear trickled down her cheek. She let it fall unimpeded. Old, hurtful memories flooded her brain. She had loved him when they were first married. An all, consuming passionate kind of love. Robert seemed to have the same feelings until they returned from their honeymoon to live in the family mansion.

"Robert, you and your bride will live in the west quarter." His mother, Louisa announced coldly when the young couple first entered the foyer.

Princess lifted her bag.

"No, dear. You are a Godfrey now. We have servants to do the manual labor." Louisa waved her hand away. She motioned for the butler to take the bag. "Robert, your father is in the study waiting for you. Dinner is at 6 sharp, Anastasia. Don't be late."

Louisa Godfrey turned away from her new daughter-in-law. She disappeared down a long hallway. Robert tossed his coat to the butler.

"I'll see you tonight. The servant will show you the way to our rooms," Robert nodded his head towards her then turned and walked away in the opposite direction.

Stunned at the coldness of their reception and Robert's quick departure, Princess stood for a long moment unwilling to move. The servants busied themselves with the mound of luggage surrounding her. Their frenetic movement didn't faze her. It seemed to coincide with her feelings now so completely in disarray.

What have I done? she thought. It was the first time she felt her marriage might have been a mistake. This thought would reoccur many times in the future. Still, there was something else that kept her from moving forward. A feeling so foreign to her, she didn't grasp it at first. Then it came to her in a ferocious rush--a pervasive sense of evil was all around her. She could almost reach out and touch it.

"This way, Madame," the butler gestured towards a grand staircase. His words startled her.

"Yes...yes of course," grasping her coat and purse, she followed the man silently to her new life.

"So long ago," Princess whispered shaking her head to dispel the memory. The sitting room was quiet now. Princess laid back in the chaise lounge. Muffled voices in the distance piqued her interest. The girls were quarreling again. She would have to deal with it later. Now all she wanted was sleep. Her mind drifted away.

"Elodie! What's wrong with you? Why do you insist on provoking her?" Dani confronted her sister in the hallway.

"This place sucks. I'm tired of that old bitch calling the shots. I need to get out of here." Elodie pulled a cigarette out of her pocket.

"And go where?"

"Anywhere is better than here." Elodie flicked a small lighter.

"Stop it," Dani snatched the cigarette out of her hand. "Don't you know this shit will kill you?"

"Don't you know we are as good as dead? Figure it out, Dani. Uncle R. P. is crazy and getting worse every day. Once he's gone, it will be

Dad's turn. Of course, we haven't seen *him* long enough to know if he's dead or alive." Elodie's last sentence was spoken in disgust.

"That reminds me. I think I saw his car pull into the drive last night."

"Dad's here? Really?" Elodie's voice became childlike.

"I said I think. I didn't see it this morning. No telling where he might have parked it. Probably doesn't want Grandmother to know he's home right away."

"Yeah, then she'll monopolize his time. We won't see him at all. What's wrong with us, Dani? Why doesn't Dad stay?" The pain in her sister's voice struck a nerve in Dani. It was at the heart of her sister's open rebellion.

"I don't think Dad ever got over losing Mom. He loved her so much." She reached out and pulled her sister into her arms. Elodie didn't resist.

"Doesn't make it right," Elodie wiped away a tear.

"No, it doesn't, but everyone grieves in their own way."

Elodie stepped away from her sister. She raised the cigarette snatched earlier, and with great ceremony put it in her mouth. "Fuck 'em if they can't take a joke."

Chapter 8

"Simon, there's a young man on the phone who says he's a graduate student from Columbia University. He's writing a story about Tempe Falls and wants to speak to you," Connie Plimpton called upstairs to her husband.

"Get his number and tell him I'll call him from my office," Simon Plimpton answered. A brief lull in the conversation followed while Connie relayed her husband's wishes.

"He says he's speaking with Princess Godfrey today. He says he wants to talk to you before he goes out to the Godfrey estate," Connie yelled up the stairs again. Another, lull ensued.

"Did you hear me?" Connie asked. "Simon?"

Slow, methodical footsteps began working their way down the hall up above.

"Hold on Mr. Cooper, I hear my husband coming this way," Connie listened to Simon's footsteps descending the staircase. His deliberate slowness irritated her. It was typical of how he handled situations he disliked. Connie refused to lay the receiver down. If she didn't put the phone into his hands, he would walk right past it. Her husband's reluctance to discuss the Godfrey family was well known.

It was why Princess Godfrey supported his Mayoral campaigns for all these years. She rewarded silence.

"Here, give it to me." said Simon when his foot touched the bottom step. The exasperation in his voice told Connie she had once again crossed the line. She didn't care. She never missed an opportunity to delve into the mystery surrounding the Godfrey family. It was worth her husband's ire.

"Be nice," she said shoving the phone into his hand.

Simon testily ignored his wife's plea.

"Simon Plimpton," he said gruffly into the phone. "Yes, I'm the Mayor of Temple Falls. What do you want?"

Connie hovered on the opposite side of the room. She was glad she hadn't gotten her way when she wanted to remove the hardwired hallway phone and replace it with a remote one. It made it impossible for Simon to talk privately which suited her thirst for gossip. At seventy years of age, her husband was not a man who accepted technological change readily, particularly when it came to telecommunications. He claimed he couldn't hear well on a cell phone although Connie knew that wasn't the entire story. A cell phone would mean he could be found even if he didn't want to be. A stationary phone couldn't follow him. His wife's eavesdropping was its only downfall. Connie, on the other hand, carried a cell phone in her pocket at all times.

"I'm not sure what my schedule is today, Mr. Cooper." Simon lied at which Connie cleared her throat loudly. "Maybe we can get together next week?"

Connie crossed the room before Simon could go any further and thumped her husband on his arm. Simon responded by turning his back on her.

"Meet with him, Simon. What do you think Queen Princess will do, have you banished from the kingdom?" she whispered sarcastically.

Simon pursed his lips and gave his wife a withering look. She responded by thumping his arm again.

"On second thought, why don't I meet you down at City Hall at 11:00? I can probably spare a half hour. Fine, see you then."

"Now was that so hard?" Connie teased.

"You are so God damned irritating. Princess warned me about you. She said I shouldn't have married an outsider. She said you would be a pain in the ass and she was right," Simon said angrily.

Connie was stunned by her husband's words.

"Princess Godfrey told you that you shouldn't have married me? Why on earth would she do that?"

Simon refused to look at his wife. Connie gently touched his arm. He pulled it away in anger.

"How does this woman control you? Does she have something on you?" Connie probed.

She would always remember the look in Simon's eyes when he finally raised his head. It was a mixture of fear, pain and love.

"Don't ask me that, Connie. Leave it alone," exasperated, he continued. "You would never understand," and with that he slowly turned away from his wife and walked back upstairs.

Whatever horrible secret you're keeping is killing you, she thought. She followed the stooped shoulders of her husband up the stairs. In the five years since their wedding, she had witnessed the gradual disappearance of the man she married. Each day a piece of him would slip away from her much like the ebbing of a tide. If she didn't do something soon, the man she knew would be gone forever.

"Maybe I should call on the high and mighty Princess myself," she said aloud. The idea of an actual plan of attack briefly lifted her mood somewhat. It gave her something to focus on rather than the disintegration of her marriage.

"I'll just give her a call right now," she announced and walked down the stairs.

Her address book was in her desk in the living room, but before she could find it she heard Simon yelling. It sounded like he was calling for help.

"Simon, are you okay?" A loud crash emanating from the master bedroom quickened her response. She bounded up the stairs.

"Simon!" she yelled. Their bedroom door was shut which alarmed her. She received a second shock when she found the door securely locked.

"Simon," she screamed pounding on the door. "Let me in!"

No amount of pushing or shoving would open the door.

"Simon, please open the door!" She received no answer. A myriad of thoughts raced through her mind until she finally announced her decision facing the door.

"I'm calling for help, darling," Connie said pulling the cell phone out of her pocket. It was dead. She reluctantly ran downstairs to the hall phone.

The 911 operator assured Connie that the police were on their way and to stay calm.

"Hurry, something awful has happened to my husband," Connie cried into the receiver. "Please hurry."

She had barely laid the receiver back into its cradle when she heard the sound of multiple sirens wailing in the distance. A huge wave of relief swept over her.

"It won't be long now, darling. They're coming, Simon," she yelled over her shoulder while she raced towards the front door. Before her hand touched the doorknob, a loud, single knock startled her. Under normal circumstances she would have opened the door immediately, but it was far too soon for the ambulance to be there. She recoiled in fear.

"Who's there?" she asked. There was no response. A shiver of fear shook her entire body. Something was wrong. She could feel it.

"The police are on their way," she yelled in the hopes her announcement would scare whomever away. Another loud knock happened instead. Connie jumped backwards.

"Go away," she screamed. She ran back to the hall phone. When she put the receiver up to her ear, she heard nothing. The phone was dead. A clicking sound returned her attention to the front door. She could see the brass knob slowly turning. Someone was trying to get in. A scream welled up in her throat. Fear had her rooted to the floor. Then a familiar voice called out to her.

"Connie, run. Get away from the door."

"Simon?" she said glancing up the staircase. Another, much stronger knock was delivered to the door followed by a single knock that turned into a steady pounding.

"Go away!" she screamed putting her hands up to her ears. She couldn't block the relentless sound.

"Connie, come upstairs," she heard Simon say.

"Simon," she raced up the staircase to her husband. The moment she turned down the hallway, the pounding stopped as inexplicably as it had started. Her relief was short lived. The bedroom door was now open.

"Simon?" she called out timidly. "Are you all right?" The house was eerily quiet.

"Simon?" she whispered. Every fiber of her being resisted moving forward.

"It's a trap. Hide until the police get here," Simon's voice instructed.

Connie silently turned away from the master bedroom. She retreated down the hallway into one of the front rooms. The closet in this particular bedroom was used for storage. It was the only place she could think to hide.

"Do it, get in the closet," Simon's voice urged.

"Okay, darling'," she said half expecting to see him at her shoulder. Quickly as she could, she moved a suitcase and a hanging garment bag until she was securely wedged up against the back of the closet. Then she waited.

Chapter 9

The phone rang on Cody Davis' desk. "Davis here," he answered. "Hello?" When he didn't get a response, Cody hung up. It wasn't more than a minute when his phone rang again.

"Hello, Davis here," he answered again.

"Cody, is that you?" A woman's voice he could barely hear said.

"Yes, this is Cody. Who's this?" he answered.

"Cody, this is Connie Plimpton. Please help me."

"Connie? What's going on? Why are you whispering?" he asked. Cody heard muffled crying.

"There's someone in the house. I'm hiding in the upstairs closet. I think Simon's hurt," she sobbed.

"Connie, don't move. I'll be there as quick as I can," and with that pronouncement Cody slammed the phone down. He picked up his cell phone and called his partner, Brian Smith.

"Brian, I just got a call from Connie...You're on your way to the Plimpton house now? When were you planning to call me? Never mind, I'll be there soon." Cody shoved his cell phone into his pants pocket. He grabbed his coat from the rack behind his desk. It annoyed him that his young partner had been called first instead of him. After all, he was the one with twenty-five years of experience. Cody put his complaint out of his mind. He needed to focus on the situation at hand. However, he made a mental note to bring the subject up with the Captain at a later time.

It didn't take more than fifteen minutes to cross town to the Plimpton residence. Cody arrived as Brian was getting out of his cruiser.

"You're just getting here?" Cody wondered out loud as he pulled his car into the driveway.

The Plimpton home was literally surrounded by a sea of flashing lights. A fire engine, ambulance and two police cars were parked at various angles with their occupants waiting outside. Brian was approaching one of the officers standing on the front stoop when Cody got out of the car. The officer nodded to Brian and deliberately walked by him in favor of the older detective. Brian shook his head in obvious annoyance at the slight.

"Cody, glad you got here so quickly," the officer said. He then proceeded to tell the detective about the 911 call.

"We believe the call came from Mrs. Plimpton, but we haven't found her yet."

"She's in an upstairs closet." Cody offered smugly passing Brian into the house. Whatever the officer said after he and Brian crossed over the threshold he never heard. Cody would later confess that it was the strangest crime scene he had ever encountered in his entire career.

"What the hell?"

The house was cold, bitterly cold.

"Do they have the air-conditioning on? I can see my breath." Cody crossed his arms. "Is that a trail of blood?" His eyes followed a line of dark stains traveling up the staircase.

Brian leaned forward. "Looks like it." His teeth chattered slightly.

Cody said grimly. "Let's get Connie."

The two detectives walked gingerly up the stairs trying their best to avoid contaminating the crime scene.

"There's more blood in the hallway," Brian noted. "Look, the thermostat says it's 45 degrees in here."

"Yeah, 45 my ass. It's below freezing. Damn, see if you can get the heat to work." Cody shivered. He hope Connie was okay.

He liked Connie. They first met socially at the Temple Falls Founders Day picnic shortly after her marriage to Simon Plimpton five years ago. He remembered how surprised he was when Simon announced he had remarried. He was even more surprised when he met the new Mrs. Plimpton. She was pretty. Barely 5' 2" tall and 100 pounds soaking wet.

At the time, he assumed she was at least fifteen years younger than the sixty-five year old Simon. He received another shock when he learned she was a well-preserved sixty. He remembered thinking what a good looking woman she was and what the hell did she see in that fat, balding slob of a husband. They became fast friends the moment she stood up to Princess Godfrey.

"Looks like it goes that way," Brian pointed towards the master bedroom.

"Let's see if the Mrs. is in there," Cody motioned towards a room in the other direction.

The door to the front bedroom stood open. The two detectives entered the room cautiously. Not knowing what to expect, they pulled their guns.

"Connie," Cody called, but he received no answer.

"Connie, it's me, Cody." He approached the closet slowly. Before he could turn the knob, the door burst open and Connie emerged.

"Thank God, you're here," the frightened woman threw herself into his arms. Cody felt her trembling before she collapsed. He scooped her up and placed her on the twin bed behind him.

"Brian, call the paramedics up here, now." He picked up Connie's hand and patted it.

Brian hurried out of the room. Once he was gone, Connie's eyes popped open immediately.

"Is he gone?" she asked.

"Connie, what are you doing? Do you realize I had my gun drawn. You might have been shot bursting out of the closet like that." Cody was exasperated.

"Is he gone?" Connie asked again.

"Who, Brian? Yes, he's gone," Cody leaned away from the elderly woman. "Hey, did you fake that collapse?"

Connie smiled slightly. "Kind of. I needed to talk to you and only you," she said.

"All right, wait a minute." Cody went into the hallway.

"Brian, tell the medics to come up in five." He called before closing the door.

Instead of sitting back down on the bed, Cody stood next to it. He studied everything about the woman in front of him. Her short grayish white hair was disheveled and sticking out at odd angles. Her blue eyes were red and slightly swollen from crying. For the first time since their initial meeting, Connie looked small, frail and vulnerable. She almost looked her age.

"What happened here?" he asked gently.

Connie sat up on the edge of the bed and told Cody everything she knew. She finished with an all too familiar statement. "Princess Godfrey had something to do with this. I know it."

"So, why couldn't you tell me this in front of my partner?" he finally asked.

"I don't trust him. He knows more about the Godfreys than he says," she said angrily.

Cody felt like he had been delivered a blow to the gut.

"Oh come on, Connie. How do you know this?" he said quietly.

If her eyes had been knives, Cody would have been cut to ribbons. "I can't explain how I know but I know," she said cryptically.

If it had been anyone else but Connie Plimpton, Cody would have dismissed that last comment unequivocally. Brian had never given him a reason to believe he fraternized or even knew the Godfrey family. That being said, Cody knew Connie to be a straight talking, extremely bright woman and not prone to making off the wall statements. Not to mention it was common knowledge that she openly disliked the Godfreys as much as he did, which was a huge plus in her favor.

She started to say something more when she was interrupted by a single knock at the door. Connie jumped violently at the sound.

"What the hell. I told them to wait," Cody said angrily. After hearing Connie's story about the odd way the intruder knocked, he was more than perturb that the medics chose that same way to announce themselves. Cody yanked the door open only to find no one was there. Although he was startled, Cody didn't let Connie see his reaction.

"Hey Brian, where are you?"

"Downstairs, can I send the medics up now?" Brian asked.

Cody looked at Connie who was visibly shaking.

"Damn," he muttered. She wasn't fooled. He shook his head and shrugged. It wasn't the first time strange things happened during a murder investigation. Connie, however, was reacting badly. At his urging, the paramedics hurried into the room and gave Connie a thorough check-up. Cody walked out when they began administering oxygen.

Once back in the hallway, the two detectives picked up where they left off. They and two other officers followed the trail of blood into the master bedroom. What was left of the body they assumed was Simon Plimpton, lay on the floor.

"Man, what got him?" one of the officers said in amazement.

The room was awash in splattered blood. Simon's pajamas and

bathrobe were shredded and also saturated in blood. One arm and leg was gone including his head.

Cody walked over and lifted the remaining arm. A gold class ring from Columbia University adorned the second to last finger.

"Well, it's Simon's ring," he said flatly. "Someone needs to search the yard for his head and other body parts."

"I'll do that," said Brian whose face was now a ghastly shade of white.

"Yeah, you go do that." Cody said hoping Brian would not heave all over the evidence. He could barely suppress his snicker when the young man hurriedly left the room. It was only a few minutes more before the sound of his partner throwing up, then flushing the bathroom toilet could be heard.

Pantywaist, Cody thought recalling one of his father's favorite expressions of ridicule. *Get out of the kitchen if you can't handle the heat.*

An hour went by before Cody could leave. Simon's head was yet to be found. Connie tentatively identified Simon's ring. Cody then instructed her to pack a few belongings and gave her his well-rehearsed "don't leave town" speech.

"This is my home. Where would I go?" she replied tersely.

He thought about asking his wife Bess if Connie could stay with them, but knew that harboring a possible prime suspect would have been nixed by his Captain. So, he called one of two hotels in town and made a reservation for her. It was the least he could do given the situation.

Connie was a little indignant when Cody took it upon himself to call for her.

"I'm not senile." She huffed. Later she forgave him with a hug before getting into the cruiser with Brian. Cody told her he would be in touch then motioned Brian to leave. Connie's eyes followed him as the car backed out of the driveway.

"You betcha, I'll be in touch." Cody watched the car disappear from view. The brief conversation they had shared intrigued him far more than the headless body in the master bedroom. It was for that reason, Cody didn't reveal the real conversation he had with Connie to Brian. Instead, he proceeded to tell his partner an alternate version in case her accusation proved to be true. Since her story involved Princess Godfrey, he was inclined to believe her. Now he would have to find some evidence and watch his back at the same time. As he was headed for his cruiser, a strong urge for a second look around the yard came over him.

"So, what line did you cross Mayor Plimpton to make one of the Godfreys kill you?" Cody mused. He followed the pristine edge of a bed of Pachysandra. Connie was a consummate gardener and it showed in her attention to detail given to every aspect of the yard. His yard was lucky if it got mowed once a week.

Cody walked with his eyes trained on the grass in the hopes of finding the slightest bit of evidence. His comment about the Godfrey family was an epiphany of sorts. Although there was nothing so far to warrant thinking the Godfreys had anything to do with this murder, his thought was an intuitive leap of judgment on his part. He knew before Connie's accusation that the Godfrey name would eventually work its way into investigation. It always did.

Another thought occurred to him. One that prompted him to pull out his check book from the inside pocket of his sport jacket and look at the calendar printed on the check register. His finger began tapping on the book in his hand. It confirmed what he was thinking; Caroline Godfrey was murdered one month ago today. Two entirely different sets of circumstances but for some odd reason Cody had the feeling the disappearance of Caroline and the death of Simon were linked.

"But how?" he thought out loud.

He snapped the check book closed and continued following the meandering ivy bed. Its end coincided with the start of the back yard and a small dirt path that led into the Reservation. Since the backyard was already searched, Cody studied the path leading into the dense trees. He felt conflicted about continuing forward. It wasn't like him to hesitate, but the same urge that made him stay behind to wander the yard was now compelling him to stop. Cody fought the feeling. He didn't want to leave. The woods looked beautiful and inviting. The leaves were beginning their change from summer green to a brilliant autumn red.

Cody remembered when the leaves were barely hanging onto the trees by Halloween when he was a young boy. At the very least, they were a riot of color by the time he and Adam went trick or treating. Halloween was a week away and the forest was still as green as ever.

"Things sure have changed, Adam. I miss you big brother." Icy cold air surrounded him.

"You're right, you know," a voice from behind him said.

Cody whirled around startled by the unexpected intrusion.

"Connie?" he said when he saw the diminutive woman standing in front of him.

"No, Connie is my twin sister, I'm Samantha Howell. Sami for short." The small woman thrust her hand into his and shook it enthusiastically.

"Like I said before, you're right about the Godfrey connection. They did have something to do with the Mayor's murder and I suspect, Caroline Godfrey's as well."

Cody shook his head. He struggled to restart his thought processes after their abrupt termination.

"How did you…What are you talking about," he stammered.

"You were thinking that this murder and the disappearance of Caroline Godfrey were somehow connected. I was agreeing with you," Sami said.

It was a rare occurrence indeed when Cody found himself at a loss for words. First, he was completely speechless because he didn't hear her coming and secondly, if he hadn't put Connie in the patrol car himself, he would swear he was now staring at a perfect replica of the murder suspect. He wondered why Connie never mentioned her identical twin in the five years he had known her.

"My sister and I are closer than you think," Sami offered.

"Wait a minute," Cody said holding his hands up like he was stopping a bus.

"You're reading my mind. How are you reading my mind?"

Sami smiled and patted the detective on the arm. "Well not exactly. I have a little help from the souls of the dead. It's like a radio you can't shut off. Damn irritating at times."

Cody let his arms flop to his side.

"The dead talk to you? Do they talk to Connie, too?" He asked without masking his disbelief.

"No, my sister wasn't blessed with all of my ability," Sami answered. "You don't believe me."

"Well, it isn't every day you meet someone who hears the dead talking," he answered sarcastically. He turned away to continue his walk up the path.

"Why are you surprised? From what I hear, you've heard from you brother once. Adam says you're being a butt head," she retorted.

Cody felt his heart jump. Adam used to call him that when he was being stubborn.

"So, Adam told you that did he? What else did my big brother have to say?"

Sami touched his arm stopping him. She turned him around and stared intently into his eyes.

"He says he misses trick or treating with you, too."

Now convinced of her power, Cody felt a twinge of jealousy.

"Why does he talk to you? Why doesn't he come to me like he

did before?" Cody said angrily .He looked around him for any sign of Adam.

"I don't have an answer for that. Neither does Adam. Some things a person, whether they are dead or alive, just can't explain," Sami said gently. "He did say you would be the one person who would believe me. Is that true?"

Cody turned away from Sami. He couldn't fall apart in front of her. When it came to Adam, his emotions were still raw even years later. It was like a hole in his heart he couldn't fill. Secretly, he always hoped Adam would visit him again. He missed him.

"Why is Adam talking to you now? Did Connie call you?" he asked studying the woman in front of him.

"Because the dead talk to me as I said before, and no, to your second question," said Sami.

"Connie never called you about Simon? How did you find out?" Cody asked looking at Connie's replica with new interest.

"As I said Detective Davis, I hear from the dead. I'll talk with her presently," she sighed wearily.

"You haven't seen her yet? You came here first?" Cody said in disbelief.

"Adam was insistent that I see you right away. He said you needed me," she said.

"He said *I* needed you?" Cody couldn't hide his surprise.

Again, Sami put her hand on Cody's arm. Cody could feel a calm strength in her touch.

"You mustn't go into the woods. He says you can't fight it alone. It's too evil, too powerful."

"What are you talking about?" Cody queried.

Sami let go of his arm with a sigh.

"I'm not sure. Even the dead are afraid. I only get glimpses every now and then of this entity. I'm not even sure what it is really. But I've figured out that it's been in these woods for a long time. It's connected to the Godfrey family in some way. I haven't been able to break their wall of silence to find out more, yet."

"Their wall of silence?" Cody asked. "You've talked to the Godfreys?"

"Not the living ones by any means. The dead don't always cooperate either, particularly the men in the family. I can't remember a time in my life when a conversation with the Godfreys either dead or alive was easy."

"You know the Godfreys?" Cody spluttered. He didn't like surprises and Sami seemed full of them.

"Yes, Connie and I both knew Robert, Princess' late husband when we were children. He and our father were in business together in New York City. I think we were about five years old when Robert married Princess. That would make Princess well over ninety if my addition is correct. Their wedding was quite something," she mused.

Cody was speechless. His mind was having a hard time digesting Sami's information.

"I guess my sister never told you about our past relationship with the Godfreys?" Sami said.

"No, she never did," Cody said this time suppressing his rising anger. A new thought crossed his mind. Sami answered it before he could express it.

"Yes, that's why she married that fat slob. To be closer to Princess Godfrey," Sami said.

"*What?*" Cody was stunned.

"Our father was murdered shortly after Princess Godfrey was married. Our mother told us years later, that Robert and my father had a huge argument at the reception. She said Robert Godfrey was responsible for his death, although she couldn't prove it. It was the beginning of Connie's obsession with finding our father's killer." Sami said matter-of-factly and then after a few moments had passed in silence added. "She didn't kill him."

"Great, that helps a lot. You tell me that your sister married a man she didn't love to be closer to the wife of the man she thinks killed her father. Her husband has been literally torn apart and you want me to believe she didn't have something to do with his death?" Cody shook his head in dismay. "Just don't tell me anymore right now, okay?"

Sami nodded her head. She followed the detective from a discrete distance. Cody walked with his head bent in thought down the path towards the trees. Something caught his eye once he reached its end. It was a piece of fabric. He took out a rubber glove and slipped it over his right hand. He bent down and picked up the small bit of evidence.

"What have we here?" he said softly as he studied the material. "What does Adam think about this?"

Sami was looking beyond Cody into the Reservation.

"Does Adam have anything to say about this," Cody repeated holding his find closer to Sami's face.

"He says you'll find what you are looking for about fifty yards from here," Sami said pointing straight ahead.

"All right, brother." Cody walked forward.

Sami grabbed him before he entered the trees.

"Adam says you can't go in there. Not now," she warned.

"Why not?" Cody asked.

"You can't…he says you must trust me," she said.

"I can't believe I'm doing this," Cody turned away from the trees. "When will it be safe to go in?"

"Adam says bring others with you and go in tomorrow," Sami said.

"I'm a cop. I can't just walk away," he said to Sami. Then he looked beyond her. "I'm a cop. I can't just walk away," he said again for Adam's benefit. He looked back at Sami then threw his arms up in resignation.

"I can't believe I'm doing this. Okay, I'll come back and lead a team into the woods tomorrow. But whatever it is I'm walking away from today, better be there *tomorrow*," Cody warned.

"Don't worry Adam said he'll make sure," Sami said.

Cody nodded in tacit agreement. He looked back and made a mental note of where he found the small bit of evidence. When he did, he would swear later that something or someone moved between the trees.

Chapter 10

"Must have been an interesting day yesterday," Bess Davis said while she poured her husband a second cup of strong black coffee.

"It could have been better." He responded curtly then immediately regretted his tone of voice.

"Another great day in the life of a Temple Falls cop, am I right?" Bess continued unperturbed by her husband's shortness. In the twenty-five years since marrying Cody Davis, Bess was immune to his cranky behavior whenever his job got the better of him. She smiled then returned her attention to a pan of scrambled eggs.

"You talked in your sleep last night," she said softly flipping the eggs over with ease. Cody put his cup down hard on the table. His response surprised her.

"You were talking to Adam in your sleep. Actually, it sounded like you were carrying on a conversation. What happened? What's bugging you?"

Cody ran his hands through his hair then picked up his cup. He gulped a big swig of the hot coffee.

"Connie Plimpton's twin sister, Sami showed up yesterday. She claims she's a medium, psychic or something. I have to admit she's pretty convincing. Anyway, she told me Adam talks to her. In fact, she claims she hears from the souls of the dead all the time."

"Connie has a twin? Wow, she never told me she had a twin. Are they identical or fraternal?" Bess asked.

"Boy, are they identical. Didn't you hear me? I said she claims Adam talks to *her*," Cody emphasized.

Bess flipped the eggs again before emptying the finished product on a plate resting nearby.

"I heard you. So, she says Adam talks to her."

"Yeah, what's with that? Why can't he talk to me?" Cody said. "I'm his brother for Christ's sake."

"Sounded like you were arguing with him last night. Maybe that's why he talks to Sami. He can tell her stuff without the sibling thing going on." Bess took the chair beside him.

Cody ignored her sarcasm. "We were arguing, huh? That figures. He *always* had to have his way."

Bess sat back in her chair and watched her husband. When they were first going together, he told her about Adam's death and his visitation. It was a story she believed Cody's young mind made up to cope with such a traumatic loss. Never once did she think it was true. Over the years, Cody's story never wavered.

"Come on, Adam, talk to me," he pleaded.

Bess shook her head. She didn't comment. There was no way she believed the notion that the dead can communicate with the living. She never expressed her disbelief to her husband although she wanted to, many times. She didn't want to spoil his illusion.

Cody dropped his gaze to meet his wife's eyes then looked at his watch.

"Sami," he said. "I gotta go." And with that pronouncement, he pushed away from the table and hurried out of the room.

Bess continued slowly sipping her coffee. "Some things never change," she said aloud.

She heard the sound of the garage door rising. Murder cases always had a peculiar effect on her husband. Sometimes he would get so wrapped up in his work, he would only come home long enough to change his clothes, grab a bite to eat before heading back to the office. Until the crime was solved, their home life was put on the back burner. Which meant their life was generally in an uproar on any given day. Everything about this investigation seemed the same as countless other investigations yet, Bess could sense a difference this time. What the difference was exactly, she didn't quite know.

"Maybe it's me," she said before drinking the last dregs of her coffee. Cody's ramblings in his sleep the night before wouldn't get out of her head. She picked up the morning paper. She focused on the headlines only to put the paper down moments later.

"This is not working. You need to get up and get busy." She told herself. She rose from the table putting the cup in the sink with the rest of the dirty dishes.

"Ghosts, you can't be serious, Cody. It's a figment of your imagination nothing more." She explained to the assortment of cups and plates in front of her.

"Damn it, you better not disappoint him, big brother. It would kill him." She threw the sponge into the water.

A young boy spoke softly. The sound was so close to her, she whirled around expecting to see an intruder. The kitchen was empty.

"Who's there?" she yelled. "Cody, if that's you playing a trick, I'm not amused."

The boy spoke again.

Without even thinking she blurted out, "Adam? Is that you?" She paused waiting for a response.

"Come on, Cody. Give me a break." she stormed to the door leading to the garage and pulled it open. "This isn't funny. Enough is enough."

Cody's car was gone. The garage door was down. The garage was empty. Bess stepped back into the kitchen. She felt numb as she let the door close slowly. It wasn't her imagination. She had heard a voice. Sweat accumulated over her lip. Her heart was racing.

"I'm not crazy," she whimpered. The house no longer felt safe. "What do you want?" she demanded to the room at large.

"Woods, it lives in the woods," the boy's voice said.

"What? What lives in the woods?" What are you talking about?" She pressed up against the door for support.

"Malsumis."

Chapter 11

"I'm coming, Sami," Connie called when she heard the knock. She crossed the room in a few strides, undid one lock and a dead bolt until she finally opened the door.

"What took you so long?" She gave her sister, Sami, a big hug.

"I had to see Cody Davis first." Sami said returning her sister's hug with the same emotion. "It's good to see you, too. How are you?"

"I'm holding up okay. Was Cody surprised?" Connie asked.

"Oh yes, he was shocked to say the least," Sami answered. "I love it when we do that."

"Me, too," Connie said then added. "Do you think Princess knows you're here, yet?"

Sami shrugged. She walked over to the bedside table which stood in between two queen size beds and put her purse down. Connie could tell her sister was upset.

"What's wrong? Something is wrong?" Connie said.

Sami frowned. "I haven't heard from Father since I got here. In fact, the only soul who is talking to me is Adam Davis. It's almost as if everyone has run away."

Connie stared at her sister with genuine fear. Although the souls of the dead didn't communicate directly with her as they did with Sami, Connie could sense their presence.

"I wondered what was wrong. I haven't felt anyone around me since yesterday. Feels strange, empty," Connie was worried.

"You know, I complained to Cody today how damn irritating it was constantly hearing from the dead. I wish I could take back that statement. Now no one is talking to me with the exception of Adam. What are the dead afraid of? They're already dead," Sami said.

The two sisters sat side by side contemplating the strange and abrupt change.

"I told Detective Davis why you married Simon," Sami said.

"Why on earth did you do that? Now he will think I had no feelings at all for the man," Connie was flabbergasted at her sister's announcement.

"No, I don't think so. He was surprised though," Sami continued.

"I guess it doesn't matter anyway. I didn't learn much in these past five years. Princess never talked about her husband's past business dealings. In fact, she never talked to me at all except when social convention demanded it. That was Simon's fault. He never should have told her my maiden name."

"Well, I found something out." Sami smiled broadly.

"Really, what?"

"I went over the old newspaper clipping detailing father's death. It mentions of course, the car accident and the fact he was Robert Godfrey's partner on Wall Street. A young friend of mine suggested I research the old business. So, I went online looking for any article about Wood, Struthers and Godfrey, Inc. I actually found one obscure article that says the firm was being investigated for fraud."

"Fraud? Not our father. He was the most honest man." Connie was indignant at the suggestion.

"Yes, and I was trying to corroborate that fact when..." Sami's smile widened. " I located an old employee."

"After all these years?"

"The internet is an amazing tool, not to mention I had other help," Sami looked upwards.

"Who was this person? What did they say?" Connie was enthralled.

"The man I discovered was a clerk who reported directly to father. He's about the same age as Princess, over 90, I believe with a mind as sharp as a tack. He remembered father and the events leading up to his death like it was yesterday. He also had some interesting insights. Apparently, right before Robert and Princess were married, father and Robert were in the middle of some kind of business deal. Father had some misgivings about it, but Robert insisted he go through with it. Well, before the wedding, the deal went awry. Somehow only father was being implicated in the subsequent investigation. He claimed he was set-up. He and Robert had several heated exchanges over this, one of which we know happened at the wedding." Sami paused in her narration.

"And...?"

"Father's soul has never been able to tell me how he died, but this old employee finally solved the mystery." Sami said triumphantly.

"What did he tell you?" Connie was becoming impatient.

"Someone tampered with the brakes. Father was drugged first, put into his car then it was shoved down a ravine. The resulting explosion was a gift to the murderer. It destroyed any and all of the evidence."

"How did this man know this?" Connie asked.

"He was the one who did it."

"What? He was? Did he say why?"

"The man told me he was caught by Robert Godfrey embezzling money from the company. Rather than press charges, Robert Godfrey made him an offer he couldn't refuse."

"We always knew Father was murdered," Connie shook her head. "Is he going to tell the police and finally clear father's name?

Sami grew quiet. The smile left her face. "No, he told me he would not tell the police. I guess telling me relieved him of some of his guilt.

I was going to go to the police myself, but I had no proof really. So, I stayed in touch with him for a while hoping to change his mind. Then he quit communicating with me."

"He didn't want to talk to you anymore?"

"Oh, he eventually did get back to me. At least his soul did."

"He died?"

"Murdered, actually, although the coroner said it was natural causes. The old man told me his caregiver didn't show up one day. A different one came instead. Gave him a shot of insulin and that was that." Sami paused briefly. "The Godfreys are still a powerful force. What I can't figure out is how they knew I was talking to him."

"That is strange. Was the old man sure he was murdered?"

"Oh yes, quite. His soul was adamant the Godfreys were as responsible for his death as we know they were for our Father's. Its proving it that becomes the problem."

"Yes, I know? What about Simon? Have you heard from him?" Connie asked.

Sami gave her sister a look of concern. "The moment Simon died, he contacted me. Actually, he was trying to warn you about someone or something in the house. Unfortunately, I couldn't make out what he was saying other than I heard your name and a few snippets of information. It's like someone is interfering with my reception."

"I wonder why?"

I don't know exactly but Adam keeps repeating a name … Sami said.

"A name?" Connie asked.

"He keeps saying, Malsumis."

"Who or what's a Malsumis?" Connie asked.

"Not sure, but it might be the reason for the silence," Sami said gesturing above her as she stood up. "They're going to find Simon's head tomorrow. Adam says we need to protect Cody."

"Protect him, Sami?" Connie felt a chill encompass her.

"Yes. I just hope we can," Sami shivered.

Chapter 12

"**O**kay, ladies and gents here's how it's going to go. Everyone spread your arms out and stand touching your neighbors fingers." Cody inspected the group of recruits he commandeered from the precinct to search for Simon Plimpton's remains. Early that morning he got permission from the Captain to pull as many officers as he needed. Even though he knew he would find Simon's head on his own, Cody decided it was best not to deviate from the normal routine. He ended up with three officers, 3 trainees, Detective Brian Smith and himself.

"Try to stay at least three feet apart as you move forward. Do the best you can getting through some of the bushes. Above all keep your head down and look for anything and everything. When you find something, give a shout. When you hear someone shout, I want everyone to freeze in place until I tell say it is okay to move. Is that understood?" The recruits vocalized their acknowledgement of his orders.

"All right, move out everyone." Cody waved his hand starting the group forward. He made sure the team was doing exactly what he told them to do before he joined the search as well. The benign expression he wore on his face belied the tension he felt in his neck.

Since his arrival, nothing had gone as planned. The recovery team he hastily put together was supposed to meet him at precisely 9 a.m. Instead they arrived a half-hour late. Brian claimed they had trouble with the police van. Then there was this odd change in the temperature even though it was a mild autumn day. While he waited for the team, Cody felt the air around him grow cold. Now as he entered the Reservation, it was downright freezing. He didn't understand why no one else seemed to notice the change.

"Hey, Brian is it cold to you?" he asked his young partner who was wearing a light jacket.

"No, actually I was thinking about taking off my jacket. Why? Are you cold?"

"Yeah, been that way since I got here. Maybe I'm getting sick or something," Cody said even though he felt fine. Shrugging off his misgivings, he waved Brian forward while pulling his jacket a little tighter.

What's up big brother? I thought you said I could walk in here today. Why is it so cold? Come on buddy, talk to me, Cody pleaded. He received no response. Cody couldn't suppress his disappointment. Adam's silence made it hard for him to focus on the matters at hand.

The team advanced at a snail's pace carefully scrutinizing every inch of ground while they walked. Cody played the game and acted like he was searching as well. He knew it wouldn't be long before Simon's remains were found. He mentally practiced acting surprised since he already knew the outcome.

Cody followed the dirt path leading from Connie's backyard. He made sure no one was within an arm's length of him. His partner, Brian was the only one walking near him however, bushes and trees obscured most of the view between them. It provided Cody some privacy. The detective moved forward slowly. He acted like he was studying the well-worn path. Every so often, he would hear Brian curse after he tripped over some downed limbs or a well-hidden rock. Cody forced himself to suppress his chuckle. It might have been him cursing, if he hadn't been in charge. A rabbit frightened by the intruders darted out in front of him. Cody watched the rabbit leap into the air then inexplicably drop over as if it had been shot. It lay motionless at his feet.

"What the hell?" Cody bent down and touched the still animal. The rabbit was frozen stiff.

"Impossible." Cody whispered quickly withdrawing his hand.

"Did you find something, Cody?" Brian asked when he overheard Cody.

"No, not really," Cody stepped over the dead rabbit. A tingling sensation at the nape of his neck put him on edge. It was a queer sensation. He looked around him with suspicion. Something was wrong. He could feel it.

Cody checked his watch. Fifteen minutes had elapsed so far. He suspected the team was near the spot Sami pointed out the other day. He wished they would hurry up so he could find something. The cold intensified with every step he took. Uncontrollable shivering racked his body. He thought about the frozen carcass behind him and wondered if he was going to end up like the rabbit when an officer to his right yelled.

"Hey, Brian, look at Cody's lips. They're blue." The officer was pointing at the shivering detective.

"Take over here, Steve." Brian relinquished his spot to the officer. He walked over to his partner. "Cody, what's going on, buddy? You're freezing."

Cody couldn't talk.

"Come here and help me get Cody out into the sun." Brian called the officer over. He turned Cody around and headed for the Plimpton's yard. Cody couldn't feel his legs. The second time he stumbled, Brian and the other officer kept him upright. Cody noticed the rabbit was gone when he passed. In a few short moments, he was out of the woods. The rays of the warm sun penetrate his jacket. Cody motioned Brian away.

"Help the team," he said through chattering teeth. By the time Brian returned with news of Simon's remains, Cody was back to normal.

"You found something, huh?" Cody asked although he already knew the answer.

"Certainly did. Simon's head," Brian answered.

"Anything else like the missing arm and leg?"

"The team is still looking but so far, nothing else," said Brian.

"What do you think?" asked Cody.

"Well, I might be wrong but it looks like his head was pulled clean off his shoulders," Brian said.

"Pulled off his shoulders, huh?" Cody grunted again. "What is strong enough to pull a man's head clean off his shoulders? Not a small woman that's for sure."

"Yes, that's for sure. Something else is odd. I never saw any blood on the path. You would think there would be some blood, somewhere." Then as an afterthought, he added. "Do you want me to call Mrs. Plimpton and tell her?"

"Tell me what?" Connie and her sister, Sami came around the corner of the house. Cody could sense Connie's tension. Sami, who was slightly behind her sister, looked upset.

"I believe we've found your husband's remains, Mrs. Plimpton," Brian said.

"I'll verify what Brian just said, Connie. Then I'll let you know definitely if it's Simon's remains. Brian, why don't you check up on the team. I'll be there in a few? I need to talk to Connie for a minute." Cody waved him back to the forest.

Brian was clearly unhappy at being dismissed so abruptly. He reluctantly followed Cody's orders.

"What's wrong with Sami? Is Adam talking to her again?" Cody asked once Brian was out of range.

"No, she…" Connie was interrupted before she could finish.

"No, I haven't heard him today. But…" Sami interjected looking towards the woods behind Cody. "There's something else. I …I can't explain it."

A cold breeze whipped around Cody then stopped as quickly as it started.

"Is Adam saying something?" Cody whispered.

"He's afraid. They're all afraid," Sami pulled her jacket around her a bit tighter.

"Sami, are you all right? Do you feel the cold? Come over and sit in a chair in the sun." Cody pulled the chair out and motioned her over.

"No, I'm fine. We need to leave, Connie. It's about Katy." Sami said as her teeth began to chatter.

"Katy?" Cody asked. "Who's Katy?

"She's someone the dead say we must visit. She lives on the other side of town. In your old house, Cody." Sami pulled her jacket again.

"She lives in my old house? How do you know that?" Cody stared at the small woman. Then he answered his own question. "Yeah, yeah I know, the dead told you."

"Will your partner mind if you leave? Don't I have to identify Simon?" Connie said as she wrapped her arms around her shivering sister.

"No, it's not necessary. I'll identify him. Stay in the sun, Sami. That's an order." Cody looked towards the trees. "I'll let Brian know we're leaving after I identify Simon."

The sisters nodded simultaneously. Cody turned towards the path again. The bitter cold that surrounded him earlier was gone. It felt like a typical autumn day. He glanced over his shoulder at the two sisters. Sami was sitting in the sun as he had instructed with her sister hovering nearby. He could tell the warmth of the sun wasn't working. Sami was rocking back and forth rubbing her arms. She looked miserable. He wondered how quickly he was really going to be able to leave.

"I better have a good story in mind to cover my tracks," he said to himself. He could see Brian in the distance. He was headed in that direction when he heard a woman's voice calling his name.

"What the…" Cody was stunned to see his wife running towards him.

"Cody, stop," she yelled. "Don't go into the trees."

Bess was at his side before he could answer. "I don't know why I am saying this but don't go into the trees."

"What?" His wife's remark stunned him.

"I don't understand it either. I…I heard someone…I think I heard someone…it doesn't matter how I know," she said softly glancing around. She didn't want anyone to hear her.

"Cody," Sami called. "We have to go."

"What do you mean, you heard someone?" he ignored Sami's pleas.

Bess looked at her husband with the most confused expression. "It was so real. I don't understand it but I know it was real. It was real. I heard a young boy. Maybe it was Adam?" Bess grabbed her husband's arm and held on. "And what he said scared me, Cody. I've never felt this frightened before."

"You heard a young boy? You think you heard Adam? Come on, Bess, you don't believe in all that supernatural crap. I know you don't. " Cody studied his wife's expression. He wondered if she was playing a joke. He couldn't remember a time in his entire marriage when his wife ever confessed to being truly afraid. It just wasn't in her makeup.

"Cody, please hurry," Sami's tone of voice was tinged with desperation.

He hated putting his wife off, but Sami's insistence that he hurry somehow outweighed her concerns. "Tell me more when we're on the road, honey. Help Connie and Sami get into the car. I'm going to tell Brian I'm leaving. Go on, Bess. I'll be there in a minute." He said turning his wife towards the driveway.

"It's okay. I promise I won't be in the trees long, I'll hurry." Cody reiterated in the hopes of pacifying her. From the expression on her face, he knew she wasn't convinced. If Adam didn't want him to walk into the Reservation, he would let him know. At least, that is what Cody hoped.

Without a backward glance at the three departing women, Cody followed the path into the thicket of trees. The bitter cold that had embraced him before didn't surround him this time. Its absence let him relax a little. However, his wife's warning kept resonating in his brain. *The boy said not to go into the trees.*

The team was in a small circle surrounding Simon Plimpton's remains. Brian was kneeling taking pictures when Cody approached. "Hey, there you are. How's Mrs. Plimpton holding up?" Brian asked when he saw Cody walking towards him.

"She's all right. Let me have a look," he said.

Brian waved his boss forward. Simon's detached head was lying face up.

"I don't remember the last time I saw a dead person wearing an expression like that." Cody said pointing to the deceased's face. "Couldn't you close his eyes or something?"

"I tried, they won't close," Brian said. "Hey, be careful over there. Excuse me Cody, I'll be right back." Brian walked away. He motioned for the rest of the team to follow him leaving Cody alone.

"Shit, what the hell happened to you, Simon?" Cody said under his breath. He reached down to close the dead man's eyes. Simon's eyelids were cold to the touch. Cody gently forced them closed, but the moment he removed his hand, the dead man's eyes flew open.

"Ah, come on," Cody said under his breath. He tried to close them again with the same results. The third time he tried, the eyes did the unthinkable, they moved.

"Whoa!" Cody jerked back in fright. He scrambled away from Simon's head until a trunk of a tree stopped him. The whole time he was moving, the dead man's eyes watched. Cody felt the numbness of fear travel from his head to his toes.

"No, no, no this can't be happening," he stammered. His heart was hammering out of control. His breath came out in short spurts. A scream was lodged in his throat. He wanted the others to see what he was seeing, but when he looked up everyone was going about their business. They were oblivious to the distraught detective.

Cody picked up a stick lying nearby. He slowly waved it to the right, then the left. The dead man's eyes followed the motion for a short time, then abruptly stopped and stared at him like before.

"What the hell is this, Adam?" Cody asked the only one he thought might be able to help him. "Come on big brother. Now is not the time to be quiet."

Cody dropped the stick. "What do you want?" he finally asked. Simon's eyes blinked then the lips curled up into a hideous grin.

"Shit," Cody felt his throat tighten as the head took on a more sinister look.

"What do you want?" Cody repeated.

Simon's lips moved. Slowly and deliberately, the lips mouthed words.

"I don't get it, Simon," Cody couldn't decipher the message. The lips continued moving. Cody glanced up at the other officers. He tried calling them but nothing came out of his mouth. A sound coming from the detached head returned Cody's attention. It was talking. Cody couldn't make out what it was saying. He inched closer. Simon's head nodded its approval of his movement. Cody kept going until he was directly in front of the grinning face. The mouth was moving more rapidly now. Cody still couldn't make out what it was saying. He glanced to his right and to his left. What he was about to do would be fodder for gossip at the station, if he was seen. He didn't want the rumor mill to run amok, especially when the rumor would be about his sanity. Cody tilted his head and eased downward until his ear was within inches of the moving lips.

"Tell me," he asked.

The stench of rotting flesh invaded his nostrils. He could feel the cold dampness of its grey skin. His stomach roiled.

"Tell me." he demanded. He stifled the urge to vomit.

"What are you doing?" Brian asked.

Cody jump at the sound of his voice.

"Nothing," Cody answered quickly lifting his head.

"I don't think he's gonna talk to you," Brian said with a bemused chuckle.

"Yeah, very funny," Cody replied testily. He stood up. "I'm done here. I'm leaving. Can you finish up without me?"

"Sure, no problem, what's up?" Brian asked.

"Nothing. I need to run an errand," Cody said deflecting Brian's question as best he could.

"Okay, see you back at the station. Hey, you over there. Wait a minute," with those parting words, Brian walked away.

Cody watched his young partner leave. Brian was irritating, but thankfully he wasn't a gossip. At least, he hoped he wasn't. Cody patted his chest. His heart was beating out of control. He felt a little lightheaded. The cloying smell of dead flesh clung to him. An involuntary shiver racked his body. He was utterly disappointed he had gained nothing in return for his misery. And where was Adam? More importantly, Cody wondered, why didn't he help? He felt a strange urge for a final look at Simon's face. He wrestled with the notion, then against his better judgment, he looked. Cody instantly regretted his decision. The look on Simon's face was sheer fury.

Demonic was the word that popped into Cody's head. He recoiled at the sight.

Why did you look, you idiot? he admonished himself. Cody made his way out of the trees. If he ever saw this part of the Reservation again, it would be too soon. The warm sun felt good on his back.

Chapter 13

"Grandmother, has Elodie told you the news?" Dani asked.

"I assume you are referring to the death of Simon Plimpton, Temple Falls' illustrious mayor?" Princess said dryly.

"Yes, how did you…," Dani stopped mid-sentence. Her grandmother had the uncanny ability of knowing everything that went on in Temple Falls, sometimes even before they happened.

"The police said his head was ripped entirely off his shoulders," Dani continued.

"Spare me the details, Dani. You're a Godfrey. It's beneath you to talk about such morbid goings on," Princess sniffed.

"Yes, Grandmother," Dani said dejectedly. "I thought I might send Connie some flowers. I'm sure she must be devastated."

Princess ignored Dani's comment. Connie Plimpton was the proverbial pain in her backside ever since she arrived five years earlier. The woman's intrusion into Simon Plimpton's business and personal affairs crimped Princess' ability to maintain a discreet distance from the city government while secretly controlling its every move. Now she must find someone as equally pliable as Simon to be the next mayor.

"Grandmother, did you hear me? Shouldn't we send flowers to Connie?" she reiterated.

Princess let out a long wearisome sigh. "Yes, I suppose that would be the correct thing to do. You can sign the card for the family."

Dani nodded. She left the room quickly. Princess picked up her tea cup and took a sip. The hot tea should have tasted better than it did. She set the cup back down on the side table. Thinking about Connie always precipitated trouble. She and her equally annoying sister had the temerity to stand up to her on more than one occasion.

Princess recalled the day Simon introduced his new wife to her. His sudden marriage had taken her by surprise. However, when she realized whom he had married, that surprise turned into shock.

"Princess, I'd like you to meet my wife, Connie Howell. Excuse me, I mean Connie Plimpton,"

"Howell?" the name immediately caught Princess' attention.

"Yes, I believe you knew my father, John Howell," Connie had answered extending her hand.

Princess had been blindsided. So much so, she let Connie's hand stay extended far too long. Her predilection for proper social etiquette prevailed in the end. However, when their hands touched, Princess knew the woman didn't marry Simon for love. Connie's entire being oozed revenge. Since that day, the two women played an ongoing game of cat and mouse; a game in which Princess found herself in the role of the mouse far too often.

A knock on her bedroom door brought her back to the present.

"Come in," she called.

Elodie Godfrey walked into the room. The air became charged with tension instantly. "What is it, Elodie?" Princess girded herself for their inevitable confrontation.

"That guy, Harry Cooper called and said he would be here around three o'clock. I told him you'd be here," Elodie replied flippantly.

"You go too far you know, Elodie," Princess said angrily. "You know you are to check with me before you accept any engagement on my behalf."

"What are you going to do, Grandmother, kill me?" Elodie retorted with unabashed contempt. When her grandmother didn't respond, Elodie continued. "Oh come on, Grandmother, it is common knowledge that anyone who gets in the way of a Godfrey ends up dead, especially when they cross the high and mighty Princess. But I am curious. How did you manage to rip his head clean off his body?" Elodie taunted.

Princes leveled an intense stare at her granddaughter. Subtlety was ineffective.

"Yes, it was the most efficient way to kill a maggot, wasn't it?" Princess looked knowingly at her granddaughter.

Her response had its intended effect. A ripple of unexpected self-doubt in Elodie's otherwise rock solid self-confidence appeared. A less audacious person would have retreated but not Elodie.

"You know, Grandmother old age has made you forgetful. You should be more careful about what you leave lying around. People are so snoopy these days." Elodie tossed the bomb back into her grandmother's court. Her words had the effect she desired. Princess let her guard down for a brief moment. Her eyes flicked over to a picture on the wall. It covered a small safe. She knew the journal was safely inside. She recovered her composure but not before Elodie followed her glance.

"This is most unfortunate, Elodie," Princess reached for her cane. Once it was in her hand, she pulled herself up from the chaise lounge. "You realize, I can't allow an insurrection." Princess nodded towards the door. Ronald, the butler, had entered the room silently. He left just as quickly. Elodie jumped when she heard the door lock.

"I'm tired of you, Elodie. Always meddling in things you shouldn't."

"Why, Grandmother, why does this family have so many dark

secrets? What's in that book that's so damning?" Elodie backed away from her Grandmother.

"Nothing that concerns you, Elodie. It's time you learned your lesson. Now, in answer to your question," Princess kept walking towards her granddaughter. "It wasn't hard to separate Simon's head from his body."

Elodie felt the hard wood of the closed bedroom door against her back. Princess put one hand up against the door. She leaned forward until she was inches from Elodie's face.

" I heard it was all in the wrist."

Chapter 14

"The place hasn't changed much. You'd think someone could have painted it by now," Cody said cheerlessly eyeing the dilapidated house he once called home. A small rusty tricycle and other assorted toys littered the weed-choked, front yard. A dog house complete with a water bucket and food bowl sat empty near the front door. A long gray metal chain attached to its side was stretched out in its entirety where it had been left by its previous captive. Tall grass made sections of the chain invisible suggesting the pet had been gone for some time.

Cody could tell Bess was nervous. She spent the entire drive to the St. Clair home engaged in small talk with Connie, who seemed equally unsettled. Cody wondered what else Bess wanted to tell him. He assumed she either forgot or changed her mind. It was Sami, however, who concerned Cody the most. Her shivering stopped shortly after they pulled away from the Plimpton home. She was withdrawn except for a few furtive glances at him. He suspected she knew about his ghostly encounter with Simon's head. He wondered what was keeping her from coming right out and asking him. It suited him not to talk about it right now anyway. His heart was still pounding.

The car turned down a familiar driveway. A persuasive sense of dread enveloped Cody.

Too many bad memories, he assumed.

A thin, young girl, perhaps fifteen years old or so, stood on the dilapidated porch watching them approach. She was dressed in tight jeans that were far too long for her. The pants bundled up at her ankles. Her straight, dark black hair hung to her waist. Her high cheek bones denoted her Abenaki heritage. A big, baggy flannel shirt all but covered her entire frame. Cody guessed she couldn't have weighed more than 90 pounds. She never moved even after the car came to a halt.

"Katy St. Clair," Sami said. It was a statement of fact not a question.

"Well, here goes nothing," Connie opened the back door of the sedan. Everyone else followed suit. When the last car door shut, the group stood in front of the silent girl.

"Hi, Katy, I'm Cody Davis. I'm a detective with…"

Katy cut him off. "You shouldn't be here."

"What do you…"

Sami touched Cody on the arm. "Let me, Cody. Katy, I believe you know who I am?"

Katy nodded. Although her face wore no expression, her dark eyes however, betrayed her fear.

"I was told by your grandfather that you could help us."

"Her Grandfather? When did Sami talk to her Grandfather?" Cody whispered in Connie's ear.

"He's been talking since she arrived. He won't stop," Connie whispered back.

Cody stared at Connie in confusion then he understood what she meant. "He's dead, isn't he?"

"Yes," came her reply.

"I should have known," Cody shook his head.

"You can't stay. It watches everyone." Katy's voice gave away her tension.

"What's watching, Katy? We need to know. Who is watching everyone?" Sami pressed.

Katy shook her head.

"What's going on out here?" A tall, heavy-set woman with jet-black hair and equally dark eyes stepped out onto the front stoop. Like Katy, she was wearing a flannel button down shirt that hung well below her waist over a pair of faded jeans. Cody guessed her age to be late thirties early forties. Her high cheek bones told Cody she was an Abenaki as well. In all, he thought she was positively stunning.

"Can I help you?" she said eyeing the odd group with outright suspicion.

"My name is Sami Howell. I..., I mean we came here to talk to Katy."

"Has she done something wrong?"

"No, but we would like to ask..." Cody felt pressure on his arm.

"No, Mrs. St. Clair. Katy hasn't done anything wrong. Rachel sent us," Sami said softly.

"Rachel?"

"Rachel and Grandpa."

Cody watched Sami and Connie exchange a knowing look. He wondered what had just transpired between the two sisters. Something in his universe changed in a matter of seconds and he felt completely left out of the loop.

Mrs. St. Clair pulled Katy towards her. She glanced with fear at the surrounding woods. "Inside." She abruptly pushed Katy through the door first. Then she motioned for the rest to follow.

Once everyone was inside, she shut the door. "Have a seat," she said motioning towards a well-worn couch. Then she left the room. The three women sat down. Cody sat in the only remaining chair near the door

"Cody, are you okay?" Bess asked concerned by the look on her husband's face.

"Yeah, I'm okay. I didn't think being here would bother me," he said sadly. *I hope I never have to come back here again,* he wished.

A sound in the hallway made Cody turn his head. In an instant, he was that young boy dreading his father's approaching footsteps. Before he realized what he was doing, Cody was on his feet.

"Honey, what's wrong?" Bess asked when she saw her husband head for the door.

Cody stopped a few feet from his goal. His wife's voice brought him back to the present. "I…I was getting away from my father," he stammered in disbelief. "I didn't want him to hit me."

"Your father is a mean man," Katy St. Clair said.

"Is? *Was* a mean man," Cody corrected the young girl.

Katy St. Clair shrugged her shoulders

"This was your home, wasn't it?"

"Yeah," he was surprised she knew.

Katy went no further. Instead she turned towards the women on the couch. She took Bess's hand. "You're his wife," she said. Bess stared at the girl in amazement.

Katy stood in front of Connie. She didn't take her hand. Instead, she stepped back. Her eyes darted from one sister to the other. She knelt down in front of them. Her eyes continued darting back and forth. Without a word, she abruptly stood up.

"I can't help you."

"That's not what Rachel told me," Sami said.

"She lies. She listens to Malsumis."

"No, she says she doesn't listen to the trickster anymore. She says she's sorry," Sami continued.

Katy shook her head. "Rachel always says she's sorry."

"Who's Rachel?" Bess whispered to Connie.

"She is my twin," Katy replied.

"You have a twin sister?" Bess looked around the room expecting to see another girl.

"She never really lived. She died at birth but she has been by Katy's side until about two years ago," Mrs. St. Clair came through the doorway carrying a tray with several drinks.

"What happened two years ago?" Cody asked.

"Malsumis made her take me to the mekwi nebi, red water. Rachel believed him when he said I wouldn't get hurt. He was waiting for me but I escaped," she said.

"My daughter was attacked and left for dead," Mrs. St. Clair said flatly.

"Red Water? Do you mean Bloody Creek? What happened?" Cody didn't remember a case of assault involving Katy St. Clair. A vision of Adam lying in a pool of his own blood in that same horrible creek crossed his mind.

Katy lifted the front of her shirt. She revealed broad scars across her abdomen.

"My God, it looks like a bear got you," Cody gasped.

Katy shook her head. "It wasn't a bear," she said. "Malsumis told Rachel he needed my help but Malsumis wasn't there."

"You mentioned that name earlier--Malsumis, the trickster. What does it mean?" Bess asked.

" Malsumis, the Trickster is a son of Tabaldak," she said.

"Tabaldak?" Bess said.

"Tabaldak is the creator. Gluskabe and Malsumis sprang from the dust in his hands. Gluskabe creates good. Malsumis creates trouble. My grandfather told me stories, stories that his great grandfather told him when he was a little boy."

"Stories about your Abenaki heritage?" Bess continued.

Katy nodded. "He told me that before the English took Abenaki land, our ancestral home was on the banks of Bloody Creek, mekwi nebi. Our families lived there for generations. Gluskabe protected us from Malsumis and his tricks."

"Tricks? What kind of tricks?" Bess said.

Cody interrupted before Katy could answer. "But you said Malsumis wasn't there the day you were hurt. Who was?"

Katy shook her head. She refused to say any more.

Mrs. St. Clair interrupted Cody at that point. "Why are you here? What do you want from my daughter?"

"Mrs. St. Clair I'm sorry to bother you today. My name is Sami and this is my twin sister, Connie. I'm like Katy. I hear from the dead, too" Sami said. "In fact, it was Rachel who told me to find Katy. That's why we are here."

Mrs. St. Clair studied the small group intently. She put her hands on Katy's shoulders and drew her close. "What do you want with my daughter?" she reiterated.

Cody answered before Sami could. "Does Katy know who or what killed Simon Plimpton or Caroline Godfrey?"

Mrs. St. Clair and Katy both looked at Cody at the same time. Mrs. St. Clair seemed surprised by Cody's statement. Katy was not.

"The mayor is…" Mrs. St. Clair didn't finish.

"Dead, Mrs. St. Clair, horribly murdered," Cody continued. "Can Katy tell me about that?"

Everyone's eyes focused on the young girl. If their stares bothered her, she didn't let on. Her face remained impassive.

"Do you think my daughter had something to do with Mayor Plimpton's death?" Mrs. St. Clair continued.

"No, Mrs. St. Clair, I'm a detective with the Temple Falls Police force. I don't believe your daughter had anything to do with Simon's death. It's just that…well, there have been…"

"What Detective Davis means, Mrs. St. Clair, is that Simon's death is one of many strange deaths that have occurred in Temple Falls over the years. We are trying to find out once and for all, what or who is doing these things. Mr. Davis' own brother, Adam was a victim of this murderer many years ago," Sami said. "The dead told me Katy can help us.

Katy took her mother's hands off her shoulders. She walked towards the petite woman on the couch. She dropped to the floor and sat crossed legged in front of Sami. Mrs. St. Clair didn't stop her, but she stood nearby.

"My grandfather said it started a long time ago. There was a French man, a fur trapper who was a friend of the Abenaki. He fell in love with a young Abenaki girl. But she didn't love him back. She was in love with someone else. One day the young girl went alone into the woods gathering nuts. An awasos with a cub charged her. The Frenchman heard her scream. He shot the awasos and saved her life. The young girl's father was so grateful, he made the Frenchman a member of his clan. He trusted him. But the Frenchman was a liar. He was in the woods that day following the young girl but not to protect her. He was following her so he could kidnap her. The charging bear surprised him, too. It worked in his favor.

When the Abenaki warriors heard the sound of his gun, they rushed into the woods. The Frenchman knew he couldn't carry out his plan. So he came up with a new one."

The girl paused in her narrative and looked at her mother. Although the exchange was brief, Cody noticed that something more than a look passed between them.

After a brief pause, Katy resumed. "Not long after he saved the girl, the English threatened the Abenaki. The Abenaki were not friends of the British. The Frenchman convinced the young girl's father that the tribe must sign a treaty with the English, if the Abenaki wanted to keep their land. All the Abenaki had to do was meet with the English in their village and it would be done. The chiefs believed him. Most of the Abenaki died that day. Only a few survived."

"Did the Frenchman get the young girl after all?" Bess said.

"Yes and no," Katy said solemnly.

"But what about Malsumis?" Cody asked.

"When the massacre was over, the Frenchman found the young girl hiding near a cliff overlooking the lake. She was so scared. The Frenchman told her that her family was dead. She didn't believe him. She wanted to go back to the village. The Frenchman said no. She tried to go back anyway. He got angry and hit her," she said. "She fought him but the Frenchman was too strong. She grabbed the knife off his belt. She stabbed him." Katy's hand went up in the air. She made stabbing motions, then dropped her hand. "He let her go. Once she was free, she tried to run towards her village. The Frenchman caught up with her and blocked her path. The only way out for her was over the cliff. She asked the spirits for forgiveness and revenge when she jumped," Katy said.

"And did the spirits help?" Sami asked.

"They punished the Frenchman and his heirs forever," Mrs. St. Clair interrupted Katy.

"His heirs? Who..?" Cody asked.

"How was the Frenchman and his family punished?" Bess interrupted him.

"Yes, the Frenchman?" Sami repeated Bess's question. "Reynard Pillion Gillett was his name I believe. How was he punished?"

Mrs. St. Clair didn't speak right away. She was taking the time to choose her words carefully before she answered. Although her face wore a benign expression, she rubbed her hands together nervously. It was clear to the group in front of her she was afraid. It was Katy who finally answered.

"My grandfather said Malsumis heard the young girl's plea but it wasn't Malsumis who answered. He said..."

"Katy, why don't you see if Gypsy's come home?" her mother stopped the girl from completing her story. She motioned her out of the room.

Her daughter gave the group one last worried look over her shoulder before leaving.

"Gypsy?" Cody queried.

"Our dog. She's been missing for a while," Mrs. St. Clair answered.

"Thank you, Mrs. St. Clair for your time," Sami said abruptly signaling the group it was time to go.

Her quick movement surprised Cody. The story was unfinished. He had more questions. Connie and Bess followed Sami's lead. Cody sighed and reluctantly stood up, too. The small group traipsed one by one out the door. Each nodded to Mrs. St. Clair as they passed. Once outside, they huddled in a small circle.

"Why did we leave so soon?" Cody was irritated by their abrupt departure.

"Mrs. St. Clair and Katy can't tell us anymore. Actually, I should say they were forbidden to say anymore," Sami answered grimly. "It's possible the loss of their dog may have been a warning."

"A warning? From who? Who's threatening them?" Cody asked.

"Rachel tells me there was something unleashed that day in the woods when the young girl cried for help. She says it's older than Malsumis and more cunning. But she's afraid like the other souls and won't elaborate," Sami said.

"This Frenchman is somehow related to the Godfreys, right?" Cody asked.

"I'm believe so," Sami said.

"Hard to imagine a family as wealthy as the Godfrey family being cursed," Bess added.

"Yes, it's hard to imagine," Connie said.

"Their wealth comes at a price," Sami said knowingly.

"So, what do we do now? Wait for another murder?" Cody said sarcastically.

"Unfortunately, yes," Sami said matter-of-factly.

Chapter 15

"Mr. Harry Cooper, I presume?" Princess Godfrey walked slowly into the room. A tall, thin man with a stock of shaggy brown hair and an even thicker mustache rose from the living room couch to greet her. There was something oddly familiar about him that struck Princess the moment she saw him. She just couldn't figure out what that familiarity was.

"I understand you are interested in writing a book about my family, Mr. Cooper. Is that correct?" she asked. She motioned for him to sit back down.

"Please call me, Harry. Yes, Mrs. Godfrey, the history of some of Vermont's oldest towns and families is the subject of my book. Your family is one of the few that has remained in the state and more specifically has been in the same town since the Revolutionary War. I'm sure you have lots of family stories passed down from one generation to another that would make for interesting reading. And, if you have any old letters, pictures, books that tell the story of how your first ancestors arrived here, what they did for a living, who they married that would be great, too." The young man's words droned on and on.

Stories. Yes, there are stories, Mr. Cooper but would you and your readers believe some of the stories I have to tell, Princess wondered.

"Mrs. Godfrey, do you think you can help me?" Mr. Cooper asked.

Princess met his eyes with an unemotional stare. Purposely ignoring his request for familiarity, Princess continued. "My family has always maintained a code of strict privacy, Mr. Cooper. Too many times in the past, we have been vilified by unkind and one-sided reporting. This has left us reluctant to speak to the press," said Princess.

"Then why did you agree to see me today?" Mr. Cooper asked.

Princess sighed. *You are the perfect pawn, Mr. Cooper.* Her eyes drifted to a large portrait of her late husband. She sighed again. *A perfect, gullible pawn.* She smiled slightly. *Wouldn't you agree, Robert?*

"Mrs. Godfrey?"

"Hmm, yes...yes, I have nothing against telling you the history of Temple Falls or that of my husband's family as long as you do not twist my words." She leaned forward to emphasize her next statement. "My lawyers are quite adept at handling libelous allegations. Are we clear, Mr. Cooper?"

"Absolutely," Harry pulled his notepad out of a small briefcase. He also removed a recorder which he set up on an end table next to a silver bell close to Princess.

Princess eyed the small recorder. "I do not wish this conversation to be recorded, thank you."

"Oh, okay," Harry took the machine back. He pretended to turn it off before returning it to the front of his briefcase.

"Mr. Cooper, have we met before?" Princess couldn't shake the nagging suspicion.

Harry shook his head and quickly changed the subject. "No, Ma'am. Can you tell me where the Godfrey family originated?"

"My husband's family came from France originally."

He's lying, a male voice hissed in her ear. *He knows you.*

"That first ancestor was..." Harry tried to ignore Princess's intent stare.

"Mr. Cooper, I don't believe you are being truthful. This interview is over," Princess pulled her cane in front of her. She then picked up a small silver bell and shook it. Ronald, the butler appeared almost instantly.

Harry was lost. "What? What did I say? What did I do? I don't understand? Why did you agree to this interview if you...?"

"Yes, Mother, why did you agree to this interview?" A male voice interrupted the young man.

"Bennett!" Princess exclaimed in complete astonishment upon recognizing the speaker.

Her youngest son, Bennett Godfrey strode purposely into the room. He hugged his mother. After this brief exchange, he turned his attention to the young man.

"Mr. Cooper, I'm sorry you came out all this way for nothing, but the Godfrey family is not interested. Thank you for your time. Ronald will see you to the door." And with that pronouncement, Bennett turned his back on Mr. Cooper in a final gesture of dismissal.

The butler moved over and stood behind Harry and Princess. When Mr. Cooper didn't stand up, Ronald cleared his throat gently. It was several more moments before Mr. Cooper acknowledged his presence with the most perplexed expression.

"This way, Sir." Ronald motioned towards the open door.

Harry Cooper rose slowly. The interview was over before it began. Without another word, he picked up his briefcase and preceded the butler out of the room. Once the click of the closing door was heard, Bennett took several steps away from his seemingly adoring mother. He glared at her with unabashed contempt.

"Why?" he said. "I had to read about Caroline's murder in the newspaper. The article didn't mention the fact she was leaving Paul.

Was she silenced for creating a scandal, Mother or did she discover something about the family you didn't want her to know?"

"Really, Bennett. Do you actually believe I had something to do with her murder?" Princess feigned surprise.

"Come on, Mother. You know as well as I do, no one ever leaves this family at least not willingly. Then Dani tells me you actually granted an interview, I couldn't believe it. And what's this about?" He threw an opened envelope down on the chaise lounge.

Princess returned her son's stare with equal hostility.

"How else could I bring you home, Bennett? You've refused my phone calls, returned my letters with the exception of my last note. You've ignored my concerns for a long time, Bennett. It was time for you to return. You cannot escape your destiny."

"Ah yes, the infamous Godfrey destiny," Bennett was livid. He walked over to a dark wood cabinet and threw open its doors. "The Godfrey destiny, that killed, my father and grandfather and numerous other innocent people. If the family history continues to repeat itself, will ultimately kill R.P. and then, me."

He reached into the cabinet and pulled out a glass decanter filled with whiskey. He poured himself a stout drink. At fifty-eight years of age, Bennett Godfrey was remarkably fit. The average person would have thought him much younger than he appeared, as his blond hair offered no hint of grey. Maybe a few small telltale flecks dotting a thick mustache over his lip might have given his age away, if he allowed a mustache to grow. A passion for physical exercise left his tanned face and body lean. The fact his weight was the same as it was in college was a source of immense egotistical pride. He was handsome and he knew it.

"So, Mother how much time do I have?" He tossed back another drink. "I believe your most recent missive said something about my brother was in, how did you put it 'in death's clutches'."

Bennett hated every inch of Pinehurst and the corresponding

drama that came with it. For generations, every male heir was expected to live on the property in order to be able to benefit from its wealth. Bennett was no different in the beginning. He followed the tradition like his father before him until his wife passed away in what he considered typical Godfrey fashion: "cause unknown". The loss of his young wife was too much for him. He rebelled against the "family tradition" and his mother's wishes. He fled leaving behind his two young daughters. Something he later regretted.

Once free from the confines of Pinehurst, Bennett slowly recovered. He threw himself into the many family businesses spending months at a time traveling around the world. Never staying in one place long enough for his mother to find him. Although he did provide her with a post office box number in case of emergency.

Every so often, he would return home for unannounced visits which thrilled his children until he left again. They grew resentful of the long absences. Today however, was the beginning of a new era.

Can't believe I'm home for good, Bennett studied the glass in his hand.

Princess glanced at the butler, then redirected her gaze to her son. For all his bravado, she could tell he was frightened. She watched in silence as he poured yet another drink.

"Ronald, that's all. You may go," she spoke sharply.

"Alcohol will not change anything," she said once Ronald was gone.

"Right, Mother but at least I won't care," he said. "I take it R.P. is gone?"

"No, your brother is alive," Princess replied then added. "For the moment. He's been asking for you."

"Asking for me? R.P. never *asked* me for anything. He just took it. Where is the fucking bastard?" Bennett asked. Princess watched more whiskey disappear.

"He stays in the east cellar most days. I'm afraid he's quite mad," she said quietly. "There is one complication."

"What now?" Bennett said with disgust.

"Your daughter is completely out of control. I had no choice but to put her in the cellar next to her Uncle," Princess said.

Bennett lowered his glass. "In the cellar? Really, Mother.? What are you going to do with her? Kill her?" He noted his mother's look of surprise. "Don't look so surprised, Mother. I know what you are capable of. Hasn't there been enough killing already?"

Princess looked wearily at her son. The slow lingering death of her philandering husband had taught her to disconnect her emotions. R.P., her oldest son, was going to die much like his father. She was prepared for that eventuality. Bennett's death however, would most likely kill her. He wasn't like the rest of the Godfrey men before him.

"How can we break this curse, Mother? There must be a way," Bennett pleaded. "Every *contract* has an escape clause. What's ours?"

"You know it is forbidden to talk about this. You don't want the servants hearing our conversation." she cast a wary glance at the door

Bennett confronted his mother. "Why? Why can't we talk about a curse that has taken every male heir in the Godfrey family since time began almost? Don't I have the right to know why, since I'm the next in line?" Bennett demanded.

The room grew cold. Princess covered her shoulders with a nearby shawl. She shivered slightly. "Your father tried many times. I let him read Reynard's journal more than once. Even when he began losing his mind, he continued looking for a way to save you and your brother, but it was all in vain." Princess noticed she could see her breath. "He wasn't strong enough."

"Strong enough? Good God, Mother. My father was the strongest man I ever knew." A thought occurred to Bennett. He slowly placed his glass on a nearby table. "That's it, isn't it. Caroline got hold of the journal, didn't she?"

"Nonsense. She didn't know anything about the journal. The girl was a whore. Nothing more. I'm sure once they figure out who her lover was, her murder will be solved. It had nothing to do with him." She stopped abruptly in her narration.

"Him? Mother, who is him and why are you shivering? It's stifling in this room." Bennett said. His mother's body began to shake uncontrollably. "Mother, are you all right?"

Princess couldn't move her lips. She felt paralyzed.

"Mother? Ronald call 911. I think Mother is having a stroke." Bennett rushed to Princess' side. He caught her before she fell sideways off the couch.

"Hang on, Mother. The ambulance will be here soon." he said but as he cradled his mother in his arms, he felt her icy hand squeeze his arm. "What is it, Mother?"

Princess struggled against the paralysis slowly overtaking her body. She mouthed a few words.

"No ambulance…Sami Howell…who's Sami Howell, Mother?" Bennett asked but Princess didn't respond. The paralysis was complete.

Chapter 16

"You were awfully quiet on the ride home this afternoon," Connie said. "I felt your helplessness."

"After hours of no communication from the dead, everyone began talking at once. It was all so confusing. Katy's sister, Rachel kept being interrupted by Katy's grandfather. He wouldn't shut up. Then Cody's brother chimed in. I could feel their fear. I just wish I knew why. Are they afraid for themselves or are they afraid for their loved ones who are still on earth?" Sami wondered.

"I can't imagine what could frighten the dead. What's left? What can possibly hurt them?" Connie said.

"I might have an answer. Adam mentioned something in passing before Katy's sister cut him off. He said there was an endless space. A place where a soul wanders alone. Its unable to talk to the living or dead, solitary confinement so to speak. It's death to the dead."

"Death to the dead. So, how does one end up in this endless space?" Connie asked.

"He never explained. Which brings up something else. Mrs. St. Clair was clearly nervous about what Katy might tell us. I swear something or someone was controlling her but usually when a spirit invades a living person, I can sense it, clearly sense it. Not this time. There was something else going on with her," Sami said.

"I wonder if she will let you speak to Katy again," Connie said.

Sami shrugged.

With nothing more to add to the conversation, Connie picked up a magazine she had purchased the day before. She crossed the room and sat in the only available chair. Sami remained where she was on the edge of the bed. The quiet lull ended with the sharp ring of the bedside telephone. Sami picked up the receiver.

"Hello," she answered. "Yes, this is she."

Her conversation with the caller took only a few moments. Her answers to whatever questions were being asked were short and clipped. Connie attempted to fill in the blanks in the conversation as best she could. When her sister finally hung, Connie peppered her with questions.

"Who was that on the phone, Sami?" The puzzled look on her sister's face surprised her.

"Do you know Bennett Godfrey?" Sami replied answering her sister's question with a question.

"NO! Bennett Godfrey was on the phone? He's hardly ever in Temple Falls. Why did he call here? I didn't think anyone knew where we were staying," Connie wondered.

"Heavens, Connie there are only two motels in Temple Falls. It wouldn't be a huge conclusion to assume we were staying in one of them," Sami said. "Bennett came home a few days ago. Apparently, Princess has had a stroke. She asked to see me." The clamoring voices inside her head grew. "There's more… stop it, you're all talking at once. Princess didn't have a stroke. What…I don't understand…"

Connie watched her sister grow more agitated. If the voices were as numerous as Sami maintained, she wondered why the noise didn't drive her sister crazy. Still, she wished she could eavesdrop on her conversation.

"Why does Princess want to see you? Dear God, how can you stand that racket?"

Sami shrugged her shoulders. "Actually Bennett asked me to come to the house. Rachel, Rachel, tell me what's going on? Wait...I hear her...Malsumis, the trickster he's upset Bennett has come home. He's punishing Princess. But...wait... Rachel says...Rachel sees another spirit, older more evil. Now Adam says it isn't Malsumis... I think..." Before she could finish her sentence, Sami took a sharp breath and fainted.

"Sami, Sami no..." Connie wailed. She rushed to her stricken twin. Sami's face was a horrible ashen grey.

"What's wrong? Stop, stop you are all killing her." Connie touched her sister's still body. "Sami, it's going to be okay." Connie brushed a tear off her face. "Wake up, Sami. Please don't leave me." Connie patted her sister's arm. Sami eyes opened with a start.

"I felt it. I felt that spirit's, no that *demon's* anger. I felt that demon's fear. It's afraid of Bennett Godfrey. Bennett Godfrey might break the curse... and the demon is afraid he will. There's something different about Bennett Godfrey," Sami looked at her sister. "This demon is extremely powerful. Adam says its power has a limit."

"So the Godfreys *are* really cursed? Is this why they're so reclusive?" Connie asked.

"Could be. Now we must see Bennett and Princess," Sami teetered dangerously when she stood up.

"You're pretty wobbly, Sis. Why don't we go in the morning?" Connie suggested

"No, we have to go..." Sami tried again. A sharp knock on the motel door stopped her.

"Are you expecting anyone?" Connie asked.

"No are you?" Sami countered.

"Who is it?" Connie called.

"It's me, Cody," Cody Davis called back.

"Cody?" Connie rushed forward and opened the door.

"Did Bess come too?" Connie looked past Cody to see if she was there.

"No, she's at home. I was on my way to the station to get some paperwork done but somehow I ended up here," Cody said. "What's going on?"

"Bennett Godfrey called for Sami. Princess is in some kind of trouble and wants Sami," Connie said.

"Bennett Godfrey is back? Do you think Adam wanted me to know this? Do you think he brought me here?" Cody said.

"I'm not sure he did," Sami said quietly. "I'm not sure of anything."

"Sami are you okay?" Cody walked past Connie into the room. Her twin looked terrible. She had aged well beyond her years since he saw her a few hours earlier. "What happened?"

Sami waved her hand in an act of dismissal. "They besieged me. I've never been besieged like this before. When the souls of the dead talk, it's normally one voice maybe two at a time not a screaming multitude. It was too much. My brain just shut down. Thank God, the noise has stopped for the moment."

"What were they saying?" Cody asked.

"It was such a mish mash. But the gist of what I think I heard was there is something else going on here. Something far more evil than we can possibly imagine." Sami let the last few words trail off. She stared straight ahead. It was several moments before she resumed. She shook her head slightly. "That's all I was able to glean from the dead," she said.

"Did any of the voices talk directly about the Godfreys?" Cody asked.

"No, not directly. Speaking of which, I guess we better go see what's going on with Princess." Sami said. "It might not be a good idea if you go with us, Cody. As a detective, you might put a damper on the conversation."

"Agreed," he said. "I will be going out to Pinehurst in official capacity anyway in a day or two. Caroline Godfrey's murder investigation is still ongoing. But call me the minute you're done."

Cody was almost to the door when his cell phone rang.

"Davis, here," he answered. "Really? Where? Got it. I'll be there as soon as I can." He ended the call. Without turning around he said, "Katy St. Clair just called 911. She found her mother outside on the ground, dead."

"Oh my God, that poor child," Connie said.

Cody slowly turned around. "The 911 operator said the phone cut off when the girl was talking, but before it did, she said she heard a dog barking."

"Didn't Katy's mom say their dog was missing?" Connie said.

"I got the impression she thought it was dead," said Sami.

"Me, too," said Cody. "I guess I better go. Be careful ladies. Watch your back. I don't trust the Godfreys."

Connie and Sami nodded. They watched the detective leave.

"Oh, that poor child. I hope she has family close by," Connie said.

"No, actually she is all alone now," Sami paused. She heard a new voice. "Her mother says her father was killed in a freak accident when she was born. Mrs. St. Clair says Katy is in danger. I have to tell, Cody." Sami rushed out of the motel room door only to find Cody was already gone. When she returned, she grabbed her purse and jacket.

"Come on, we need to go to the St. Clair place. I'll talk to Cody out there. Call Bess, she has to be out there, too. I don't know why, but Adam says Cody will need her. Come on, come on we have to go," she repeatedly waved her arms to emphasize the urgency.

"What about Princess?" Connie said juggling the phone and her purse at the same time.

"She will have to wait," Sami rushed ahead of her sister.

Connie did her best to follow her.

"Come on," Sami snapped her fingers to empathize the urgency.

"I'm hurrying," Connie yelled back. As she was locking the motel room door, she saw someone moving out of the corner of her eye. A hunched figure of a man was walking towards her. Something about his presence made Connie feel uncomfortable. That slight uncomfortable feeling turned into an intense sense of fear as his slow steady footsteps approached. The sound propelled Connie. She fussed with the door. The key refused to turn. Connie struggled with the lock while she listened to the approaching man's footfall. Panic welled up in her throat. Finally, the key moved. She breathed a sigh of relief. It was then she noticed the silence. A quick glance towards the approaching stranger produced an empty sidewalk.

"Good, he's gone." She relaxed. "You're letting your imagination run away with you," she admonished herself. She threw her keys in her purse. When she turned towards the parking lot, a pair of icy hands grabbed her around the neck. The cold fingers tightened like a hangman's noose.

"Sami…" she uttered in a strangled whisper. The fingers pressed their murderous grip harder. Connie fought her unknown assailant.

At the end of a distant row of cars, Sami felt a tingling sensation rush through her body. *Strange,* she thought. "Hey, Connie do you feel…" she thought her sister was right over her shoulder. When she realized she wasn't there, Sami looked towards their motel room door. Connie was all alone on the sidewalk in a violent struggle against some unseen force. With one hand, she was scratching her neck. The other was reaching for something behind her. Her sister was in serious trouble.

"Connie!" Sami screamed racing towards her. "Stop, make it stop." She screamed at the multitude of voices bombarding her brain. "Rachel, Adam, do something. Make it stop!"

Sami reached her sister in time to see Connie's eyes roll back into her head. She caught her as she fell.

Curious motel dwellers hearing Sami's screams opened their doors. Some rushed to help the stricken woman.

"What's wrong?" A man yelled.

"I think the woman is having a heart attack," another man yelled back.

"She's turning blue. She's choking," another yelled.

"Call 911," a woman urged.

More people came out of their rooms. The crowd swelled. Their loud conversations made it impossible for the voices of the dead to reach Sami. She extended her arms in an attempt to keep people back from her struggling sister.

"Connie, what's wrong?" she cried. A voice entered her head. She didn't recognize it.

Stay away. This is a warning, the voice threatened.

Sami felt an intense cold surround her. She closed her eyes. The souls of the dead were silent.

"Stay away from whom?" She whispered.

She heard Connie gasp. The pale blue around her lips faded into a more normal pink. She took several more breaths. Her eyes blinked several times. The large group of strangers hovering above her bewildered her at first, but she managed a feeble smile. She smiled again when she recognized Sami. Sami smiled back and patted her sister's shoulder.

"I'm so glad you're okay," she said letting relief cascade over her.

Connie nodded and with Sami's help sat up.

"What happened, Connie? Can you tell me?

"There was a man, a crooked man. I couldn't see him very well but he frightened me. I thought he was gone. I finished locking the door then cold fingers wrapped around my throat. That's all I remember until I saw you." Connie smiled weakly at her sister.

Sami smiled back. Then, it disappeared quickly.

"What's wrong, Sami? First you, then me." Connie noticed the change in her demeanor. "Can the dead tell us who is doing this?"

A lone voice had entered Sami's head. He was laughing maliciously.

Chapter 17

"What's up?" Cody asked the lone police officer kneeling over the body.

"Looks like a possible heart attack or something. There were no marks on her body or anything." The officer said scribbling in a small notebook.

"Where's her daughter?" Cody asked.

"She's in the squad car," The officer nodded to a vehicle parked near a large tree.

"I hope she's not alone…?" Cody let his words trail off. A quick glance at the distant cruiser answered his question. He could see more than one person in the car. He was about to ask the officer who was with the young girl, when he realized the man was gone. It surprised him the officer could walk away so quickly and so quietly.

Man, where'd he go so fast, he thought. He shrugged off his misgivings and headed towards the vehicle.

The past several days had taught him to expect the odd occurrence or two. When they happened, he had to move on immediately. Right now, he was focused on Katy in the back seat of the squad car. The sun was below the ring of trees surrounding him. Its demise allowed long shadows to blanket the cruiser. Still, he could see the head of a woman in front of Katy in the front seat. He could also see the head of a black and white dog next to Katy.

That must be Gypsy, her missing dog, he mused. He walked up to the passenger window and rapped on the glass. The woman jumped at the noise.

"You doing okay?" he asked but he received a shock when the woman turned around. "What…hey, why didn't anyone tell me you were here?"

Bess shrugged. She gave him a sorrowful look. Cody pulled the door open. He bent over to look at Katy. The young girl had her chin on her chest weeping softly. The seat next to her was empty. Cody immediately stood up and looked around the car.

"Where's the dog?" he asked.

"What dog?" Bess answered.

"The dog I saw sitting next to Katy just a moment ago," Cody looked over the top of the cruiser.

Bess gave him a strange look and didn't answer. Cody bent down. He looked at Katy again. She was still weeping but she turned her head just enough for him to see a slight, unnerving smile.

"Bess get out of the car," Cody demanded.

"What's the matter? What's wrong with you?" Bess exclaimed.

"Bess, you need to get out of that car now!" Without waiting for Bess to say anymore, he reached in and tried pulling her out by the hand.

"What's wrong with you? I told you before, I'm not Bess!" the police woman exclaimed pulling her hand out of his.

Cody stepped back. He looked at the woman in front of him. "How could you…you looked like…I mean…shit." He was flabbergasted at the sight of a policewoman rather than his wife.

"Katy?" he said ignoring the glowering police woman in front of him. He looked inside the car again. It was empty.

"Katy! Where is she? Where did she go? What the hell is going on?" Cody screamed. The police woman ignored his outburst while quietly writing down notes on a piece of paper attached to a clipboard. She acted like he wasn't even there.

Cody stepped away from the car. He scanned the yard around him. About fifty yards away, right at the edge of the woods, he saw the black and white dog and Katy. Cody slammed the car door and took off running towards them.

Brian heard a car door slam and looked up in time to see his partner running towards the woods. He put his notepad in his pants pocket.

"Hey, when did he get here? Where's he going? Cody's on to something. You and you come with me." Brian pointed to two officers standing nearby.

"Let's go and be prepared." Brian warned as he drew his gun before sprinting to the trees himself. In a few moments, he had broached the tree line. He slowed his pace down to a quick walk. Brian lowered his gun motioning to the other officers to do the same, but he remained prepared to use it. The dense New England forest coupled with the many twists and turns the path took plus the rapidly setting sun made it difficult for Brian to see too far ahead. The lack of visibility made him nervous and more cautious.

It wasn't long however, before he saw his partner standing in the middle of the path with his feet squared and his arms up.

He's drawn his gun. He's got something, Brian realized. "I'm coming up behind you, Cody," he said softly.

Cody didn't answer. Brian moved slowly towards him. He was amazed at what he saw when he reached his partner's shoulder. "Cody, lower your gun. You're scaring her." He looked at a cowering Katy St. Clair trembling in front of them. "Hey, looks like her dog came home. Cody, Cody…?"

Cody didn't move. Brian glanced at his face. Sweat was slowly dripping down his partner's forehead into his eyes although Cody didn't seem to notice nor did he blink.

"Cody, I said lower your weapon. It's Katy." When he still didn't move, Brian reached up and gently tapped his arm. His touch broke his partner's trance. Cody blinked several times then looked at Brian as if for the first time. He blinked again before returning his gaze to Katy and her dog.

"Katy, speak to me. Tell me you're really Katy," Cody's voice trembled.

"What are you nuts?" Brian looked at him in disbelief. "Of course it's Katy. Lower your weapon, man. We've been looking for her since we got here."

Cody swallowed then gasped. "What? One of your men told me she was in the car." He claimed still pointing his gun at the girl.

"Cody, what are you talking about? Listen to me, lower your gun," Brian insisted in a stern, quiet voice. He motioned for the officers behind him to come closer then stopped them when they were about an arm's length away.

"I'm Katy," Katy whimpered. "Malsumis is tricking you."

When he heard the name Malsumis, Cody blinked several more times. He looked at Brian then back at the frightened girl. It was several more moments before he lowered his gun. "Oh my God, the trickster. Katy? I'm so sorry." He motioned for the young girl to come to him.

She hesitated at first, then ran into Cody's arms sobbing uncontrollably.

"I'm so sorry," he said again. He had no energy left. His arms fell limp to his sides. It all seemed so real. *What if I had pulled the trigger,* he let the seriousness of the moment sink in. He looked at his partner helplessly.

"Sorry, man," he said. Katy clung to him. "I'm so sorry, Katy," he said slowly letting his left arm wrap around her to console her. Her dog, Gypsy was busy circling the three of them wagging her tail in happiness.

Brian put his gun in his shoulder holster and ran his hands through his hair. "I gotta tell you, you scared the hell out of me. What was that all about? What's a Malsumis?"

"I'll try to explain this all to you later, Brian but for now, would you mind calling my wife and asking her to come out here?"

"Yeah, but I want an explanation or I'm telling the Captain what happened here. You scared the shit out of me." Brian shoved his pistol into its holster before he stormed away taking the two police officers with him.

Cody with his arm still around Katy began walking out of the woods. "Katy, would you like to come home with me?" Cody asked although he already knew the answer. "Bess makes a mean apple pie." He added to lighten the mood.

"Okay," she said softly. "Can Gypsy come, too?"

"Sure, why not. Come on down, Gypsy," he said. The dog woofed it's approval. Daylight was all but gone. A dim grey aura remained.

"Let's go home," Cody gave Katy's shoulder a quick squeeze. They were almost at the end of the path, when a bitterly cold breeze whirled around them. Gypsy yelped and charged ahead into the back yard. Her tail tucked securely between her legs. Cody glanced over his shoulder. He could see nothing behind them. The cold breeze slapped the two of them in the back once more. The darkness rapidly descended. Cody hoped they would reach the backyard before all the remaining light disappeared.

"Sun sure is going down fast," he said for want of something better to say.

Katy stiffened when another gust hit her. "It's angry," she said.

"Malsumis is angry?" Cody asked.

Katy looked up at him with the most worried expression but didn't answer.

"Okay, let's move it." Cody tightened his grip on the young girl. It suddenly became imperative to get the hell out of the trees. Then he felt it. The same kind of urge that propelled him to the motel. The same irresistible urge that made his look at Simon's head again. He looked back one more time and when he did, he was shocked to see the dark shape of a man. A bent, crooked man.

"Walk faster, Katy." He said forcing her forward until they came to the edge of the woods. Gypsy was waiting for her at the end of the path. Cody took Katy by her shoulders and looked directly into her eyes. He had to make sure she heard what he was about to say.

"Take Gypsy over to Officer Smith and wait for me," Cody said pointing to his partner next to the cruiser. "Don't look back."

Katy nodded. "Come on Gypsy," she said. The dog happily followed behind the running girl. Cody turned around and looked into the trees. Whatever or whomever he saw was no longer there.

"So where'd you go," he retraced his steps. A familiar voice stopped him before he could enter the trees. He felt his knees weaken.

"Adam?" He said softly.

Stop. It's a trap. The voice warned.

"What does he want, Adam?" Cody asked.

What he always wants, Adam answered.

"And what is that exactly?" Cody asked again.

A life, came the answer.

Cody peered into the now dark woods. "You can't have her, you son-of-a-bitch. Not now, not ever."

A stronger, much colder gust of wind met him this time. It didn't faze him. Instead, Cody merely turned around and walked away. As he walked, he lifted his right hand and gave the woods behind him the finger. "Yeah, you too, buddy."

Chapter 18

Bennett Godfrey waited until his mother fell into a paralyzed sleep. When her breathing became relaxed and steady, he gently lifted her into his arms. It surprised him how light she felt as he carried her up the grand staircase to her room.

Nothing but bones and flesh, he thought. Guilt tapped at his conscience which he quickly brushed it aside.

Sorry, Mother, he apologized silently. *I guess I wasn't a very good son.*

He ruefully noted the elaborately carved banister. It ascended majestically to the second floor. Every day it was polished meticulously by the servants to Princess' precise instructions. Many times in the past, the family pleaded with his mother to install a lift to carry her up the steps. She adamantly refused. She couldn't stand the thought that some kind of mechanical contraption would be physically attached to that magnificent balustrade. It was sacrilege to even consider it. No amount of arguing could convince her it was for her own good.

"Maybe a good spill down the staircase would change the old bitch's mind," R. P., his older brother declared after a particularly nasty discussion with Princess. "Maybe it would knock some sense into her."

It struck Bennett that he didn't understand his brother's comment then or now. He never heard of his mother falling down the staircase whether by accident or otherwise. The idea seemed inconceivable, but he knew his family was good at keeping secrets, especially dark secrets. He meant to ask Ronald about that one of these days. The old butler was a wealth of information particularly after a few glasses of Sherry. Bennett reached the top step and found himself somewhat out of breath.

Stubborn old woman, he thought. *I don't know how you manage that climb everyday Mother. R. P. was right, a lift would definitely help you.* His brother's cryptic comment crossed his mind again.

The master bedroom was situated at the end of the East wing. Five other bedrooms each with their own bath, and a small library completed the floor plan. Only his parents and occasional guests inhabited this wing of the mansion. Its rich Victorian trappings virtually unchanged since their installation.

The opposite side, the west wing was reserved for the children. It boasted six bedrooms and baths, a playroom, a classroom and a room for the governess. That end of the mansion always seemed to be in a state of decorating flux depending on the whims of the current generation. The east wing remained constant. Its splendor untouched and revered. As Bennett walked, he felt as awestruck now as he did as a child. A deep red carpet with its fussy ornate pattern stretched the depth and width of the hall. Dark mahogany panels covered with period art work adorned the walls. A Renoir here, Rembrandt there and in their only nod to an American painter, a lone Childe Hassam was hung next to the door to the library. The hallway spoke of the wealth, taste and breeding of the Godfrey family. Bennett found it to be the most suffocating part of the house.

The door to the master bedroom stood open in anticipation of their arrival. A faint scent of lilac from his mother's favorite perfume was in the air. Ronald had performed his magic once again. Bennett marveled at the butler's quickness and stealth. It took him five minutes to carry his mother upstairs and in that time, Ronald managed to do what he did and leave. Bennett truly believed as a child that the servants were ghosts. They appeared and disappeared at will. He was almost eight years old when R. P. showed him a secret panel near the master bedroom. This panel opened to a small narrow staircase that allowed the servants to attend to the family's needs silently and unseen. It became Bennett's favorite hiding place.

Princess's bed was already turned down and waiting. Bennett gently placed her in the center of the huge four-poster. Her thin frame barely sank into the soft mattress. Ronald appeared at the doorway and stood waiting for instructions.

"I'm going to the cellar, Ronald. If mother wakes up or Sami Howell arrives, call me," he handed the butler a cell phone. Then as an afterthought, "Don't wait for me, if you need to call 911," he added with a nod at his sleeping mother. Ronald acknowledged him solemnly.

Bennett kissed Princess on her forehead. "I'm going to see R. P. and free Elodie." He said then paused to see if his announcement would arouse her. Nothing changed. A sigh of resignation escaped him. He secretly hoped she would suddenly rise up and stop him. With a slight nod, Bennett left the bedroom leaving Ronald in charge.

At the sound of the closing door, Princess' eyes flew open. She looked around until her gaze came to rest on the butler. A small, knowing smile creased her face.

Chapter 19

"Rich assholes," Harry Cooper said out loud once the servant was out of range. The sting of his dismissal from the mansion gnawed at him. None of his plans had gone the way he wanted since his arrival in Temple Falls. It was as if someone was always two steps ahead of him thwarting his every move. Harry pulled a small picture out of his wallet. He gazed lovingly at the image of a young woman in her bridal gown.

"I told you, Sis. I told you there was something rotten about these people. You wouldn't listen. But I promise you I will find out who killed you and they *will* pay. As God is my witness, they will pay."

He looked back through the gates at the enormous stone mansion. He was only ten when his older sister married into the Godfrey family. Then she slowly disappeared from his life. Every so often he would receive a note or a little gift Caroline picked up on one of her many travels, but he never saw her again. The joy his mother expressed at her daughter's good fortune turned to abject grief when contact with the family dwindled, then disappeared not long after the wedding. Harry looked down the expansive driveway. This was only the second time he had been on the Godfrey property. The first was during Caroline's wedding reception.

That day was indelibly etched in his mind. An enormous white tent had been erected near the garden behind the mansion. Its bright white color was in stark contrast to the emerald green lawn and dark forest that lay beyond. He remembered how insignificant and irrelevant he felt during the wedding ceremony and the party that followed. Harry only managed to talk to his sister briefly during the reception before she was whisked away. If he had known then that he would never see her again, he would have never left her side that night. Now all Harry had was the memory of his beautiful sister in her magnificent wedding gown.

Harry pulled a notebook out of his briefcase to jot down some thoughts. He wasn't about to give up the idea of interviewing the Godfrey family. If anything, he was more determined than ever to find another way to gain their confidence. Harry paused in his writing. His stay in Temple Falls so far had been frustrating at every turn. First the mayor stood him up, then he was abruptly dismissed by Princess before he could ask a single question. He glanced at the almost bare page in front of him.

Several early mornings eating breakfast at the Maple Leaf Café with some of the locals produced a few interesting notes but nothing substantial. Harry chuckled at the memory. It didn't take much prodding to get the old timers to gossip. They loved gossiping although Harry noticed that the Godfrey name never came up directly. Instead, they were called the "family" or just "them". Even that inference caused a ripple of concern amongst the group. To talk about "them" outright produced a distinct chill in the air. As if the mere mention of their name invited calamity to fall on one's family or person. He could sense the group's fear.

Harry snapped his notebook closed. With a quick toss, he threw it back into his briefcase. He noticed the small recorder thrown hastily inside earlier. He pulled it out and laid it on the seat next to him. He tapped the play button.

"That's funny." He heard nothing on the recorder. "I could have sworn it picked up some of the conversation." Disgusted, he returned the recorder to the briefcase.

In the end, his multiple conversations at the café were titillating but lacked substance. He wanted proof. He *needed* proof that the Godfreys were responsible for his sister's death. Only then would he be able to move on with his life. Harry let out a sigh. Money was beginning to run low. He glanced at the gas gauge.

Half a tank, he thought. *At least I don't have to worry about that for a while.* He put the car in gear and pulled away from the main gate.

The sunlight was all but gone. The dark veil of night had descended. The several miles he needed to travel from the Godfrey estate to town went directly through the dense forest of the Temple Falls Reservation. The road itself was barely two car widths wide. The hilly, serpentine course was treacherous even in broad daylight. Now driving under the claustrophobic canopy of trees, Harry anxiously leaned forward trying to see just a little better. Even on high beam, the headlights did little good. His limited view of the road was confined to a narrow band of light.

"Damn, it sure is dark. Is it going to rain, or what?" He rolled his window down part way. The scent of rain was definitely in the air. However, there was no wind shaking the trees that foretold of a coming storm. Harry put the window back up. He was tense and uncomfortable.

It wasn't only the drive that was making him anxious. A singular thought that he might have been recognized nagged him.

"There's no way that old man knew who I was," he said aloud. Yet, he couldn't quite dismiss his apprehension. "I'm probably imagining things." And with that declaration he pushed his aging car a little faster down the road.

Ronald's glimmer of recognition had been fleeting and quite by chance. Had it not been for one well-place mirror, Harry might not have seen it at all. It shook his composure for a mere millisecond at the time. Now the memory behaved like an annoying fly he wished he could eliminate with a commanding swat.

"Shit." His assumption had been correct. An intense rain shower began pelting his car. The ferocity of the sudden storm surprised him. Leaves and small limbs dropped onto the hood. Within a matter of minutes, visibility was reduced to zero. Harry slowed his car down to a crawl then he stopped completely. His world was enveloped in an impenetrable shroud of black.

A fearful tingling at the back of his neck sent a shock wave through him. "Calm down, Harry. It's just rain. There's no boogeyman in the woods." He murmured. Fog covered the windshield. He strained to see beyond the blackness. The tingling sensation refused to abate.

Then a noise other than rain startled him. It took him a moment to realize that the sound was coming from his briefcase. He felt his heart plunge. The sound was coming from the small recorder.

. "That's impossible," he whispered. He lifted the recorder out. The instrument was definitely on. "It couldn't have been...." Before he was able to finish his thought, a man's voice coming from the recorder could be heard laughing. Harry threw it down on the floor as if it was on fire.

Suddenly, a hunched figure dashed in front of his headlights and disappeared to his left.

"Whoa. What the hell?"

It happened so quickly. Harry wasn't quite sure what he actually had seen. Now he knew not to dismiss the warning his body was urgently delivering. Without another glance, he stepped on the accelerator. The car lurched forward just as another figure dashed in front. The sickening sound of an impact sent a horrifying chill through him.

"God damn it," he watched helplessly as the body fell away from the car. It lay motionless in glow of the headlights. Harry told himself to get out and see who he hit, but his body refused to budge. The tingling sensation at the back of his neck was racing up and down his spine. His "inner alarm" as he called it came upon him only when he was in extreme danger; a premonition of sorts that saved him more than once in the past. It was screaming at him to go.

The windshield wipers were overwhelmed and useless. His rapid breathing created an even thicker layer of fog on every window. Harry reached forward and wiped a small hole.

"Shit." The body wasn't moving. He could see the soles of two shoes and nothing more.

"Women's shoes," He noted. Still, he couldn't bring himself to get out of the car. Finally, he put it into reverse and backed up several feet until the soles of the shoes were out of the headlights. When he put the car in forward gear, he heard a soft thump on the trunk. His eyes flew to the rearview mirror. Harry swallowed hard. His eyes flicked from the side mirror to the rearview mirror in rapid succession.

"Shit, did I hit someone else?" His neck felt achy and stiff. He didn't know whether to drive forward or backwards. Then a sound riveted his attention. Someone was tapping slowly on the trunk of the car.

"What do you want?" Harry screamed. The tapping stopped briefly then resumed as a loud pounding. They were beating on his car. It was the push he needed. Harry stepped on the accelerator. The car jumped into action.

He did nothing to slow down or stop its forward motion. Body or no body, he was getting the hell out of there. Fear propelled him recklessly down the road. He was almost to town when it dawned on him that he never ran over or passed the body. Relief coursed through him.

"Temple Falls, Vermont. Population 5,200," Harry read on the passing road sign. The tingling sensation was gone.

Chapter 20

"**A**re you crazy? You could have been killed." Bennett bent over and helped his daughter. The steady downpour continued with a vengeance. If there had been more time, he would have dressed more appropriately. He shrugged off the chill numbing his body.

Why did I bother to come home? Nothing ever changes, he thought.

His impromptu trip to see his older brother and release his daughter from captivity went instantly awry the moment his feet touched the cellar floor. The dank confines of the lowest portion of the house reeked of human waste. There was also an unfamiliar foul smell he couldn't make out. When Bennett turned on the single overhead light, rats rummaging through the remnants of leftover meals scurried out of view. Only their telltale feces remained as evidence of their encroachment.

In any of the other older houses in Temple Falls, this room was used to store perishables but not in the Godfrey home. This was the room where the condemned Godfrey men spent the latter part of their lives. Old decrepit furniture and an even older television set lined the walls. A tattered braided rug covered the uneven stone floor.

"Discarded furniture for discarded lives," he sighed at the sight.

Two halls intersected the room. One led to a series of small rooms and the other was a tunnel to a door leading to the outside. Bennett turned towards the left hall leading to the small rooms. Ugly memories of a single forced confinement as a child overwhelmed him. Each heavy door was equipped with an enormous bolting mechanism securely locking a person within the confines of a windowless room. Only a light switch placed outside every door adorned the hallway walls.

Elodie's room or "cell" as Bennett preferred to call them was at the end of the hall. Her door stood open. Each step he took towards that open door catapulted his mind back to that one dreadful childhood memory.

It was a punishment for some minor infraction. After his father beat him with a belt, he then sentenced him to spend a night in prison. Bennett thought he was banished to his own bedroom, but when his father descended the stairs to the cellar, he realized his fate. He was being taken to hell. Hell, in the dark, dank bowels of the house. The room, R. P. had spent untold hours deliberately scaring him with stories; stories of ghosts and demons waiting for their next victim to arrive. There was no place on earth scarier to the young boy.

"Quit crying Bennett, or I'm turning off the lights," his father had said dragging his son downwards.

Bennett couldn't stop. So his father followed through with his threat and left him in that dark room, now Elodie's room without so much as a glance backwards. Bennett believed his life was over. He fainted.

Hours later, he remembered waking up to a room illuminated by a single overhead bulb. He was tucked into the small bed between two crisp sheets and a mound of gray blankets. A glass of milk and a plate of cookies sat on the bedside table. The only other piece of furniture in the room was a simple wooden chair left a few feet from his bed. The naked, dark gray stone walls smelled old and musty. A locked door stood between him and the rest of the world. The Godfrey's own private prison with an inmate of one young boy: Bennett.

He remained in that room for what he thought was an eternity until Ronald, the butler, set him free. Then he fled vowing never to set foot there again, an unbroken vow until now. The fact he survived his imprisonment in spite of R.P.'s dire warnings gave Bennett a newfound inner strength. Years later, he couldn't help but wonder if that had been the real reason his father punished him that way; a shock treatment or sorts to toughen up his youngest son. It was a question he never asked and an explanation his father never offered.

Bennett stepped into the room of his childhood nightmare. Its chaotic appearance alarmed him. Dirty clothes, plates and rumpled empty packages of chips covered the floor and bedside table. An assortment of eye shadow and lipsticks were strewn across the top of the bureau. Bennett picked up a hair extension laying on top of unopened makeup boxes.

"Elodie must be trying a new look?" he muttered. He tossed the hair extension back and turned away from the bureau. He studied the rest of the room. The blankets and sheets were pulled off the mattress. They lay at the foot of the bed. The mattress was askew. The disheveled room gave the appearance that someone was looking for something. He wondered where Elodie was. Bennett stepped into the hall.

A cold draft of air touched him.

The tunnel door must be open.

When the mansion was built, a small earthen tunnel leading from the cellar to the grounds outside was added. His mother told him it was designed for the gardeners to bring the food inside without tramping through the house. It wasn't until he was older that Bennett realized there may have been a far more sinister purpose for its construction.

An entrance or escape route for the damned, was his conclusion.

He hesitated at the mouth of the tunnel. The air streaming in was cold and a scent of rain was evident. He wasn't dressed for either eventuality. He contemplated going upstairs for a raincoat when he noticed a large flashlight with a thin jacket strategically placed on the sofa.

Odd, I don't remember that being there before, he thought.

Another blast of cold air interrupted his thought. He wasn't going to worry about that now. It was time to go.

Bennett picked up the flashlight and before donning the jacket he gave it a good shaking. Rats were nasty creatures in his mind. In any other instance, he would never have worn a jacket he thought a rat might have touched without thoroughly washing it first. He pushed the possibility of contacting some kind of disease out of his mind and pulled the garment on. He flicked the flashlight on several times to make sure it worked then proceeded to the tunnel door.

A deluge greeted him outside. It shocked him.

"Damn," he cursed. He could have left the jacket on the couch for what little protection it offered. By the time he found Elodie sprawled on the road, his assumption was correct: he was soaked.

"Are you hurt?" Bennett wrapped his arms around her. Elodie shoved her father away.

"What do you care?" She said angrily.

Bennett anticipated his daughter's rejection. He couldn't remember the last time he saw her. Guilt visited him again.

"I'm sorry. I know I deserve that. What's going on? What are you doing out here in the rain?"

Elodie didn't immediately respond to her father's query.

"Give me that." She snapped snatching the flashlight out of his hands.

Bennett was left standing in pitch blackness. "What are you looking for?"

"My flashlight," came her curt reply.

"I saw your room, did R. P. do that?" Bennett asked again.

"There it is," Elodie rejoiced ignoring his question.

A second beam joined the first.

"Here," she said shoving the first flashlight back into his hands.

Bennett reached out and grabbed his daughter's arm. The rain coupled with the exceptional darkness surrounding them made Bennett feel too exposed, vulnerable. To what exactly he wasn't sure but a nagging sense of uneasiness had followed him since he left the tunnel door.

"Answer my question," He demanded.

Elodie tried to pull her arm away from her father's tight grasp.

"Uncle R. P., he's crazy. He tried to kill me." Her voiced trembled.

"My brother tried to kill you?"

"Did I stutter?" She answered rudely.

Bennett gave his daughter's arm a jerk forcing her to walk with him.

"Why would R. P. want to kill you?"

"She has something I want," a raspy voice answered.

The man's voice elicited a scream from Elodie.

"R. P., is that you?" Bennett swung his flashlight back and forth but saw no one.

Bennett felt Elodie step behind him. She put her hand on her father's arm and held it tightly. She was absolutely terrified.

"R.P.?"

"The prodigal son returns. Your turn is next," replied the voice a little louder and closer.

Bennett and Elodie both jumped simultaneously. Bennett moved his flashlight around again until it located a hunched figure standing a short distance from the two of them. A familiar rotting smell assaulted his nose. It was the same smell he couldn't account for in the cellar. He took a step backwards. He pointed his light towards the stench. Bennett couldn't suppress the gasp that escaped his lips.

"Oh my God, R.P., is that really you?"

A wail emanated from the exposed man. It was the most anguished, agonizing sound. Bennett reached out to console his brother. His hand met no resistance. His brother wasn't there.

"R. P.? Where are you?" he asked fanning the air with his outstretched hand.

The rotting smell hit his senses with full force just as the man lunged forward. Unable to stop his backward fall, Bennett let go of the flashlight and grabbed at the foul smelling hands wrapped around his neck.

"R.P., no…" The hands tightened.

"Stop, let him go," screamed Elodie.

The two men struggled violently by the edge of the road. Elodie danced on the periphery searching for a way to separate them. She strained to see what was going on in the abject darkness. The small circle of light emanating from her flashlight was useless. She tried her best to follow the struggle anyway. When the two men rolled to the right forcing Elodie to jump out of the way, she felt her foot dislodge a large rock jutting out of the ground. She bent down and picked it up. She juggled it along with her flashlight waiting for the right moment to land a blow.

"Uncle R. P., stop," she screamed holding the weapon over her head. The two men continued their struggle until Elodie saw her uncle roll over and sit on her father's chest. His hands still wrapped around Bennett's throat.

"Stop Uncle R. P. or I'm going to hit you," she screamed.

A burst of wind blew towards her at that particular moment. Its coldness shocked her and she was no match for its powerful push. She narrowly missed falling on another large rock when she tumbled down. She kept the flashlight clenched in her hand. She wasn't going to let it go no matter how hard she landed, but the rock tumbled away into the darkness. She heard someone running away..

"Daddy, are you okay? She said regaining her footing. She pointed her light at the side of the road. Her uncle was gone.

"Daddy," she called.

The silence was deafening.

"Daddy," she cried when her flashlight exposed his still body.

A moan followed by several coughs greeted her ears. Elodie rushed to her father's side. The rotting smell from her uncle's touch lingered in the air around them.

"Daddy, say something. Are you all right?"

Pelting rain renewed its assault adding more misery to their plight. Elodie put the light directly into her father's face. He squinted against the glare. She breathed a sigh of relief. At least he wasn't dead.

"Come on, let's get out of here." She jerked his arm.

It took several tugs before her father sat up. It took several more to get him on his feet.

"Dad, we can't stay here. We've got to go." She urged.

Not much in this world truly frightened Elodie. The family considered her their resident daredevil. She rarely back down from a challenge or a dare. But tonight it was too dark, too miserable and something else was in the woods. She could sense it.

"Daddy, please we *have* to get out of here." She tugged on his arm more forcefully this time. "Here lean on me," she urged.

"I'm okay," Bennett replied weakly. "Where's my flashlight?"

Elodie swung her light up and down the road. She did not see it.

"I think we better find the light tomorrow. Let's go." A strong breeze made the cold rain slap against her face. It also brought with it that nasty rotting odor.

"You're right," Bennett conceded.

He smells it, too, she thought

They fell in step side by side. "I wish we were a little closer to the house." Elodie said pulling her wet jacket a little tighter.

"I'd suggest going back through the tunnel but I don't think I want to meet up with R.P. just yet." Bennett said rubbing his throat. "How long has he been like this?"

Elodie picked up her pace to match her father's long stride

"I'm not sure. I didn't see him that often until *your* mother locked me in the cellar. I think he tried getting into my cell several times but Ronald made him go away."

"Ronald? Why would R.P. listen to him?" Her comment puzzled him.

Elodie gripped her father's arm a little tighter.

"I don't know Dad? I think the other night Uncle R. P. brought a woman into the cellar. I don't know who she was but I think he did something awful. I could hear her screaming for the longest time. Then I heard Grandmother yelling at Uncle R. P. Right after that Ronald came into my room with some hot tea. He said I *had* to drink it. He even stood there until I did. I don't remember anything more. I woke up the next morning."

"Who let you out of your room?" Bennett stopped her before she could answer. "Did you hear that?"

"No, hear what?" Elodie's eyes searched in the darkness but to no avail.

"I hear voices."

"Oh great, now you hear voices." She said sarcastically.

"It's coming from over there," he whispered ignoring her sarcasm. He touched her arm pulling her to the right.

"I don't want to go, Daddy. Come on let's get out of here," she cried.

The rain came down harder.

"Please let's go back to the house," she pleaded.

"I think the voices came from…do you hear that?" Bennett said again. "It sounds like a girl crying. I think it's coming from over there."

Bennett moved towards the sound coming from across the road. Elodie refused.

"Daddy, please. You can't help her," she pleaded.

He stopped. "I can't leave whoever it is out there. I have to help."

Elodie pulled him back preventing him from walking forward again. Bennett persisted. He took her flashlight.

"Stay behind me."

Elodie grabbed the bottom of her father's jacket. Something inside her told her not to let go. Bennett pointed the flashlight into the trees ahead.

"There must be a path around here somewhere. Ah, there it is." He said pointing his light towards a narrow dirt strip between the trees. He put his hand on his daughter's and gave it a squeeze. It was ice cold. "Come on."

They were twenty feet from their starting point when the rain came down again in torrents. The dense trees did little to break the rain's fall. It was impossible to see more than a few feet ahead.

Bennett and Elodie stopped. Her father shook his head. It was impossible to go any further. He turned around and pushed Elodie towards the road. She wasted no time leaving. In a few moments, they were back where they started.

"Do I hear a car?" Bennett said in disbelief.

"Thank, God. Who would be coming out here at this hour?" Elodie said.

Before Bennett could answer, lights from an approaching vehicle rounded the curve. It was moving slowly giving the impression the driver was looking for something or someone. Elodie and Bennett crossed the road. They stepped off the pavement onto the narrow shoulder. Even if they wanted, they could go no further. A steep embankment was at their back. The relentless downpour prevented a quick getaway anyway. The car slowed in its approach then it stopped altogether. A door opened.

"Can we be of help?" A woman's voice called.

The sound of a window rolling down came next.

"Miss Elodie and Mr. Godfrey, I think you need to get in, now," another woman's voice called.

"How did you know…?"

"It doesn't matter, dear. Time is of the essence. I think you know what I mean," the woman said again.

Bennett took Elodie's arm. "It's okay, come on."

He put his hand on the small of Elodie's back and pushed her slightly towards the awaiting car. The back door was already open. Bennett let her climb in first. Two elderly and remarkably similar women were in the front seat. Bennett hurriedly closed the door. He snapped on his seatbelt then leaned back against the seat.

"I wondered how long it was going to take before you found me."

"You certainly didn't make it easy," the woman on the right retorted.

"Do you two know each other?" Elodie asked.

"Well, yes and no. We've communicated in the past, yet we've never actually met face to face," said Bennett. "Elodie, this is Sami Howell and her sister, Connie Plimpton."

"Mayor Plimpton's wife?"

"Widow, I'm afraid but yes," said Connie.

"I think we should move on, Sis," Sami urged with a wave of her hand. "We can talk later."

Connie stepped on the accelerator making the car tires slip slightly on the wet pavement.

"Let's not skid off into the trees, please." Sami chided.

"Well, you said to move." The two sisters began quibbling back and forth as siblings are apt to do. Elodie listened in amusement to their banter. It brought back fond memories of a time when she and Dani actually got along.

"You know your sister does love you," Sami said.

Elodie didn't respond right away. Sami's declaration caught her off guard. "Can you read my…"

Bennett let out a chuckle. "Oh, it's going to be interesting when we get home. Who is talking to you today, Sami?"

Sami didn't answer Bennett right away.

When he didn't get a response, Bennett leaned forward and put his hands on the headrest in front of him. "Who is talking to you?"

"Giselle," Sami said softly.

"Mother, *my* Mother?" Elodie exclaimed. "How can that be? She's dead!"

Bennett sat back again. "I'm not surprised. She's always looking out for me," he said sadly.

"What, I don't understand. Is mother alive?" Elodie asked.

"No. Ms. Howell has a gift. She hears from the souls of the dead."

Elodie was about to ask another question when the car lurched to a stop. Her seatbelt kept her from bumping into the back of the driver's seat.

"Who is that?" Connie whispered nodding to a dark figure standing squarely in front of the car.

"My brother, R.P.," Bennett said.

"No, I'm afraid it's not R.P. anymore," Sami offered.

Chapter 21

Cody ran his hand through his rumpled hair. *When will this day be over*, he thought as he shuffled through the mound of paperwork stacked on his desk.

He cast a quick glance to his left at the strategically placed computer, then looked down at the array of folders. It would be so much easier to put the information into the computer if he could type rather than "hunting and pecking". He sighed and picked up the top file. After he made all his notes, he'll get his assistant to put it on file for him.

"Godfrey, Caroline." He picked up another folder. "Plimpton, Simon." He threw both back down. Reaching into the bottom drawer of his desk, he pulled out a clean manila folder.

"St. Clair." He wrote in big block letters. It struck him at that moment, he didn't even know Katy's mother's first name. "Poor kid. It's going to be a drag growing up without a mother."

With a sigh, he tossed the empty folder on top of the file. He pulled a small note pad out of his pocket followed by his check register. Flipping open the note pad, he jotted down the day's date. Then he opened the check register and studied the circled date. Caroline Godfrey was murdered one month ago.

"Two murders and one suspicious death all within the space of one month," he muttered. "Why?"

Voices out in the hallway interrupted his thoughts. "Who's here at this hour?" He glanced at his watch. His question was answered with a sharp rap at his door.

"Cody?" It was his partner.

"I thought you called it a day two hours ago?" He said when Brian walked into the office.

"I tried to, but on my way home I heard that a 15 year old girl was abducted near the Temple Falls Reservation. Her friends claim someone in an old white pick-up truck took off with the girl in it. It was seen going towards Pinehurst?"

"Lots of people drive white pickups." Cody had no desire to drive out to Pinehurst.

"Yeah, well her friends got the tags." Brian threw the information down in front of Cody. "Says the truck belongs to Robert Paul Godfrey."

"Shit, R. P.," Cody ran his hand through his hair again. He rocked back in his chair. "A couple of murders and now an abduction. What the hell is going on in this town?"

"Want to go out there?"

Cody reached down to the lower drawer of his desk. He pulled out another manila folder, then he stuck it and the note pad into a briefcase. "Guess I'm going to have to now."

"I've called for backup. My cruiser is outside. Let's go." Brian opened the door.

"On second thought, you go on. I've got to finish up Mrs. St. Clair's file. I'll catch up," Cody waved him off. "Remember, lots of people at the Godfrey estate drive that pick-up. Be careful how you approach 'ol lady Godfrey. Piss her off and she'll feed you to her attorney for breakfast."

Brian frowned. Cody's lecture irritated him. He never gave him any credit for having a brain. "Guess I'll see you later."

"Yeah, see ya." He dropped his head giving the appearance he was working. He didn't raise it until he heard the door click close. "Yep, things are heatin' up around here. I wonder...?" A thought occurred to him. He turned on the computer and typed murders in Temple Falls, Vermont in the search bar.

"Wow, I didn't realize how many there were," he whispered as he read the list. "There has to be a connection." Deep in thought he never heard the voice when it whispered.

"Malsumis."

Chapter 22

R.P. stood menacingly in the glare of the headlights. His back was bent at an odd angle. His spine looked like it had been wrenched at the waist. His left shoulder hung forward dangling uselessly. Nothing more than rags covered his body in a quilt of haphazard patches. Long, straggly grayish-brown hair and an equally shaggy beard covered the majority of his face. It was impossible to see any of his facial features or eyes.

"He's hurt. He's covered in blood," Elodie's voice was strained.

"That's not his blood," Sami said flatly.

"Then I did hear someone," Bennett said. "Another victim?"

"She's young, maybe fifteen years old. Her body is nearby." Sami concurred.

"We were so close." Bennett said.

"You couldn't help her, Bennett. It was all quite thorough and quick," Sami said.

"Oh my God. Uncle R. P. killed a fifteen year old," Elodie whispered.

"Not sure R.P. was responsible, my dear," Sami offered.

Bennett pointed at the figure in front of the car. "What does he want?"

Sami leaned forward until her face almost touched the windshield. "There is only a small portion of R.P.'s mind that is his own. He has something for you, Bennett. Something you need."

Bennett reached for the door handle. Sami whirled around and grabbed his hand. "There is more. Giselle says…Giselle says… No! She's gone. I can't hear her anymore. She's been silenced." Sami peered out the windshield. R. P. was gone. Suddenly, a rock landed on the hood of the car.

"Connie, move. Drive away, now," Sami screamed.

Another rock crashed on the hood of the car. Connie flinched at the sound of the impact.

"Don't stop. No matter what," Sami demanded. To make sure Connie did what she requested, Sami added her foot to her sister's on the accelerator. The man's tortured scream was drowned out by the roar of the engine. The car flew forward.

Connie negotiated the first curve successfully. Her grip on the wheel became a death grip when the vehicle fishtailed violently on the wet pavement as she attempted the second.

"Sami, get your foot off," Connie demanded struggling to keep the car from careening completely out of control. She jerked the wheel to the left barely avoiding a collision with the hillside. When she did, the car leaned dangerously to the right throwing Sami against the door. The movement however, dislodged her foot just in time. The car righted itself and slowed down.

"Are you out of your mind?" Connie screamed at Sami once she regained control. "We could have been killed."

"You drive like an old woman. We had to get out of there fast," Sami countered.

"I AM an old woman. And getting older by the moment, no thanks to you," Connie snapped. "My heart will never be the same." She wiped her face with the back of her hand. "Why? Why did we have to get out of there fast? Shouldn't we call someone about R.P.? What about the murdered girl?"

Sami looked past her sister through the driver's side window, then to the right. "The police are already on their way. Adam says Cody knows. That's one of the reasons why we needed to get out of there."

"What's the other reason?" Bennett asked.

Sami stared out at the road ahead. "I'm not sure. Connie, pull off the road at the next turn."

"What next turn? There's a road around here?"

"There's a small dirt road, there… right there," Sami said emphatically pointing to the left. "Turn now or you'll miss it."

Connie crimped the wheel hard. The car bounced over several pot holes before stopping in front of an old metal gate.

"Turn off the lights, now!" Sami again demanded.

Connie didn't hesitate. They were immediately plunged into darkness. As if on cue, the entire group turned around and stared out the rear window. Several minutes elapsed before a caravan of police cars with sirens blaring whizzed by.

"They're headed towards the house," Bennett said. "If we show up now, they're going know we were out and about tonight. We better wait here for a while."

"You know, Daddy we aren't that far off the road. They might see us when they come back this way. Maybe we should go through the gate." Elodie gestured towards the front of the car.

"She has a point, Bennett. Where does this road go?" Sami asked as she reached into the glove box.

"Do we have to? This road leads to a family retreat. We call it the "cabin". Not sure what kind of condition it's in. It's been there forever. It was built close to a bluff overlooking the lake. My grandfather loved to fish there amongst other things."

"Works for me," said Sami. She switched on a small flashlight and stepped out onto the dirt road. The souls of the dead were clamoring in her head. They all started talking at the mere mention of the cabin.

Connie watched her sister walk towards the rusty gate. The tilt of her head told her the dead were talking. She wasn't necessarily sure that was a good thing.

"I don't think she can get the gate open." She noticed Sami struggling with the latch.

"I'll help her," Bennett opened the door just as another car pulled in behind them. "Damn, now what?"

Sami turned towards the incoming car. She put her hand up to shield her eyes from the bright lights. "Cody, is that you?"

"Yep, as always." A man's voice called before turning off all of the lights on his car.

Bennett got out. He hurried to Sami's side. "You were expecting him?"

"Yes. I told you, I heard the detective was on his way."

"Detective? Are you going to tell him about R.P. and the …?" Bennett said.

"Shhhh, relax the dead are telling me to wait." Sami answered.

"Wait for what?" Cody's walked briskly to Sami's side.

"Nothing," Sami said.

"Why are you out here?" Bennett asked.

Cody studied the man next to Sami. "Police business. You are?"

"Forgive me. Where are my manners?" said Sami. "Cody, this is Bennett Godfrey. Bennett, this is Cody Davis. He is a homicide detective with the Temple Falls Police department."

Cody extended his hand. The two men shook. Cody vaguely remembered Princess Godfrey's second son. It had been years since he last saw him.

"What is a homicide detective doing on the road to Pinehurst?" Bennett queried.

He didn't want Bennett to know the real reason for his official visit so he answered with a question. "What are you doing out here?"

"I think we better talk about that at the cabin. First, you two boys open this gate. I can't get it open." Sami waved the two men forward.

It took the men only a few moments before the gate fell away easily.

There should be a padlock. Wonder where it went? Bennett couldn't see beyond the gate without his flashlight.

Cody put his hand on Sami and pulled her back. He held on to her until Bennett was back in the car before he began talking. "Cabin? What cabin? What are you doing out here with Bennett Godfrey?"

"The dead told me he needed help," Sami said.

"Yeah, I bet he needs help. Who's in the car?"

"Elodie Godfrey and Connie."

"Elodie Godfrey? What's she doing out here? Where's their car?"

Sami put her hand up and stopped Cody's barrage of questions.

"Cody, I don't have all the answers. We must go." Sami massaged her forehead. "Your partner couldn't pass up the opportunity, eh?"

"Yeah, he's a little eager beaver. How did you...never mind. Head hurt?"

"Sometimes it's too much," Sami whispered.

"How far is this cabin?

"I don't know but it certainly has the dead talking."

"Look, I'm coming along. I don't trust anybody in the Godfrey family right now. " Cody looked back at the awaiting car. "This should be interesting."

"That's fine with me. Let's get going," she said briskly.

Once Sami was back in the car, Connie switched on the headlights and drove through the opened gate.

"The road twists and turns. You will need your brights," Bennett offered.

Connie flipped on the high beams as Bennett suggested. The headlights exposed a narrow, twisting gravel road between the trees and little else. The first sharp curve surprised Connie. After the second one, she drove even more slowly with her nose inches from the steering wheel. Sami was impatient with the car's slowness. Every now and then she would sigh and shift in her seat. Connie ignored her sister.

Cody closed the gate behind him. By the time he was back in the driver's seat, Connie's car had disappeared around the first curve.

"Yep, ought to be interesting," he hurried to catch up.

For the next hour, the small caravan navigated the steep hills and plunging ravines of the Temple Falls Reservation. The rain's continued onslaught made the drive hazardous. Connie inched along much to her sister's annoyance.

"Where *is* this cabin?" Sami could no longer hide her growing impatience.

Bennett answered in his most assuring voice, "Not far."

Bennett couldn't remember the last time he saw the cabin. He was surprised however, that the dirt road was unusually clear of normal debris with few, if any potholes. It was apparent someone graded the road on a fairly regular basis. He knew his mother was anal about maintaining the grounds, however she never bothered with the cabin in the past. In fact, she resisted the family's attempts to pave the road. She claimed it cost too much money. Bennett suspected she loved every pothole and anything else that made the drive more difficult. He knew the cabin held too many bad memories for her.

Connie stopped the car. "Is this bridge safe?"

The "bridge" amounted to nothing more than six thick planks of wood stretching across a now swollen stream. Connie eyed the short span with suspicion.

"It's been here forever, Connie. It's fine," Bennett assured her.

Connie was unconvinced.

"The cabin is just on the other side. We're close," he continued.

"For heaven's sake, Connie, go! I've got to get out of this car," Sami demanded.

Connie sighed loudly. She inched the car over the bridge. Once on the other side, a small wooden sign heralded the entrance.

"Casa de mi suena," Elodie read.

"What does that mean?" Connie asked.

"House of my dreams," Bennett snickered. "It was for my father anyway. He used this cabin for, shall we say, romantic getaways and not necessarily with my mother."

Connie negotiated the car down the long driveway until the headlights illuminated a large dwelling . "Wow, this is some kind of cabin."

"The Godfreys never spare any expense when entertaining." Bennett snickered again.

The "cabin" was in fact a large five bedroom, three bath ranch style home with separate guest quarters over an attached three car garage. It was nestled up against the hillside surrounded by an assortment of trees. When the cars pulled up to the front sidewalk, small lights hemming the path automatically came on.

"Well, I guess there have been some improvements since I left," Bennett noted the lit driveway ruefully.

Cody pulled up. The two cars parked next to each other. The group disembarked one by one until they were all assembled in front of the house with the exception of Sami. Instead of following the rest, she stood next to the rear passenger side door of Cody's car. She rapped on the window and said, "I don't think you want to spend the rest of the night in the back of this car."

"Who is she talking to?" Cody asked.

Sami's first request received no answer. She rapped on the window again. "Let's go!"

The car door opened slowly. A small figure emerged with a dark blanket over her shoulders.

"Are you kidding me? Katy St. Clair, What are you doing in my car?" an exasperated Cody declared.

A new round of rain began in earnest. "Let her answer once we were in the house," Sami instructed. "I'm sure she has an interesting explanation."

The group huddled under the eaves while Bennett tried the front door. It was locked. "Great. I don't have a key and I have no idea where a spare key might be. Any suggestions anyone?"

"Check the windows. Maybe one isn't locked."

"Good idea, Cody. Elodie you check the ones on the left. I'll go right. Can I borrow someone's flashlight?" Without another word, Cody passed his light to Bennett.

"Let's do it," Bennett nodded to Elodie. They left the group huddled in a small tight circle at the front door.

"I'm cold," Connie complained. "What if we don't find a way in?"

"I'm sure Bennett will..." before Sami could finish her sentence. Katy St. Clair delivered a strong squeeze on her arm. She was pointing down the driveway.

"Do you hear something?" Connie looked off down the driveway.

"We must get into the house, Cody," Sami urged.

"We will when..."

"No, we need to be in the house now. Pick the lock," Sami demanded. Her voice was tense.

"What do you mean, pick the lock? I'm a cop. I'm not supposed to..."

Sami grabbed his arm. "Adam says pick the lock."

Cody knew arguing was useless. He shrugged. "All right, I'll pick the lock. I have a tool in my car. It will just be a minute."

"Here, use this." Sami said handing him a nut pick.

"Man, you come prepared," he joked.

"Never mind, just hurry."

"Okay, okay give me a minute," Cody turned towards the door.

"Point your light over here." He was picking the lock when he heard heavy footsteps approaching from the other side of the door. They echoed loudly giving the impression the house was devoid of furniture. Then the door swung open.

Bennett stood in front of the group with a huge smile on his face. "It was a lot easier than I thought. Maybe I was a cat burglar in another life," he quipped.

"Don't get carried away," Sami said. "You had help."

"Help?"

Sami didn't respond. She brushed past him into the darkness.

"Isn't your flashlight working? Why don't you turn on a light? " Cody followed Sami into the dark house.

"My flashlight wouldn't work for some reason," Bennett thumped his it on the palm of his hand.

"My flashlight isn't working either." Connie said smacking the light several times against her hand, too. "Is anyone's working?"

"Guess not," said Elodie as she too tried her switch several times.

Connie walked out the front door. She tried her light again. She was pleasantly surprised when it turned on. However, when she crossed the threshold back into the house, the light quit.

"Well, isn't that the stupidest thing?" She was clearly annoyed at the malfunctioning torch. Her sister's, on the other hand, beamed brightly. "Sami, how come your flashlight is working now and mine isn't? Sami? Sami, what's wrong?"

Sami stood a distance away from the group. She was guiding her light around the room.

"When did you say this "cabin" was built?" Sami asked Bennett.

"I don't think I did, but as I recall, my grandfather built this about 1903. My father updated it, added a wing and the garage. I think he even took off the wraparound porch. Why?"

"There was a different house here once upon a time, wasn't there?" Sami asked quietly.

"Yes, some kind of cabin that my grandfather said was built right around the Revolutionary War. He said it burned to the ground. This house was built in the same spot. I guess that's why we refer to this place as the cabin."

The beam from Sami's flashlight dimmed then went out. "Does anyone have a match?" Sami asked.

"I think I have a lighter in the car," Cody replied. He took the flashlight from Bennett and stepped outside. The flashlight's beam came on immediately. Several moments later, Cody returned. He stood in the center of the room and flicked the small lighter without any luck.

"Why won't it work?" Cody lamented.

"I believe there are some matches in the kitchen. I'll be back in a minute," Bennett felt his way through the house. He returned using a single wooden match to light his way. When it burned out, he struck another one. It cast a small circle of light.

"It seems colder in here than it is outside," Elodie shivered.

"Seems that way doesn't it?" Connie concurred.

"Where's Sami?" Katy huddled close to Cody to stay warm

Before he could respond, Sami entered the room carrying two brass candle holders with two candles. She held them out for Bennett to ignite. Once that was accomplished, she set one candle down on a small table. With the remaining candle still in her possession, Sami walked around the room lighting any other candles as she found them. Soon the room was awash in a dim light with Sami in the center again scrutinizing her surroundings.

"When did you say your grandfather built this house," Sami asked again.

Bennett noticed the intensity of her stare. A slight gasp escaped him when he began appraising the room himself. "1903 but this isn't the house he built."

The once opulent room appointed with fine antiques was gone. A different, far more rustic room appeared. The room was empty with the exception of a wooden table, a few chairs and a rocker. A large stone fireplace with a black kettle suspended in its center was on the right. A pile of wood along with a broom made of some kind of twigs rested nearby. The floor was covered with wide rough, hewed planks. There was a simple door at the back and a single window facing the driveway. It was not the sprawling home they entered a moment ago.

"What's going on? What is this place? Am I hallucinating?" The astonishment in Bennett's voice was clearly apparent.

"I don't know but right now all I want to do is get warm. Someone get that pot out of there. Let's throw some wood in the fireplace and get it going. I'm going to get some paper from the car," Cody was clearly shaken. He hid his fear from the group with a task.

Bennett and Elodie tackled the large pot, while Connie began stacking the wood.

"Do you suppose there's a damper on the flue?" She asked feeling around for a lever. Finding none, she backed away from the fireplace. She stood next to her silent sister. Cody returned and stuffed paper under the neatly stacked wood. Soon the popping sound of burning logs filled the room. Warmth followed shortly thereafter.

Sami remained standing while the others helped themselves to the few available chairs. Cody sat on a small stool while Bennett sat on the floor. The bright glow from the burning wood allowed everyone a chance to really survey the room.

The first comment came from Bennett. "This must be the original cabin my grandfather told me about," he was perplexed. "What the hell happened to the house we walked into? You all saw how big it was from the outside. What happened to the carpets, the Victorian couch, the chairs and the lovely old clock that sat right there." He pointed at the empty wooden mantel. "Why is this happening?"

Sami surveyed the primitive room. "The dead are showing us something."

"What did they do. Take us back in time? Is that why our flashlight wouldn't work? Is Adam doing this?" Cody asked.

"No, not Adam. It's someone else… a young girl…Cody…did you know there was a girl murdered down the road in the reservation a few hours ago?" Sami said..

"What? No! No one said anything about another murder. What girl?" Cody reached for his cell phone. His mind was on the last conversation he had with Brian. He hoped this wasn't the girl abducted earlier although his heart was telling him otherwise.

"It won't work. Not now," Sami said pointing at his cell.

"I need to talk to Brian?" Cody pushed the buttons anyway.

"I told you, it won't work. It's not our time. But it all began here. The dead want to help us. There is something here they want us to find. I wish I knew what. But it all began here." Sami's voice dropped to a whisper.

"What began here? Bennett asked.

"The curse, Bennett, your family's curse," Sami said.

"Ah, the infamous Godfrey curse; rich, powerful and damned. How many times have I've heard that." Bennett scoffed.

"You don't really believe in this family curse, do you Bennett?" Sami narrowed her eyes.

"Absolutely not." He shook his head. "At least not completely. It's the choices everyone made not some ridiculous curse."

"How do you explain your brother's current condition? Didn't your father die under rather suspicious circumstances? Then there was your grandfather…" Sami prodded.

"My brother has a drinking problem as did my father. My grandfather died of a heart attack like his father did before him. All explainable. Certainly not because of some stupid curse."

Sami gazed into the now roaring flames. "How do you explain this room?"

Bennett shook his head. He looked down at his hands.

"I can't explain this," He waved his arms at the room. "Maybe it's an elaborate joke?"

Sami looked up at him. "Didn't you recently have a discussion with your mother about trying to break this stupid curse as you put it?"

Bennett's mouth dropped open. Again, he shook his head. "I should have known. Every time someone died in my family, the "curse" was blamed. If someone died mysteriously in Temple Falls, every finger in town pointed at us. The Godfreys did it. They're cursed. I've hated this place for as long as I can remember. My wife and I almost got away once." His voice cracked with emotion.

Elodie moved towards her father. She stopped short of touching him.

"When Giselle died, my mother insinuated the "curse" did it. She told me in so many words that our attempt to leave the family caused her death. She said if I ever tried to take the girls away, they would die, too."

He could hear Elodie gasp.

"If you didn't believe in the family "curse", why did you leave the girls in your mother's care?" Connie asked.

"Because, I guess, part of me did believe it was true. I refused to risk my daughter's lives in the event it was true." He extend his hand to Elodie. "Then there were the stories,"

"Stories?" Elodie finally broke her silence.

"Yes, stories my father told me when I was a young boy. I think he was preparing me."

"Prepare you for what?" Cody asked.

"For today, tomorrow, the future. I don't know," Bennett stared in the fire.

"What kind of stories?" Elodie asked again. She held his hand.

"My father told me about our ancestor who came here from France shortly before the American Revolution. He made his living as a fur trader. Father said the cabin was built on the site of his original dwelling. Maybe this room is some kind of weird time portal. It doesn't make sense." He looked at the room around him.

"What else did your father tell you about this ancestor?"

Bennett shifted in his seat. There was no doubt the question made him uncomfortable.

"Not much. But I remember one night, my father came into my room long after I had gone to bed. I must have been about eight years old. I could tell he was drunk, so I pretended I was asleep." Bennett said softly.

"You were afraid of your father, weren't you?" Sami asked.

"He was tough. He hated it when I cried. I spent more time with the governess than I did with him. I don't think he liked me very much," Bennett said sadly.

"What happened that night?" Cody thought of his own miserable father.

"He talked to me like I was awake. He told me to run. He said to get as far away from this house as I could. Then he said something I didn't understand and I guess I still don't. He said, 'the debt will never be repaid. The monster will never let us go.'"

"The debt will never be repaid. The monster…" Sami repeated letting her voice trail off.

"Sounds like your family owes someone money," Cody said.

"Or souls," Sami added.

"That's crazy." Bennett said.

"Is it? How many unexplained deaths have there been in Temple Falls over the years? Why do the women in your family grow old but the men never do? Why have the dead shown us this room?" Sami asked.

"I don't know. I don't know. I refuse to believe that my family is responsible for every unexplained death in Temple Falls." He grabbed his head. "No, I won't believe it…I…"

A piercing scream interrupted their conversation. Katy St. Clair was pointing out the solitary front window. The group rushed to her. Against the black backdrop of night, an image of a slight thin man could be seen. He was walking slowly towards the house carrying a heavy sack over one shoulder. He held some kind of tool in his other hand. They watched in silence as the man approached the front door. No one moved when they heard the single knock.

"Oh, God," Connie said in a hoarse whisper. "I've heard this knock before."

Cody drew his gun out of his holster.

Another knock was delivered, then another.

"Isn't anyone going to answer that?" Connie whispered.

There was no immediate response from the group. "Anyone?" she reiterated.

Bennett finally broke the stalemate.

"This is ridiculous." He strode with confidence to the front door and threw it open without any hesitation.

"Uncle Bennett, is that you?" a voice called.

Paul Godfrey breezed past his uncle followed by Bess Davis and Harry Cooper.

"What are you all doing by the window?" Paul asked once inside the house. "Damn it's dark in here. Something wrong with the lights?"

Paul Godfrey flipped a switch on the wall. The group gasped as the hall light came on. The primitive room was gone.

"Close the door, Uncle Bennett. You're letting all the cold air in," Paul continued adjusting the thermostat to a more comfortable temperature. "There. It should be warmer in no time, Uncle Bennett."

Bennett was staring at his nephew with his mouth slightly agape.

"What the hell is wrong with everybody?" Paul asked returning his uncle's stare.

Bennett let go of the door knob. The front door closed slowly behind him.

"Bess, what are you doing here?" Cody was clearly surprised by the appearance of his wife.

Before she could answer, Bennett turned to Harry Cooper. "I thought we told you we weren't interested, Mr. Cooper."

"Harry Cooper? You're the man who wanted to interview my late husband," Connie chimed in.

"Harry Cooper? You're the kid from Columbia University?" Paul added.

Soon the entire group was talking at one time.

"Stop, everyone, stop talking," Sami demanded. The noise ceased.

"Thank you," Sami said. "Apparently there is a reason we have all been brought together. What that reason is, I don't know, but I'm sure we are going to find out whether we want to or not. Let's hear from you, Bess. Lovely to see you again, my dear. Why are you here?"

"I got a message from Cody's partner that Cody needed some files he forgot at the house. Brian said to bring them out to Pinehurst. I thought the request was odd, but every now and then Cody asks me to do something out of the ordinary. I was on my way out of the house, when Mr. Cooper showed up at my door." She turned and motioned for Harry to continue the story.

"I had a message at the hotel that Bess, Mrs. Davis, wanted to talk to me about the murder of Caroline Godfrey. The message said she had some important information. So, I immediately drove to her place. Mr. Godfrey was pulling up as I arrived." Harry, in turn, passed the story to Paul.

All eyes were on Paul Godfrey. The intensity of their stares clearly unsettled the man. He fidgeted with his cufflinks. He was dressed in an expensive three-piece suit. The buttons on the vest were straining under the stress of the additional weight he had put on since the murder. His face was puffy and pale. Dark circles encompassed his brown eyes indicating many sleepless nights. A slight smell of cigarettes and Jack Daniels surrounded him. Although he was only in his mid-forties, he looked much older. Streaks of grey were evident in his short cropped brown hair. A slight stoop to his shoulders made him seem shorter than his normal six foot height.

"I just left a meeting with my solicitor when I got a message from Grandmother telling me to pick up Bess Davis. I was told Detective Davis was going to meet us at the house to discuss my wife's murder. I thought it seemed strange that we would have a meeting with a detective at night, let alone picking up his wife, but to argue with my Grandmother is useless." He straightened his tie and coughed slightly.

"But you didn't go to the main house. You came here." Connie said.

"Have no idea how I got here. I could have sworn I was coming up the main drive to the house. I even thought I went through the gates. Thought I was home until Uncle Bennett opened the front door. What the hell is going on?" Paul demanded.

"Malsumis," Katy said softly. "The trickster."

"Malsumis? What's she talking about?" Paul asked.

"In the Abenaki culture, Malsumis is one of their gods. They call him the "trickster"." Sami offered.

"Oh, come on. You're telling me that some Abenaki god tricked the three of us into coming here?" Paul said. "What for?"

"Maybe this god is helping us find out the truth," Harry interjected.

"The truth about what?"

Harry opened his mouth only to be silence by Bennett with a raised hand. Bennett nodded towards Katy staring out the now big bay window. She was transfixed and visibly shaking. Bennett walked over to her. He looked out the window and was immediately shocked by what he saw.

A hunched figure stood in the driveway. It looked like R.P.

"Quick! Someone hand me a flashlight," Bennett yelled.

Connie reached him first. She pushed her flashlight into his awaiting hand. Bennett directed it out the window. The beam barely reached his target. It wasn't strong enough to illuminate the figure completely.

"Here let me help," said Sami. She pointed her light at the figure as well. Soon everyone in the group who had a flashlight was pointing it out the window.

"Oh my God, it's my brother, R. P. He's carrying a body," Bennett said.

"He sure is," said Cody. "It looks like a girl."

Cody turned away from the window. He pulled his gun out of his holster. Sami stopped him on his way to the front door.

"Cody, I don't think that will do much good," she said looking at his gun.

"I have to do my job, Sami. He's a murderer."

She nodded for Cody to look out the window. "Is he?"

He gave Sami a strange look then proceeded back to the window. The hunched figure was gone and in his place stood a young boy.

"Adam?" Cody said. "It's Adam!"

Thrilled at the sight of his brother, Cody bolted towards the front door.

"No, Cody, wait!" Bess yelled. It was too late. Cody was gone.

Frigid air struck him in the face the moment his foot touched the front stoop. He felt it pierce his clothing like so many sharp knives. Cody didn't stop. The desire to see his brother was overwhelming.

"Adam?" he walked towards the vision. "I've missed you, buddy. Why didn't you come back and see me?"

Adam turned towards Cody. A sad, crooked smile appeared on his face. He didn't say anything, instead he extended his hand.

Years of suppressed emotions erupted within the detective. He reached for his brother's hand. When they touched, his body convulsed. A foul, wretched odor overwhelmed him. Cody watched in horror as Adam's face changed. The crooked smile broadened into a thoroughly evil grin. His eyes turned coal black rimmed in an eerie red glow.

"Let me go," Cody wrenched his hand. His strength failed him. Something else was now in control.

Chapter 23

"The police are in the foyer, Madame." Ronald announced with no emotion.

"What in God's name are they doing here at this time of night?" Princess said with disgust. "Have Dani attend to them. I am in no mood."

Ronald took a step forward. "A Detective Smith says he will only speak to you. It is of the most urgent nature."

"Honestly Ronald, what good are you to me, if you can't do your job." Princess Godfrey continued. "I suppose he wants to speak to Bennett as well?"

"No, Madame. He only asked for you," Ronald hesitated then continued. "You must go, Madame."

Princess sighed loudly. She threw her butler an exasperated look. It was an unwanted intrusion, she wished she could refuse. She waved the butler away only to realize he was already gone.

Brian Smith, she remembered his name coming up in a conversation with Mayor Plimpton. Simon thought he might be able to buy his silence on the Caroline Godfrey murder. He found out, however, that the young detective was an honest cop, like Cody Davis.

"Damn nuisance," she said aloud.

Detective Smith fiddled with the buttons on his jacket. Even with two police officers standing behind him, the large foyer of the Godfrey home intimidated him. It was more than the mansion that was making him uneasy. Since leaving Cody at the station, a deep sense of foreboding invaded him. He couldn't shake the idea that something wasn't right. The moment he entered the Godfrey foyer, the feeling intensified.

A noise on the grand staircase caught Brian's attention. Ronald, the butler was standing on the top step staring at the small group at the bottom. Brian returned the elderly man's stare. He calculated the butler's height to be around five foot, five inches if he stood completely upright. There was a distinctive stoop to his shoulder. He calculated his weight to be about 120 pounds. Dark brown eyes, abundant white hair and old, extremely old. His face was narrow. His eyes were sunken trimmed with wild white eyebrows that stood up in various directions. His skin was deeply wrinkled to the point of being craggy.

I bet the old geezer is pushing 100, Brian thought.

As this thought crossed Brian's mind, Ronald's eyes met the detective's. A slight knowing smile creased his thin lips.

Brian felt a ripple of shock. *Shit, he heard me.*

"Madame will be down directly. Please adjourn to the salon." Ronald said directing the small group to the right. He continued staring at Brian.

"Thank you," Brian replied motioning for the other officers forward. He found it hard to look away. Before he entered the room, he glanced back. Ronald was still staring at him with a simpering grin. Brian was relieved when he crossed the threshold of the salon and was out of the butler's sight.

"Kind of creepy, wasn't he?" One of the officers commented.

"You might say that," Brian agreed. He wiped his forehead with the back of his hand. His stomach was a little queasy.

"Is it hot in here?" He asked as he undid his tie slightly.

The other two officers shrugged simultaneously and shook their heads no.

"Seems kind of hot to me," Brian said removing his coat. The queasy feeling was still bothering him when Princess entered the room. He extended his hand in greeting. Princess looked at him like he was a coiled viper about to strike. Entrenched good manners made her respond in kind. Her handshake was brief, limp and definitely unenthusiastic. She motioned him to a chair.

Brian and Princess sat across from each other while the two other officers remained standing. Neither spoke for several moments adding a layer of tension to the exceedingly quiet room.

"Why are you here at this late hour?" Princess' voice was firm.

Brian cleared his throat. Princess Godfrey's haughty stare made him even more uncomfortable. He took a clipboard from his fellow officer and read from the report. "Our office received word tonight that there was a disturbance at the entrance gates. Can you tell me about that?"

"Utter rubbish," Princess said haughtily. "There was no such thing."

Brian's own words surprised him. The document said nothing about the truck and the abduction. He continued reading aloud. "The call came from …a…Caroline Godfrey…" He stopped reciting the moment her name was spoken. "What the hell?"

"Is this a joke, Detective?" Princess said icily. "My daughter-in-law is no longer living. How could she have possibly made that call?"

Brian looked at one of the two officers. "What's with this report?"

The first officer shrugged. Brian studied the paper in front of him. He refrained from saying anything to Princess about the alternate reason they were there.

"The call came in around 8 p.m. A woman who identified herself as…Caroline Godfrey… said a young girl was being assaulted at the front gates. That's it?" Brian handed the clipboard back to the officer.

The officer nodded yes.

Princess stood up. "I assure you, Detective, if a young girl was being assaulted at the front gates my security would have notified me. I believe you've been duped."

"Yes, well that may be, Mrs. Godfrey. I would like to talk with your security, if you don't mind." Brian stood up as well. He couldn't help but notice a subtle change in Princess' demeanor. She was definitely rattled.

"Certainly," Princess walked to an intercom on the wall. Before she could speak into it, Ronald appeared in the doorway. "Oh good, you're here. Please ask Mr. Blanchard to come to the salon, Ronald."

"He is out on his rounds, Madame. I believe he is in the vicinity of the stables," Ronald said.

"Call him, please." She continued

"Yeah, tell him to meet us at the front gates," Brian interjected.

Ronald left the room after bowing stiffly.

"Thank you, Mrs. Godfrey. We'll speak with Mr. Blanchard at the front gates," Brian put his coat back on. "Oh, one more thing, where were you the night of Caroline's murder?"

Princess was taken aback by his question. It was several moments before she spoke. "Where I always am… here at Pinehurst."

Brian didn't bother asking if she had any witnesses. He already knew the answer.

"Let's go," He waved at the two officers. "Good night, Mrs. Godfrey."

"Good night, Detective Smith. I will leave the gate open. When you are done, call over the intercom for us to close it, if you don't mind."

Brian nodded and followed the officers. The cold air revived him once he was out of the house.

"How could I have missed Caroline's name in that report? I swear it wasn't on there." He grabbed the clipboard and re-examined the report. "Shit, I must be blind. It says here the call was about a young girl being assaulted at the front gates. There's nothing on here about the abduction." He threw the clipboard into the car. "Let's go to the front gates. Not sure if we will find anything in this rain."

The cruiser wound its way to the front gates of the estate. The three men got out of the car each holding a large flashlight.

"You go that way, you go that way and I'll check the middle. Call out if you find anything." Brian instructed.

The officers separated. Lamps secured on the stone supports for the entrance gate cast a dim glow on the driveway. The light did little to help Brian's search as the rain continued its relentless downfall. He meticulously walked in a side to side pattern covering every inch of the driveway until he reached where it intersected the road. He was on his way back when his light shown on a pair of black rubber boots. Their appearance startled him.

"Mr. Blanchard?" He said shining the flashlight into the face of the new arrival. Mr. Blanchard was wearing a uniform from Capital Security. The big heavy-set man raised his hand against the light.

"Yes, Sir," Blanchard answered.

"Can you tell me…," Brian pummeled the guard with a stream of questions.

In the end, their conversation provided no new information. Brian thanked Mr. Blanchard who promptly got into his golf cart and whizzed away.

"Funny, I didn't hear him pull up," Brian said aloud.

"Hey, Brian over here," One of the officers yelled.

Brian hurried towards the first officer. "Wha'cha got?"

The officer pointed his light to the ground. The dissected remains of a young girl were strewn over a small area.

"Holy shit." Brian gasped. He felt his stomach roil. The sight was worse than Simon Plimpton's headless body.

"I found these nearby." the officer said handing Brian a wallet and a large flashlight. Brian opened the wallet and looked at the driver's license.

"Well, well Bennett Godfrey." He said snapping the wallet closed.

Chapter 24

"Cody!" Bess watched in horror as her husband fell to the ground. She bolted for the door, but Katy intercepted her.

"No, Malsumis is playing tricks. Don't leave," She cautioned. "Stay here."

"But he needs me," Bess cried. She pushed the young girl aside.

"Bess stop!" Sami urged. "She's right."

Connie took Katy's place in front of the door blocking Bess again.

"How can you all just leave him there?" She pleaded.

Sami didn't answer. She was standing still with her eyes closed. Connie watched her sister. She wished she could hear what the dead were telling her. They were obviously communicating in full force.

"What's she doing? Taking a nap?" Paul said rudely.

"Shut up, you ass." Harry said.

"Who the hell are you to tell me…," Paul snapped back.

"Quiet, the two of you," Bess commanded. The men stopped bickering. She was watching Sami, too. Suddenly, Sami's eyes flew open. She walked over to the picture window. Bess joined her. Katy, Paul, Connie, Bennett, Elodie and Harry crowded behind her.

"Oh Cody," Bess cried. Her husband lay crumpled on the sidewalk. "Cody, please get up."

"He can't, my dear. But I will tell you he is in good hands. Adam is protecting him," Sami said.

"Protecting him, from whom? What?" Bess asked.

"From him," Katy said. She pointed out the window.

A hunched figure stood on the opposite side of Cody.

"R. P.?" Bennett whispered.

The hunched figure lifted his head. He stared into the picture window. Although the darkness made it difficult to see the details of the figure's clothing, his glowing red eyes were unmistakable.

"Caroline?" Harry and Paul said at the same time.

"Caroline? That's R.P." Bennett countered.

"No, it's Simon," Connie added.

"Mother?" Katy whispered.

"Who is it, Sami?" Bennett whispered.

"Someone evil," Sami said solemnly.

"What does it want?" Elodie asked.

"I'm not sure. Except for Adam, the dead have run away. They aren't speaking right now," She said.

"Why are we each seeing a different person?" Bennett asked.

"Malsumis, he doesn't want us to see what it really is," Katy whispered.

"What the hell is it?" Bennett said.

The hunched figure stood a little more upright. A thin wisp of vapor emanated from its mouth.

"It's breathing. I can see its breath. This thing is alive?" Bennett was bewildered.

"This "thing", I believe, has been controlling your family for generations. But it has always remained hidden until now. Something has forced it into the open. Something has changed." Sami stared back at the figure intently.

"Did that "thing" bring us here?" Bess asked.

"It told Malsumis to do it for him." Katy said softly.

"Why? Why does it want us all here?" Bennett asked.

Sami stared at the hunched figure. "It's afraid. I can feel its fear. After all these years of existing virtually unmolested in these woods, it's suddenly afraid. There is a chink in its armor. What that chink is I don't know. The dead don't know either or else they are afraid to tell me."

Sami watched as the hunched figure backed away from Cody's listless body. It kept moving until it blended into the darkness.

"Cody, oh my poor Cody," Bess rushed to the front door and flung it open. No one stopped her this time. When she crossed over the threshold, she stopped.

"What's going on? I can't walk out of the house. What the hell is this?" She screamed pushing against an invisible wall. Again and again her attempts were rebuffed.

Paul rushed forward. He too, tried leaving the house. "Hey, what gives? I can't get out either. This is impossible."

Soon everyone, with the exception of Sami and Katy, tried crossing the threshold. It was several moments before they collectively gave up. A defeated Bess returned to the window. She looked outside and saw Cody sitting up.

"Cody, in here," Bess pounded on the window.

Cody looked towards the house. He pushed himself up off the ground and stood facing the window.

"What the hell," he said. The house was dark. It looked empty. He noticed one of the cars was gone--Sami's. His was still parked where he left it.

Bess pounded on the window, but Cody wasn't looking towards the house anymore.

"He can't hear me. Why can't he hear me?" she screamed.

"Malsumis," Katy offered quietly.

"No, this is impossible. Cody, Cody. He's walking towards his car. Don't leave me, Cody," She screamed.

Sami put her hand on the distraught woman's shoulder. "You might as well stop, Bess. There is nothing we can do."

Bess quit pounding on the window. Deep, uncontrollable sobs racked her body.

"What do you mean there is nothing we can do?" Harry asked. It was the first time he had spoken since his discourse with Paul.

Sami wrapped her arms around Bess. She gently guided her towards the awaiting sofa. Calmness enveloped her.

"The souls of the dead have been my constant companion for as long as I can remember. Why it is I can hear them and others cannot is as much a mystery to me as it is to you. What I have learned from them over the years is that we are all born with, for want of a better word, an energy or soul. When we die our soul is released into the universe so it can continue on. All our memories of the good things we did and the bad are retained. So, there are essentially good and bad souls. These wandering souls coexist with us. That's why we sometimes feel that a departed loved one is near us. Every so often however, a soul returns to the living."

"It returns?" Harry questioned.

"Yes, it returns to inhabit another form and not necessarily a human one. Its memory is merged with the new one. It will live another life until death releases it again." Sami continued.

"How many times can a soul be reborn?" Harry asked.

"I didn't have an answer to that question until tonight. Apparently some souls can return many times as long as it has a willing host." Sami said.

"A willing host?" Bennett asked.

"Striking a deal with the devil you might say," Sami said. "The details are still vague but if I'm right this particular soul has survived many transformations. The Godfrey family has provided the means for its survival for years."

"Through its male heirs?" Bennett suggested.

"Among other things," Sami nodded.

"Oh come on. You don't believe that do you, Uncle Bennett?" Paul interjected.

"I didn't. How do you explain it otherwise, Paul? No male Godfrey heir has lived past their sixty-fifth birthday. Sami, you said this entity is afraid. That something has changed. Do you know what that change is?" Bennett asked.

Sami looked at Bennett then at Paul formulating her answer. "Have you ever noticed the difference between you, Bennett and the rest of your family? The Godfrey men have all been born with dark complexions, dark eyes and a heavy frame. You, on the other hand are blond, blue eyed and rather lanky. You're different. You're not of the same mold."

Bennett and Paul looked each other over carefully.

"That doesn't mean anything. There must have been someone who married into the Godfreys who brought the blond hair and blue-eyed gene. It's not unusual for a genetic trait to skip generations." Bennett shook his head. "No, it's not unusual."

"You are almost sixty Bennett but you are showing no signs of any degeneration. Didn't your father and your grandfather begin changing long before their death? Look at R. P. He's dying. So if the past repeats itself, this entity should have already begun transferring itself to you. But it hasn't or it can't and there is only one reason why."

"Why?" Bennett asked.

"You're not a true Godfrey," Sami declared.

Chapter 25

The house was quiet. The physical effort it took for Princess to walk downstairs left her drained of most of her energy. Her life was unraveling before her. It was only a matter of time before her most guarded secret would reveal itself. She silently chastised herself for believing, even for a millisecond, she could alter the impending consequences of one rash decision. That one foolish decision which will ultimately destroy her name, her life, everything.

Princess walked wearily to the chaise lounge. She was lowering herself into its comforting softness when she was startled by a figure standing in front of her.

"Good heavens, you scared the wits out of me. How dare you intrude without knocking," she said angrily.

"The Master has a message for Madame," Ronald said in an emotionless tone.

Princess shifted in her seat. Her heart was racing uncontrollably. She maintained a calm outward appearance, however.

"A message?"

Ronald moved closer. His white jacket hung loose over his withered frame. The white hair on his head still stood out at odd angles. Deep wrinkles crisscrossed his face like so many elongated scars. His thick bushy eyebrows framed black penetrating eyes—eyes that rarely missed even the smallest change in the daily household routine.

"Yes, Madame," He leaned forward. Princess couldn't avoid his stare or his rancid breath. "It is time."

Princess hung her head. A single tear left her eye. It rolled down her cheek. She brushed it away quickly. "My son is dead then?"

"No, Mother not yet." The voice came from the other end of the room.

Ronald stepped away from Princess allowing her to see what was left of her oldest son. The stoop in R.P's shoulder was more pronounced than before. Its severe tilt forced his right arm downwards until it almost dragged the ground. His body was draped in tattered bloody rags. His long scraggly hair fell forward with the tilt of his shoulder covering that part of his face his beard did not. Princess looked into her son's eyes with cold detachment.

"What did you do?" R. P. demanded.

"Do?" Princess replied calmly.

R. P. let out an agonizing scream of pain. It was as if invisible hands began twisting his bones all at once. He stood up straight then flopped forward. His back was wrenched to the right. It was several moments before R.P. stopped moving. He stepped menacingly towards his mother. It wasn't his voice she heard next. "The line has been broken. The second born is tainted." Another horrific scream followed as R.P.'s body twisted again.

"Grandmother, what is going on?" Dani exclaimed coming into the room at a run. "I heard screaming all the way down the hall. Are you all right?"

"Yes, my dear. I am fine," Princess said staring at the now empty space where R.P. had been. "It was only the television."

Dani accepted her Grandmother's explanation without complaint even though she knew she was lying.

"Okay, as long as you are all right." She gave her Grandmother a quick peck on the check. Princess took her hand making Dani stand in front of her.

"There is something I need to tell you, Danielle. Don't leave just yet," Princess ordered.

Her Grandmother rarely used her full given name unless she was in trouble. She sat down on the chaise lounge prepared for the inevitable thrashing she normally received.

"Yes, Grandmother?"

"In my desk drawer there is a journal. Would you get it for me?"

Dani did as her Grandmother instructed. Far in the back of the desk drawer, she found a small leather journal bound tightly with a black ribbon. Once she handed the journal to Princess, she sat down next to her. She waited for her Grandmother to begin.

"This journal was written by our ancestor, Reynard Pillion Gillett. He was among other things, a fur trader and an original settler of Temple Falls." Princess stopped in her narration. She placed her hand on the journal. It was several moments before she resumed speaking. "Reynard did many things in his life. Most of them to benefit his pocket. As a child, I heard stories about the Godfrey family and the curse that seemed to follow them. When you are young, you believe all sorts of wild nonsense." She sighed looking down at the tattered journal. "Little did I know that the stories were true."

"Grandmother, are you honestly telling me that you believe this family is cursed?" Dani was surprised by her revelation.

Princess placed the journal in Dani's hands. "I know it and I believe it. Caroline is gone. You, Dani are the oldest female in the family. This family's survival will ultimately depend on you. Before I die, you must be prepared for any eventuality. Your life will change rapidly very soon."

"Grandmother, you're scaring me. Can't you tell me what's going on?" Dani pleaded.

"No, it's all there in the journal of your ancestor but a word of caution, Danielle. Reynard had many secrets. Secrets that protect this family. It will be your responsibility to see to it that no one outside the family touches this journal except you. Now go. I need my rest." Princess waved her away.

Dani rose slowly. She backed away from the chaise lounge. Her mind was whirling in confusion. She had so many questions, but knew she didn't have the courage to demand the answers. So she walked away like she always did.

"Oh, one more thing, Danielle, the world is an imperfect place. Caroline found that out when she married your cousin. She didn't listen when I warned her. Her stubbornness got her killed."

"Elodie believes you killed her, Grandmother. Is that true?" Dani asked.

"Caroline was quite simply a whore. She humiliated the family more than once. She was going to again by running away with some young man she met at the country club. She sealed her own fate." Princess said calmly.

Dani looked away from Princess. "You did it? You killed her?"

"Let's just say the decision was taken out of my hands. In answer to your question, no, I did not *have* her murdered nor did I murder her myself," Princess said.

"But you know who did. Was it Paul?" Dani continued.

"There are some things better left unsaid, Danielle," Princess leaned forward. She grabbed her granddaughter's hand forcefully. She pulled her close and whispered. "Read the journal, Dani. There is a secret somewhere within its pages. It will end this horrible curse. Do it before it is too late. I couldn't find it but I'm hoping you can." Princess gave Dani an additional tug. "Whatever you do, don't let this journal get into anyone else's hands. Protect it with your life." She then let Dani go and fell back onto the chaise lounge.

Dani took a step back from her grandmother. She studied the woman she had feared for so long. *What have you done old woman?*

"Ronald will be your responsibility now. He is invaluable in running the household. He will help you move your things into this room. It belongs to you now." Princess' voice trailed off at the last sentence.

"What are you saying, Grandmother? That you're going to die? Oh come on, no one knows when…"

Princess put her hand up. She stopped Dani from talking any further. Her granddaughter obliged. With a deep sigh, Dani pressed the book against her chest. She bent down and gave her Grandmother another kiss.

"I love you, Grandmother," She said before turning away.

Princess merely nodded. Once the click of the door was heard, Princess pulled a shawl around her shoulders. She laid her head back and addressed the empty room. "I've protected this family since the day I married you, Robert. Even after you traipsed your many whores in front of me. I kept my silence." Princess thought about the picture she slid into Reynard's journal earlier that morning. "I never mattered to you. You only cared about yourself. The line is broken. Bennett isn't yours. I can say that now. Revenge, dear Robert is a picture worth a thousand words."

"Stupid, selfish bitch."

Princess inhaled sharply at the sound of her late husband's voice right behind her. She sat up abruptly.

"Robert?"

Cold, icy hands grabbed her around the neck. She felt them squeeze. Panic overwhelmed her. She gasped for air as she tried loosening their grasp. Then a calm resignation took over. She quite struggling. The room took on a grayish tint and began to fade. She thought of Bennett. A slight smile turned the edges of her mouth upwards for the last time.

Chapter 26

The car stopped within inches of the metal gate. Cody stared in wonder at his surroundings.

"How the hell did I get here?" He said aloud. He couldn't make sense of his situation. "Okay, I was in the house. I saw Adam then…how the hell did I…? Cody put the cruiser in park. He released his grip on the wheel. He had no memory of the long ride from the cabin to the gate. He patted the side of his chest and felt his revolver. It was still in place but the coldness of his shirt surprised him.

"Why am I wet? I don't remember being outside." He patted his pants. They were just as soaked as his shirt and jacket. "Damn, what the hell is going on?"

"He knows."

Adam's voice shocked Cody. He clutched his chest. "Shit, don't do that. You almost gave me a heart attack."

Cody wiped sweat off his brow. "Whew…who knows? What are you talking about?" He turned towards the sound of Adam's voice.

He could barely see the faint image of his older brother next to him on the front seat. Amazed, he watched as Adam's image grew stronger.

"Adam, you're here. I've missed you." Cody reached out without thinking. His hand passed through cold air. He shook his head in disappointment. "Who knows what?"

Adam stared into his brother's face. "Reynard".

"Reynard, who is… Reynard? The Godfrey's Reynard?" This revelation took Cody by surprise.

Adam nodded his head.

"What does he know?" Cody continued.

"There's no more." Adam said.

"No more? No more what? Food, money…come on, Adam, can't you do better than that?"

Adam's distressed look bothered Cody.

"What's going on, buddy? You look miserable," Cody said softly.

In a flash, Adam disappeared.

"Adam, ADAM!" Cody fanned the air searching for his brother. "Damn! Come back." Cody thumped the steering wheel in frustration. "This is nuts. I'm talking to a seat. Where's Bess? I need Bess."

He pulled out his cell phone. It was dead.

"Ah, great, what else?" he lamented.

A gust of air rocked the cruiser. This was followed by a weird sound that riveted Cody's attention to the opposite side of the car. "What the…"

The dim outline of a small man appeared. Cody reached under his jacket and released the handgun from its holster. He drew it out and rested it on his leg.

The diminutive figure stood within fifteen feet of the car.

"So what do you want?" he muttered. The incessant drizzle combined with the darkness made it difficult for Cody to see. Yet, something about the image of the stranger captivated him. Then Cody saw his eyes. They were red, an eerie red color with a distinct black dot in the center. And they were focused on him.

Cody was terrified. "What the hell are you?"

An intense cold seeped into the car in response. It revived his memory of the recent encounter in front of the cabin. His fear intensified.

"Adam, who is that?"

The familiar glow returned. Adam was mouthing words but Cody heard nothing. Adam reached out as if to shake his brother's arm. He pointed at the dark shape moving towards them. His frantic motions finally made sense.

"Oh baby, I guess you're telling me to get the hell out of here." Cody said.

"Cody, run!" Adam's voice finally screamed.

"Adam!" Cody screamed back at the empty seat. Then he saw him. The dark shape of someone with the red eyes standing at the passenger side window. Cody was paralyzed by the sight. It was a man or at least it had been a man. Loose, decaying flesh hung from its face exposing intermittent bits of a white skull. Tufts of dark hair in various lengths whipped one way then the other by the wind seemed alive. The sunken red eyes glowed maliciously. Cody felt his throat tighten around another rising scream. The man smiled a wide, satanic grin. Cody's scream was released.

"Shit! Holy Mother of God," He threw the car in reverse and stomped on the accelerator.

The tires spun on wet leaves before hurtling the car backwards. In his terror, Cody let the car careen out of control. He knew without looking the demon was still there, at the window.

"Get off you son-of-a-bitch," Cody screamed. Bitter cold seeped inside the car and intensified. Cody's wet clothes stiffen. His body shivered uncontrollably. He didn't stop. Fear propelled him.

"Cody, stop!" Adam's voice warned.

Cody stomped on the brakes inches away from a tree. He slammed the car into forward gear while he gunned the engine at the same time. He ignored the passenger side window. He knew the demon was still there. He could feel it. He could smell it. The car leaped forward.

"Go back, Cody," Adam's said.

"Go back? Go back where?" Before Adam could answer, the putrid smell of rotting flesh assailed Cody's senses. It was so horrible, he looked right without thinking. The man was no longer on the outside of the car. He was next to him on the seat.

"Oh, hell no!" Cody stomped on the accelerator again.

The man smiled a slow demonic grin. He made a slight gesture with his hand.

The car careened to the right. Cody wrenched the wheel fighting for control. The man flicked his wrist. The car swerved to the left. Again, Cody countered the demon's move.

"It's going to kill me, Adam. Help!" Cody felt the accelerator depress. The car lurched forward towards a series of curves. He negotiated the first, but the second was too sharp. The car veered out of control. Cody helplessly held onto the wheel unable to stop its motion. He felt it swerve on the wet ground. When the car tipped dangerously to the right, he let the wheel go. The deadly sound of crunching metal was the last thing Cody remembered as the car rolled.

The intense smell of gasoline woke him. His seatbelt held him upside down making his head touch the roof of the car. Pain coursed down his neck. It was an effort turning his head. The cruiser was resting at a sharp angle. The driver's side window was half the size it should have been. Something wet was filling the car. In his daze, Cody couldn't tell if it was gas or water.

"Get me out, Adam," he had little strength left.

He thought he heard his brother answer him. He wasn't sure. Blood rushing to his head made it throb.

"Gotta get out," he told himself. He pulled at the seatbelt. It was stretched tightly against him. He traced it with his fingers trying to find its end.

"Oh no," he said. The smell of smoke jarred him.

"Shit, the car's gonna blow," he realized. His fingers found the button that held the seat belt in place. He pushed it several times until it finally let go. Smoke poured into the car. Cody held his breath. He was taking too long getting out of his seat. He took another breath. Acrid smoke filled his lungs immediately making him cough and gag. It stung his eyes forcing them closed involuntarily.

Where's the damn handle, he couldn't feel anything. When he finally found the handle, he braced his feet against his crushed door and pushed. The door held fast.

"Come on," he coughed and inhaled more smoke. His lungs rebelled. He grabbed the lapel of his coat and covered his mouth and nose. He took another breath. It was no use, the smoke penetrated his jacket.

It's over. I love you, Bess.

He knew he couldn't take much more. Cody pushed one more time against the unyielding door. It didn't move.

I love you Bess, He thought. He slumped down prepared for the end, when he felt something soft, warm touch his wrist. He jerked his hand only to feel it being held tighter. Unable to see through the smoke and unable to breath anymore, Cody gave up.

The first gulp of fresh air surprised him. The second revitalized him. Cody awoke to the sound of a crackling fire. Cold, freezing dirt dug into his face.

What happened? How did I get here? Dazed, he pushed himself upright. He felt weak, although the fresh air was reviving him quickly. He patted himself down.

"Nothin' busted," he said with relief.

A loud popping sound caught his attention. It sounded like bullets exploding.

"Shit." Cody touched his empty holster then looked forlornly at the blaze. Several more popping sounds made him duck. He hugged the ground until the sound quit. The car and his gun were a total loss.

An uncontrolled shiver wracked his body. He scrambled to his feet. He had no idea where he was.

"Man, I need you, Adam," he pleaded. He peered nervously down the pitch black road. One thing he knew for sure, if a bear didn't get him, the freezing cold would.

"Adam, I need your help. I can't see my way. It's too dark."

"Akwi sagezo." A soft voice answered.

"What? Who said that?" Cody jumped at the sound of a woman's voice. Instinctively, he reached into his empty holster for the gun that wasn't there. "Damn it."

"Akwi sagezo," the soft voice said again.

"What are you saying? I don't know what you mean. Who …who are you, where are you?" he said turning in circles. "Adam, what's going on? I don't understand. Help me, please, help me."

Through the veil of rain, a dim narrow path of light appeared. Cody's stared in wonder and disbelief. "You want me to walk into the light, right? Are you kidding me?"

Another dim light appeared next to the path then grew brighter. It was Adam.

Cody felt himself relax. "Hey, big brother, what took you so long?

Adam raised his shoulders in a familiar shrug. There was a smile on his face.

"Akwi sagezo," he said.

"Yeah, yeah I heard that. What does it mean?"

"Do not be afraid," Adam said.

"Right, who said that?" Cody questioned. "Don't leave."

The vision of his brother disappeared leaving Cody alone on the road.

"Akwi sagezo, do not be afraid," Cody repeated. "Tell that to my heart." The words had little effect on his fear.

A cold breeze whipped around him. It reminded him of his wet clothes. It also reminded him of the demon. He looked towards the light. The path patiently waited for his decision.

"Do not be afraid," Cody repeated. He willed his feet forward. He felt his body move. When he reached the edge of the light, he took a deep breath. Then a much stronger blast of frigid air slapped him backwards. Cody stumbled. He caught himself before he fell. The demon was near. He could sense him.

"You don't want me to go there, do you, you son-of-a-bitch?" Cody no longer hesitated. He leaped into the light. Warmth enveloped him immediately. He knew he made the right decision. The road, the woods, the rain and most of all the darkness faded away. Only the path lay in front of him. He felt safe and protected.

An unearthly scream penetrated the stillness. The demon was angry. Cody smiled, lifted his middle finger and gestured towards the sound. Then he ran.

Chapter 27

"Stay on the path," Adam cautioned.

Cody stopped at the sound of his brother's voice. "Thanks, Adam."

Running long distances was never his strong suit. He was thankful for the brief recess. Within the three foot band of light, Cody could see every bit of brush, every small pebble that lay in front of him. Beyond the edges of the light lay an opaque darkness and the unknown. He peered into it. He could swear someone was running next to him the entire time. They were unseen, close. The sound chipped away at his confidence.

"Am I close to the cabin?" Cody asked in between catching his breath. He searched the void for any sign of Adam.

A twig snapped in response. Cody froze in place. "Adam, I sure hope that's you out there."

A small rock fell into the path. It was followed by several bigger rocks. They slid onto the path in front of him. Before he could react, a small boulder tumbled down knocking him off his feet. This was followed by a barrage of stones pelting him. Unable to prevent his fall, Cody put his arms up in self-defense. When he fell, he twisted his body to stay within the light. His feet fell off into the void anyway. They weren't out of the light more than a few seconds, when something grabbed them in a painful viselike grip.

"No, let go!"

His body jerked violently towards the darkness.

"Adam, help. It's taking me off the path…no…stop," a pain shot up his leg. "It's biting me," Cody twisted his body again until he was on his stomach. He looked around for something to hold onto. There were only the rocks thrown into the path. Another tug took his legs further into the void. The pain was excruciating. Cody flailed his arms grabbing at anything within reach. He felt another tug. It took all his willpower not to touch his legs.

"Adam, please…I'm not going to make it…"

Whatever was pulling him was far too strong. Cody dug his elbows into the dirt. It was useless. His body inched towards the darkness.

"Adam!"

A rock lay nearby. He picked it up and heaved it in the direction of his feet. There was no sound of an impact. Another much bigger rock lay several feet away. Cody extended his arm but he could only touch it with the tips of his fingers. Then, something grabbed his outstretched hand.

"NO!" He recoiled at the touch. "Adam?"

His brother didn't answer. Cody felt himself being pulled in two directions. He was the rope in a deadly game of tug-of-war. Pain coursed through him. His legs were on fire. For every inch he moved into the light, a corresponding tug pulled him back. He thought his back was going to snap under the pressure. The pain was intolerable.

"Adam!"

The world began to fade away when inexplicably his feet were let go. Cody quickly pulled them into the light. His hand dropped onto the ground. There was no energy left within him. He curled up in a ball exhausted. A cold steady rain tapped on his jacket. It began saturating his clothes. Cody didn't care. He didn't hurt anymore. A close inspection of his ankles revealed no damage. Not even his pants were torn. It had been an illusion albeit a painful one.

"How close am I, Adam?

Cody gasped. The Godfrey cabin stood in front of him. He glanced at his wrist.

"Impossible." His watch claimed an hour had elapsed. It seemed like a few minutes to him. Cody looked back at the brightly lit path.

"Impossible," he repeated.

Chapter 28

"Cody, is that you?" Bess cried.

A yellow shaft of light coming from the cabin momentarily blinded him. He could hear his wife, he just couldn't see her.

"Cody, I'm here. Follow the sound of my voice. Hurry," Bess's voice sounded frantic.

Not sure if he should step away from the safety of the path, he hesitated.

"Cody, it's all right. Listen to Beth," Sami urged.

"Do it!" Adam's voice was the push he needed.

Cody ran towards the yellow light. When he crossed the threshold into the house, he collapsed on the floor.

The group surrounded the shivering detective.

"You look like you've been in a fight," Bess embraced her husband. She held his face in her hands and kissed him gently.

Cody shook his head. He returned her kiss with fervor.

He glanced at the darkness beyond the open door. The lit path was gone.

"It was a fight, that's for sure," he let Bess help him up.

The warmth of the cabin was a welcome change. Cody pulled his wet sport coat off and threw it on the sofa. Bess covered his shoulders with a small throw. She took the seat next to him on the couch. The group followed. No one spoke until Sami broke the silence.

"What happened?" she asked.

Cody was surprised by Sami's question. "I figured you probably knew."

"I only know your thoughts are terribly jumbled. What have you learned?" She continued.

"There's a whole lot in this world I don't understand."

Bess caressed his shoulder. Cody could feel Sami's stare boring into him.

"All right, all right, I remember being in my car at the gate to the main road. I don't remember how I got there. Adam came to me. He told me that Reynard knows there are no more. Then I remember trying to get away from this evil thing with weird red eyes. I think it was Reynard. Anyway, he...it tried to kill me. Then Adam and another spirit helped me get here. They put me on a lit path. I followed it. Something was chasing me. It almost got me. I heard Bess. That's all I know."

"Reynard? Did you say the name, Reynard?" Bennett asked.

Cody turned his attention to Bennett. "Yes, and Adam said he knows, whatever that means."

"What was the name of the other spirit that helped you?" Sami prodded.

"I...I don't know. I only know it was a woman, an Abenaki woman," Cody was surprised by his own statement. "Yes, it was an Abenaki woman. How the hell do I know that?"

"Do you remember anything she said?" Sami asked.

"She told me not to be afraid. That's all I remember. Except this Reynard fellow is pretty pissed. What's going on?" Cody noticed the change in the cabin for the first time. "What happened to the old cabin?"

Sami waved her hand in irritation. She didn't answer Cody's last question.

"What'd I say?" Cody asked. "Was it something I said?"

Bess shook her head. "No dear, she's been like that since you left."

Sami paced in front of the fire. She was clearly upset. The rest of the group stood silently nearby. Cody noticed they all looked worried, afraid.

Elodie entered the living room carrying a cup of hot tea. She handed it to the Detective.

"Why is Reynard chasing Detective Davis, Ms. Howell?" Elodie watched the Detective take a sip.

Sami paused. She opened her mouth to answer then chose otherwise. She shook her head instead.

Elodie shrugged her shoulders.

"Yes, why is the detective being singled out, Sami?" Bennett asked.

"It's because of Adam," Katy offered. She hesitated when Sami looked at her.

"It's all right, Katy," Sami let Katy continue.

"Adam loves his brother. He will do anything for him," Katy said. "Even if it means his spirit will die."

"What do you mean his spirit will die?" Cody said. "How can someone already dead, die?"

"It's death to them. They drift in an endless void unable to come back, unable to communicate. Solitary confinement for all eternity," Sami said.

"Can this mean spirit do that to him?" Cody said.

"I don't know. I guess if it's powerful enough."

"What are you people talking about? Ghosts, demons really? I can't believe you buying into this crap, Uncle Bennett. This is horseshit," Paul Godfrey stood up pulling his keys out of his pocket. "You all can stay here if you like but I'm leaving."

No one in the group made any effort to stop him. Paul yanked the front door open so forcefully, it hit the wall with a loud bang. He put one foot on the threshold and was greeted by a huge blast of frigid air. It punched him backwards. Paul fell hard striking his head on the flagstone entryway. His body went limp. A thin trickle of blood pooled under his skull.

Connie rushed to his side. "Paul, Paul can you hear me? Someone get a towel. He's bleeding." She raised his head off the ground. She cradled it in her hands.

Elodie dashed off down the hall. The group crowded around Paul.

Cody knelt down and picked up his wrist. It was several moments before he put it down. "He's dead."

The group gasped.

"No, he can't be dead. I need to know about Caroline," Harry Cooper rushed to Paul's side and grabbed his lapels. "You can't be dead, you son-of-a-bitch. What did you do to my sister?" Harry shook Paul's lifeless body until Cody and Bennett pulled him away.

"Your sister? Stop, stop. He can't answer you." Cody stood between Harry and Paul's body.

"I vaguely remember you. You were just a kid when Paul married your sister. Harrison, your name is Harrison." Bennett looked at the young man coldly.

"You called the house and talked to Simon. I thought you were some kind of reporter?" Connie looked Harry Cooper up and down.

"The whole interview thing was a hoax? A ruse?" Elodie said.

"The Godfreys think they're so high and mighty. Someone in this family knows exactly what happened to my sister. He knew what happened to my sister," Harry pointed at Paul. Tears of frustration welled up in his eyes. "I came here to find out and I will, if I ever get out of this hell hole." Harry stomped away to the far end of the room.

Connie gently laid Paul's head down. "Is it true? Are we captives, Sister?"

Everyone looked at Sami. She had her arm around Katy St. Clair's waist. She was staring at Paul's lifeless body. "It appears so."

Cody tapped Bennett on the shoulder. "Let's wrap him up in the rug. If we can't leave the house, he can. Let's put his body in the garage."

Bennett nodded woodenly.

Cody and Bennett removed Paul's body. While they were out of the room, Connie and Sami cleaned the stone entryway. The rest of the group talked amongst themselves with the exception of Harry Cooper. He remained at the opposite end of the room--alone. When the men returned, the group returned to their various positions in front of the now extinct fire. Only a bed of embers remained. No one bothered to throw on any more wood. It took too much effort. Paul's sudden death cast a frightening pall over them all. A mixture of grief, fear and anxiety hung in the air. Everyone wondered who would be next.

Bess sat next to Cody with her arm linked around his. Cody rested his arms on his legs. Since he returned from the garage, he had been trying to contact Brian. He held his cell phone in his hands. Every so often, he would tap its face hoping for a signal.

"Any luck?" Bess asked.

"Nope, not even one bar," he answered clearly annoyed. Then he heard a cell phone ringing. Cody looked at his phone but it still read no service.

He watched as Bennett pulled his phone out of his pocket.

"Hello?" Bennett said tentatively after a long pause. "Yes, the cabin...thank you."

"That was Ronald. Mother has died." Bennett voice broke.

"Grandmother?" Elodie pulled a cigarette out of her pocket. She put her hand out to Sami. "Can I use the lighter?"

Sami obliged.

Elodie gave the cigarette a tap against the lighter, then put it in her mouth. She took a huge drag once it was lit. "Too bad the old bitch is dead."

"Elodie!" Bennett exploded. "How dare you speak of my mother that way."

"What? You're going to tell me that she was some kind of Goddess?" Elodie came right back at her father. "You left me and Dani with her and you knew what she was like, didn't you?"

Bennett hung his head. His daughter's words stung. She was right.

"Yes, I knew what she was like. I was afraid to take you away. I was afraid I would lose you, too. It was a mistake," Bennett didn't look at his daughter.

Elodie studied her cigarette. She flicked it into the fireplace. "Never liked the taste anyway."

She felt the urge to hug her father. Years of resentment held her back. Instead, she took a seat in a nearby chair.

"So, Princess is dead?" Cody reiterated.

"Yes."

"It just doesn't get any better, does it? Did Ronald say how she died?" Cody said.

"No, he didn't," Bennett said. "He did say Dani was asking for us and that he was coming to the cabin to pick us up."

Cody kept looking at his cell phone. Then he got up and motioned for Bennett to give him his phone. Cody studied the face of Bennett's cell. He gave it back.

"Strange, your phone has no service either. How did Ronald know you and Elodie were here?"

"I...I don't know?" Bennett looked stricken by the question.

"What can we do, Sami? Can the dead tell us what we can do?" Cody asked.

"Yeah, I want to get out of here," Harry said.

"I bet you do. Can this worm be charged with impersonation or entering someone's home under false pretenses?" Bennett directed his question to the detective.

"As if a Godfrey never lied to get what they want. I bet your mother…" Harry stopped mid-sentence. A noise caught his attention. He walked away from the group towards the opposite end of the house. He stared down the hall that led to the garage. "Did you hear that?"

"Hear what?" Bennett asked.

"That" Harry said.

In the distance, a distinct scrapping sound emanated from the garage.

"Daddy, the garage door is down, isn't it," Elodie asked.

"Yes. Wasn't it? He was dead, wasn't he?" Bennett asked Cody when another loud scrapping sound happened.

Cody didn't hear him. He was looking at the revolver he held in his hand.

Where did you come from? He could have sworn he lost it when his car burned.

"He was dead, wasn't he?" Bennett repeated loudly.

"Yeah, yeah it's hard to fake that sort of thing. Yes, I'm sure Paul Godfrey was dead." Cody couldn't take his eyes off his revolver.

"Maybe a bear's in the garage. They are all around here you know," Bess offered.

Cody shook his head. "I don't think that's a bear. Are there any weapons in the house, Bennett?" He pushed the issue of the revolver out of his mind.

"Should be some hunting rifles in the den. I'll go check," Bennett departed down another hall. He returned moments later without a gun.

"Sorry, the gun cabinet is locked. I have no idea where the key is," he said. "But I did find this." He displayed a wooden baseball bat.

"That ought to do. Follow me," Cody instructed. "You ladies and Harry stay here. Get out of the house if something happens to us. Oh yeah, right, we can't leave. Just stay together."

He nodded to Bennett. The two men walked slowly towards the garage. Half way down the hall, a loud thud made the men stop. This was again followed by the now familiar scrapping sound.

"They certainly don't care if we hear them," Bennett whispered.

Cody nodded in agreement. He continued towards the garage. Once he was within a few feet of the door, Cody extended his hand to grab the knob. It turned before he could touch it.

Surprised by the motion, Cody froze. He took a deep breath then swallowed. He pointed at the moving knob then put his fingers up to his lips cautioning Bennett to stay quiet. He motioned for him to move back down the hallway. Once he was about six feet from the door, Cody put both hands on his revolver and straddled the hallway. As the door knob continued turning, he slowly raised his gun and took aim.

A single click announced the door was disengaged. Cody flexed his fingers then tightened his grip. The door popped open slightly then stopped. Beads of perspiration formed on Cody's brow. He felt uncharacteristically nervous. He swallowed hard again and waited for something, anything to happen. A thin trickle of sweat rolled into his right eye causing it to burn.

Come on. Let's go. What's the hold up? He didn't budge refusing even to wipe his face. He wasn't going to be the one to blink first. He waited.

The door creaked then moved a few inches. It creaked again then opened a few more inches. A draft of cold air spilled into the hallway. With it came the nasty odor of death. Its smell was worse than a punch to the face. A cough rose in Cody's throat. He resisted the urge.

Bennett on the other hand, gagged the moment the foul odor reached him. He couldn't maintain his composure the stench was too much. Nausea overwhelmed him. He could barely remain upright when the door finished its journey.

Bennett felt his heart plunge. He didn't feel sick anymore only the need to run.

Chapter 29

Dani held Reynard's journal in her hand. Various items that had been stuck within it pages lay strewn on top of her bed: an old indenture, a map of Temple Falls dated 1846 and a single black and white photo. It was the picture that interested her the most. She put the journal down and picked up the picture again.

"Robert's christening, 1918." She read on the back. She flipped the photo over and studied it. It was taken in the living room of the mansion. Her grandfather, was dressed in a frilly, flowing white christening dress complete with a white bonnet. Her great-grandfather stood beaming next to her great-grandmother whose expression looked anything but happy. Next to her, holding a tray, stood the butler.

"Wow, that really looks like Ronald," she said to herself.

She was so engrossed in the photo, Dani didn't hear the first knock on her bedroom door. The second knock pulled her away from the picture. She gathered all the pieces of the journal.

Where should I hide this? She thought. Her grandmother's warning still fresh in her memory.

It was several moments before she found a safe place.

"Come in," she called.

The door opened revealing her visitor, Ronald.

"Yes, Ronald."

"I have unfortunate news, Madame," he said.

"What is it?"

"Your Grandmother is deceased," Ronald said bluntly.

Dani looked at Ronald in disbelief. *You're a cold bastard,* was her first thought. Stunned by the news, she felt a host of emotions and thoughts assaulting her brain. She didn't know whether to cry in sorrow or relief.

"Ronald, please find Uncle Bennett and Elodie. They must know the news," She waved her hand to dismiss him. Ronald hesitated in the doorway.

What are you waiting for? She thought.

"Is there anything else?" she asked.

"No, Madame," he said bowing before he left.

Dani checked the safety of the journal one more time before leaving the room. Something about the photo of her grandfather's christening struck her as odd. However, she couldn't quite figure out why. She forced it out of her brain for the moment.

Her Grandmother's bedroom door stood open. Dani steeled herself against what was to come next. She hated dead bodies, funerals and such. She wished her Uncle R.P or her father were there taking care of their mother rather than she. Unfortunately, she had no choice. She was now the oldest female in the family.

Her grandmother's room smelled stale and musty. Infused with the faint odor of Princess' favorite perfume. Several of the servants huddled nearby whispering.. They stepped away when Dani entered. Her grandmother lay on the chaise lounge much like she did every day. Although she knew she was dead, Dani expected Princess to say something when she walked in front of her. Therefore, it was a shock when she finally saw her face. Princess's eyes were wide open in a look of surprise. Her head was tipped backwards. Her lips were blue and slightly raised in a frozen smile. Her boney hands gripped the shawl around her neck. Under her chin, Dani could see bruises in the shape of fingers. Dani realized her grandmother had been murdered.

"Pat, call 911. Tell the police my grandmother's been murdered," she said to one of the servants.

"Madame, I think they're still at the entrance," the maid offered.

"Then tell Mr. Blanchard to drive to the gates and inform the officers what's happened. Now go!" Dani knelt down next to her Grandmother. Alone in the room, Dani reached out and touched Princess' hand. It was still warm. "Who could have done this?"

"Where's the journal, Dani?"

Dani whirled around at the sound of her Uncle's voice. "Uncle R.P?"

The sight of him terrified her. Even as a child, she recoiled from his touch. At that moment, it struck her that her Grandmother was always in the room with her when Uncle R. P. was near. She had never been alone with him, until now. She looked at her Grandmother.

"She can't help you now, Dani. Ding, dong the old bitch is dead," he sneered.

Dani felt trapped. Her escape route was the way she came in and she wasn't sure she could outrun him.

The police will be here soon. I've got to stall, she thought.

"What journal? What are you talking about?" she stammered.

"You never were a good liar, Dani. I know my mother passed Reynard's journal to you. Since she is dead, you are the oldest female. It is your responsibility to watch over the family." R. P. turned away from her. He walked in a small circle and as he did, he began pulling out pieces of his hair.

"You know, my mother thought my father was possessed by some evil spirit: the ghost of our dead ancestor or some such thing." A hair extension fell to the floor. "She really believed his slow death was because of some family "curse"." R. P. took off his bloodied jacket and let it drop. "Stupid woman, there is no family curse." He walked by the end of the chaise lounge and pulled several Kleenex tissues out of a box. He wiped his face. "There's only me."

"You, Uncle R. P.?" Dani said.

"Yes, me," He stretched his arms out as if to encompass the entire room. "I am responsible for it all."

"How could you be…?" she started to rebut his last statement. She knew his claim of responsibility was ridiculous. He wasn't alive when his grandfather and great-grandfather died mysteriously. What she did know was her Uncle was dangerously insane.

"So," he said. "I repeat. Where's the journal, Dani?" He continued wiping off the stage makeup smeared on his face.

"I truly don't know what you are talking about," Dani bluffed.

"Dani, Dani, Dani what am I going to do with you?" He said sighing heavily. The dresser mirror caught his reflection. R. P. paused to admire himself. His tirade stopped.

Dani couldn't take her eyes off of him. His preening was almost comical. She watched as

his initial glance turned into an intense inspection of his face. He turned one way then another.

"Why isn't this makeup coming off," he said rubbing his cheeks furiously. A bit of skin tore loose and exposed his cheek bone. He didn't seem to notice or care.

"It's not coming off!" he screamed again. His mouth sagged in one corner.

This can't be. Am I insane? Dani watched in horror as the drama unfolded.

Uncle R. P. grabbed his hair. He yanked out more than just extensions. Screaming at his image in the mirror, he tore at his face with renewed vigor. He forgot there was anyone else in the room.

Dani saw her opportunity. She bolted out the door and into the hallway. She could still hear Uncle R. P. screaming at the mirror as she ran. Thankfully, the hallway was empty. She raced down the staircase towards the front door. Her hand barely touched knob when it opened on its own. She ran right into Mr. Blanchard and Officer Smith. She fell into Brian's arms.

"He's crazy. He's ripping his face apart," she screamed.

"Who? Slow down. What are you talking about?" Brian held Dani at arms' length. He shook her gently until her eyes met his.

"Who's ripping their face apart?"

"Uncle R. P.. He's crazy," she sobbed.

"I've heard that a lot about the Godfreys. Where's your grandmother?" Brian held on to her.

"She's in her sitting room. She's been murdered. Someone strangled her," Dani could barely talk.

"Take me to her," he looked at Mr. Blanchard.

"No sir, won't do it. Place is evil. I'm leaving," with that pronouncement, Mr. Blanchard turned on his heels and left.

"You stay here," Brian told Dani

"No, I better go with you. I don't want to be alone," She straightened herself. "I'm okay. I am sure everyone has gone. News travels fast in this house."

I bet it does, Brian let Dani walk past him. The feeling of dread he felt earlier in the evening hit him with a wallop when he crossed the threshold. He stayed close to Dani as she walked up the huge staircase. He pressed his walkie on his shoulder. "Going to investigate Princess Godfrey. You copy?"

He received no response. "Do you copy?"

"Guess they're busy," he continued up the staircase. His stomach knotted. "Yeah, they're busy."

Chapter 30

"I thought you said he was dead," Bennett said clearly upset at the current situation.

"He was. I swear," Detective Davis didn't move from his stance. His legs straddled the hallway. His hands were wrapped tightly around his revolver pointed at Paul's forehead.

"If he was dead, he wouldn't be standing there," Bennett pointed frantically at the doorway.

"No shit. What's that…What's that in his hand?" Cody eyes flicked between Paul's forehead and his right hand.

"He's got a hatchet," Bennett warned.

"Drop it, Paul. I mean it. I'll shoot," Cody commanded. His eyes darted back and forth.

Paul didn't move.

"Hey, look at his eyes." Bennett said.

Cody looked up. Paul's eyes were open but there was no recognition, no life, dead.

"He *is* dead," Cody said.

"If he's dead, what's making him move? Watch out!" Bennett pointed to the hatchet as it moved slowly upwards.

"I don't know. Adam, Adam can you help me here?" Cody called.

"Malsumis," Katy said falling in behind Bennett.

"No, my dear, it is not Malsumis," Sami said stepping in front of Katy. "This is something else. A demon more powerful than Malsumis. Move out of the way gentlemen." Bennett stepped aside. Cody was harder to convince.

"Are you nuts, Sami? Get away. He has a weapon."

"So, do I," she countered pushing Cody aside. In her hands, Sami held a push broom. She charged past the detective with the head of the broom pointed at Paul's mid-section. Before Cody could react, Sami rammed her weapon into Paul knocking him out of the doorway and into the garage. She then slammed the door and bolted it.

Cody stared at the small woman with unabashed respect. "Well, I'll be damned."

Sami smiled briefly. "We have work to do gentlemen. I don't think Paul will be bothering us for the moment. Let's convene in the living room." Sami walked briskly away towards the living room. She grabbed Katy's hand in passing.

Bennett merely shook his head. He fell in step behind Katy. Cody hesitated. "I'll be there in a moment."

He was unconvinced Sami's maneuver had contained Paul. He touched the garage door, then pressed his ear against it. The garage was silent.

"Hope this holds," he whispered patting the door.

Cody and Bennett returned to the living room. The entire group was shaken by the latest development.

"Cody, I'm scared. What's happening to us?" Bess wrapped her arms around Cody.

"I wish I knew," Cody took a seat on the couch. He patted the seat for Bess to follow. The rest of the group did the same with the exception of Harry Cooper. Harry was pacing in front of the picture window.

"Mr. Cooper, now that Cody is here, why don't you join us?" Sami said.

Harry shook his head. He ignored Sami's invitation. He continued pacing.

Connie sat on the edge of the sofa. "Why are we being held here, Sister?" she asked.

"I'm like Cody. I wish I knew. The dead have quit talking, again," Sami said.

"I thought you said this Malsumis god wasn't particularly evil. He only played tricks." Bennett said.

Katy nodded her head.

"Yeah, this Malsumis guy brings us here then tries to kill us. Sounds evil to me," Cody added.

"Listen to you people. You all sound crazy. Voices from the dead stopped talking, do you think I was born yesterday? You're all in on this. All of you!" Harry pointed his finger at each of them. "Paul isn't dead. This is a trick to cover up the fact he murdered my sister. I'll prove it to you," Harry stomped away from the window towards the hallway and the bolted garage door.

"Stop him," Cody yelled.

Bennett leaped out of his chair. He tackled Harry before he got half way down the hall. Cody pulled a pair of handcuffs off his belt and promptly snapped them on the young man's wrists. He pulled the struggling Harry up and forced him onto the couch.

"Sit down and shut up," Cody commanded. "That thing out there is not alive. Believe me."

Harry snorted his response.

"What now, Sami? Do you have any ideas?" Cody asked.

"You were right when you said we were all brought here for a reason, Cody. Each of us has been touched in some way by this being. I'm not necessarily talking about Malsumis." Sami stood up. She walked over to the picture window.

"So what are you saying? That this thing wants to kill us because we know about it?" Cody looked at the group.

"Possibly," Sami shrugged.

"Sister, is there a way we can force the dead to talk to us?" Connie asked.

"Force them?" Sami looked a Connie.

"Yes, can't we contact the dead in some way. Like a séance?"

"I don't know why I didn't think of that before. Yes, a séance might do the trick. Let's all get in a circle. That means even you, Mr. Cooper."

Harry turned away from Sami. "This is ridiculous."

"That may be, Mr. Cooper. However, if you want to get out of here, I suggest you play along or we may leave you behind."

Harry thought for a moment. He huffed several times. "Fine, but I have to be out of these." He motioned to his handcuffs.

"Yeah, well promise me you won't open the garage door and I'll take 'em off." Cody said.

"Fine," Harry said again. "I promise".

Cody undid the handcuffs. "What do you want us to do, Sami?"

"Let's adjourn to a large table. Can you take us to one, Mr. Godfrey?"

"Certainly, follow me," Bennett proceeded out of the room.

The group followed Bennett down the hall to a set of French doors. He opened them then motioned for everyone to go inside.

"Wow, this is some kind of dining room," Cody was impressed. Dark mahogany wood panels covered the walls. An even darker mahogany dining table and twelve matching chairs filled the room.

At the far end of the room, behind the head of the table was a large stone fireplace with a simply carved mantel. A tray with an array of half-filled crystal decanters and a set of short glasses sat on one end of the mantel. A large painting of the Temple Falls reservation was above the mantel in the center of the wall. Beneath the painting was a tall, brass clock.

Although there were two windows on either side of the fireplace, the room was designed to be dark and intimate.

Bennett remained at the door while everyone took their place. He studied the surroundings. "Yes, sometimes my father held business meetings here amongst other things." He sighed and closed the doors behind him before taking a seat.

Sami sat at the head of the table. "Okay, everyone join hands." Sami said.

She offered her hand to Connie. Connie did the same to Bess and so on.

"Now what," Harry said. "Don't we need a candle or crystal ball in the middle?"

"Shut up, Harry," Elodie snapped.

"Please everyone, we need to direct our energy to the dead. Close your eyes and concentrate on a departed friend or family member. Maybe we can coax one of souls of the dead to break through," Sami closed her eyes.

"Yeah, right. Then what?" Harry asked.

"*Now* we wait. *Quietly,*" Sami emphasized her last word. "Concentrate please."

Harry sighed loudly. He opened his mouth then stopped when Cody jerked his hand. The detective dropped his gaze to the handcuffs strategically placed on the table. Harry took the hint. Soon the only sound that could be heard was the slow, methodical tick-tock of the mantel clock. Several minutes elapsed. Then a few more. It was too long for Harry.

"Well, has anyone talked, yet?" Harry said sarcastically.

"Shhhh…" Connie warned. "If you keep talking…" she stopped mid-sentence. Her eyes opened wide. She squeezed her sister's hand. "I can hear a voice." She whispered in awe. "It's a woman's voice."

The air in the room grew cold.

"Hey, I can see my breath," Sami cut Harry off before he could talk any further.

"Go on, Sister."

"My name is…I don't understand?" Connie stopped talking. A change came over her. She fell into a trance.

"Connie, Connie?" Sami couldn't get her sister's attention.

"What's happening to her? Is she possessed or something?" Elodie whispered.

"I don't know. I can't hear anything. The souls of the dead aren't talking to me," Sami was worried.

"Connie, who's talking to you?" she spoke softly to her sister.

"Akwi sagezo."

"I know what that means. It means "don't be afraid"," Cody said.

"We're not afraid," Sami answered.

"Speak for yourself," Harry added.

Cody pulled his hand again.

"Akwi sagezo," Connie repeated.

"We're not afraid. Who are you?" Sami prodded.

"He has many faces." Connie said.

"Who? Who has many faces?"

"The trader," Connie said.

"The trader?" Sami repeated

"My ancestor, Reynard. He was a fur trader." Bennett offered.

"We need to know more." Sami said. "Are we dealing with the Godfrey's ancestor, Reynard?

"He hides among you. Find him. Expose his deception. It will destroy him," Connie continued.

The room grew colder.

"Reynard died in1802. You want us to kill something that's already dead?" Bennett looked at Sami in confusion. "No, no." He pushed slightly back from the table. "I agree with Harry. This *is* nuts."

"Don't let go," Sami demanded. "Go on, please tell us more."

Bennett hesitated then did as Sami wanted.

A tear rolled down Connie's cheek. "So many lies." Her eyes rolled back in her head. She fell back against her chair. Water trickled from her open mouth. She began to gasp and choke.

"What's going on? She looks like she's drowning," Bess screamed.

"Don't let go," Sami demanded when she saw Bess's hand move. "Are you the young woman Reynard wanted? The young Abenaki woman who died leaping from the cliff?"

Connie's body jerked forward. Water spilled from her mouth onto the table. It turned a horrible crimson color.

"Mekwi nebi, red water," Katy declared.

"Oh God, what do we do?" Elodie wailed at the sight.

"Akwi sagezo." Connie gasped as the water ran down her chin.

"Yeah, we know. Don't be afraid. That's hard to do right now," Cody shouted.

The water from Connie's mouth stopped as abruptly as it started. Her head snapped violently backwards as the rest of her limp body fell against the chair. Her chest swelled with a draught of precious air. Then her head pitched violently backwards again only to be suddenly thrust forward until it stopped within a few inches from the table. No one moved. The room became deadly quiet. All were horrified by the sight. Bess squeezed Cody's hand.

"What's happening? Is she all right?

Cody looked at his wife. He shrugged his shoulders slightly and whispered. " I don't know."

Connie's back arched. She took another huge breath.

"Thank God," Bess said.

It was several moments before her breathing returned to normal. Then her head rose until she was once again sitting upright. All were relieved at her revival.

"Mekwi nebi, red water," Katy said softly.

"He must follow me into mekwi nebi," Connie blinked several times then closed her eyes.

Sami squeezed Connie's hand. She softly called to her sister. "Connie? Connie?"

"Wait a minute. We have to find him? Kill him then have him follow her into mekwi nebi?" Cody shook his head. He looked at Katy. "Didn't you tell us Bloody Creek was mekwi nebi? I thought the young girl jumped from a cliff? We're a long way from Bloody Creek."

"Not really. There are dozens of small creeks that spill into Lake Champlain. Maybe Bloody Creek is one of them. Maybe it meets the lake near the cliff where she died," Bennett said.

"Okay, so if Bloody Creek falls into the lake. How do you propose we kill this demon then make it follow her over the cliff into mekw nebi?" Cody asked. "Can she tell us how?" He looked towards Sami.

"I'm done. You're all a bunch of crazy nut jobs." Harry wrenched his hand out of Cody's.

"No! Don't move," Sami cried.

It was too late.

"You've broken the link. She might have told us how."

"Smooth move, you idiot. I ought to cuff you to the table and leave you there," Cody picked up the handcuffs and shook them at Harry.

Irritated, Sami looked at her sister. She was slumped over in her chair. "The spirit is gone."

Warmth returned to the room

"Connie can you hear me?" She tapped her sister's hand.

Connie sat up. She looked around the room. "What happened?"

"Do you remember anything?" Sami asked.

"I heard a woman's voice. She sounded young. Oh Sami, I heard a voice," Connie was elated.

"Find him?" Cody ran his hands through his hair. "Kill him. How when we really don't know what this Reynard fellow looks like now. Did she give you any clues about that?"

"I don't remember." Connie couldn't hide her disappointment.

"Great, we're back to square one," Harry pulled a small picture out of his back pocket. "Sorry Caroline."

"Is that a picture of Caroline?" Bennett felt an odd urge to look at the picture.

"Yes, it was taken at the wedding. It was the last time I saw her," Harry said.

"Can I look at it?" The urge grew stronger.

"Sure, why not," Harry said passing the picture to Bennett.

"I can't explain why. I just have the strangest feeling this picture is important," Bennett said.

Elodie got behind her father and peered over his shoulder. She studied the picture, too.

"Wow, that was some dress. Caroline looks beautiful. There you are Daddy. There's Grandmother and... is that Ronald?" Elodie's voice was surprised.

Bennett brought the picture a little closer to his face. "Sure looks like him. Can't be Ronald though. This was taken twenty-some years ago. Even if it was, the man avoids cameras like the plague." He brought the picture even closer. "Still, I have to admit it does look like him. He hasn't changed a bit."

Bennett's comment caught Sami's attention. "Let me look at that," she said holding her hand out.

Bennett passed the picture to her. She scrutinized it carefully. "Twenty-some years ago, huh? You said he hates having his picture taken?"

"Yes, I don't think I've ever seen him in one."

The clock on the mantel gonged.

"This was taken twenty years ago?" She repeated

"Yes," said Bennett.

The clock gonged again.

"Yes," Harry sat up in his chair. His eyes traveled to the clock.

"And he hasn't changed a bit?"

The clock gonged.

"Yes, what the hell is wrong with that clock. It's not supposed to be..." Bennett looked up at the mantel.

By now everyone's eyes were fixed on the old clock.

The clock gonged again, then again.

"She's telling us something..." Connie pointed at the mantel.

Bennett and Cody jumped up from the table. They raced for the clock at the same time.

"Are you thinking what I'm thinking?" Cody asked Bennett.

"Well if you're thinking this clock has the answer, then yes. Maybe it has a hidden drawer?" Bennett lifted the clock up gently. "Don't see anything."

"Look underneath," Cody said.

"Nope, nothing there."

"Change the position of the hands," Cody said.

"Then it should have opened on its own at some point." Bennett put the clock on the table.

"Let me look," Connie stood up. Her legs wobbled unsteadily when she attempted her first step.

"Don't," she said when Cody reached out to her. "I'm fine."

Once she was in front of the clock, she grabbed the closest chair and sat down. She pulled the clock towards her. Then she opened the front of the clock and stopped the pendulum. Everyone crowded around her. No one spoke as Connie inspected every inch of the brass clock.

"Wait." Something caught her eye. There was a fine line cutting across the base. "I think there is a hidden drawer after all," She exclaimed. "Now how do I open it?"

Bennett pulled a small knife out of his pocket. Connie got up and allowed him to take her place.

"Let's not waste any more time." Bennett thrust the thin blade of the knife into the seam and pushed down. A drawer popped open.

"What have we here?" he said pulling out a small photo.

"What? What is it?" Cody asked trying to peer over Bennett's shoulder.

"It's a wedding picture—an old wedding picture taken about the turn of the century. It's not very clear. I can't quite make out who is in it." He held the picture up under the light of the candelabra. "Now I can. The bride is my Grandmother Louisa. My Grandfather is the groom. They were married in 1903. The man next to my Grandfather is a cousin. The other person is the but...ler," He stopped mid-sentence and looked at the picture again. "It's Ronald. The butler looks just like Ronald."

"Ronald? Let me look," Elodie took the picture from her father.

"Wow, it does look like Ronald. Even his clothes are the same. But you said your Grandmother was married in 1903. Ronald is now what, 70, 80 years old. He looks the same age in this picture. He couldn't have been alive today, if he was 80 years old then." Elodie was completely bewildered.

"How is that possible?" Harry asked peering over her shoulder. "Maybe it's a relative of his?"

The clock gonged.

"What the hell?" Cody startled by the sound.

Bennett returned his attention to the clock. "I guess someone wants us to look further."

He lifted the clock up to get a better look inside the compartment "What do you know. There's another piece of paper stuck in here. I can't grab it. Does anyone have a pair of tweezers?"

"I do," Connie said. It's in my purse in the living room. She left and soon returned with a small pair. "Here."

It was several moments before Bennett removed the piece of paper. It was brown and fragile with age. When he unfolded it, bits of the edges fell off.

"It's a note written by my grandmother," He said. "It says: "His life is contained in its memory.""

"What does that mean? " Elodie asked.

Bennett studied the note. "I wonder why Grandmother didn't write something more specific."

"Maybe she was afraid Ronald might find the note," Cody said.

"What do we do now?" Harry said.

"Well, the spirit told us several things we have to do," Sami said rising from her chair. "First, we must discover what this demon's deception is. Second, he must die for us to be free. Third, he has to follow her to return." She took the photo from Elodie then the note from Bennett.

"Maybe it's just a coincidence that the butler in the wedding picture looks like Ronald." Cody said.

"Or maybe…" Sami became lost in thought.

"Wait a minute. I remember something." Bennett took the small picture from Sami. "I'll be back in a minute.

Bennett returned to the living room. He walked up to a large bookcase. The top of the bookcase was enclosed within a set of glass doors. Each pair of doors had its own key. Bennett started on the left. He unlocked the first set of glass doors. Below the three rows of books in front of him were a set of drawers. Bennett went through each drawer. When he was done, he moved on to the second set of doors. This continued until he reached the third and last set of doors.

"Finally," he exclaimed. He pulled out a small leather case and opened it. He smiled broadly. "I thought so."

"What is it, Daddy?" Curious, Elodie had followed her father.

"When I was a small boy, my grandmother showed me a miniature on ivory of our French ancestor, Reynard Pillion Gillett. I think this will be of interest to all of you." He handed the picture to Elodie.

"Oh my God," Elodie gasped.

Bennett took the miniature back. He smiled. "First, we expose his deception."

Chapter 31

Dani escorted Detective Smith to her grandmother's room. She let him walk in first. With the exception of her grandmother's remains, the room was empty. She looked around nervously. It would be like her Uncle to appear without warning.

"Where do you think your Uncle might be?" Brian asked noting her nervousness.

Dani hesitated then took a step into the room. She remained, however, near the door.

"I don't know where he went. He's crazy," her voice trembled.

Brian nodded. *All the Godfreys are crazy.*

He walked around the edge of the chaise lounge. Princess was lying on her back against several large pillows. Her head was tilted back as if she was staring at the ceiling. Her eyes were open. Her lips had a distinct bluish tint. They were turned up in a slight smile. Brian could see red imprints of a pair of hands encircling her neck. He spent several minutes taking notes. In that time, Dani stood silently by the door.

"Would you mind calling the servants here?" he kept writing as he spoke.

"Certainly," Dani promptly did as she was told. The small group arrived. They huddled next to Dani at the door.

Brian noticed one person was missing. "Where's the butler? "

"I don't know. I'll ring for him again," Dani was genuinely surprised at Ronald's absence.

Brian circled the couch. He walked over to the mirror where R. P. had thrown bits of hair. He pulled latex gloves out of his pocket and a small baggie. He slipped on the gloves then plucked some of the hair off the floor and deposited them in the baggie.

Whatever trips your trigger, Buddy, He thought wryly.

When Ronald still did not appear after several minutes, Brian turned his attention to Dani.

"Where do you think the butler might be?" he asked.

"I don't know. He's always here. I can't remember a time when he didn't come immediately when he was summoned. I...I could go look for him," Dani posture belied her fear.

"No, better you stay here." Brian pulled his cell phone out of his pocket.

"That's funny," he said. "My battery is dead. I could have sworn..." his voice trailed off.

"Would you like to use the house phone?" Dani asked.

"Yeah, sure," Brian scribbled again in his notebook.

Dani went to the table next to the chaise lounge and stopped. The phone was not in its cradle. "That's odd," She noted.

"Hmm, what?" Brian looked up from his writings.

"The phone is always returned to the base. Grandmother demanded it. Have any of you seen the phone?" Dani poised her question to the servants. They shook their heads in unison. She then presented another question: "Have any of you seen Ronald?" Again, they shook their heads no.

"I don't know what to tell you, Detective Smith. Ronald is here.

In fact, he is always here It's unlike him not to answer." Dani was genuinely perplexed.

"Ma'am, beg your pardon," A young servant girl shyly spoke up. "Mr. Ronald drove away from the house a little bit ago."

"Why didn't you say so earlier? Never mind. Do you know where he was going?" Dani annoyed at the girl's omission.

The girl shook her head.

"What was he driving?" Dani asked a different question.

"He left in the truck, Ma'am?" a different servant offered.

"You, too? Is there anything else any of you're not telling me?" Dani glowered at her staff. She looked at the Detective. "I can't imagine why he left in the truck,"

"Why? What's special about the truck?" Brian asked. He thought about the white truck and the abducted girl.

"Nothing really, except it is used for maintenance on the house and the cabin. I can't recall a time when I ever saw him drive the truck." Dani continued.

"So, you think he is somewhere in the vicinity?" said Brian.

"I guess so. He should be." Dani said.

"No, Ma'am he drove out of the gates," the young servant said.

"He drove out of the gates? Why on earth is he going to the cabin?" Dani was clearly annoyed.

Brian pulled out his cell phone again then snapped it closed just as quickly. He pointed at Dani. "You come with me. Lock this door. It's a crime scene and until I get through to the station, I don't want anyone in here."

He charged out of the room. Dani dismissed the staff with a wave of her hand. She locked the door and hurried after the detective. She caught up with him at the front door.

"Where are you going?" she asked.

"My men are still at the gates. They can tell us more. You need to give me directions to the cabin. Let's go." Brian charged down the staircase and was almost out the front door when Dani grabbed his arm

"Wait. My car is right around the corner."

"Great," Brian let Dani take the lead. He followed her around the opposite side of the house. A small compact car was parked just out of view. Dani jumped into the driver's seat. She pulled the visor down to retrieve a set of keys. Brian joined her on the opposite side just as the motor jumped to life.

They arrived at the front gates in a matter of minutes. Dani stopped the car a few feet from the entrance. The metal gates stood wide open. The police officers were nowhere in sight.

"That's odd," Dani said. "Why are the gates open? They close automatically."

"Stay here. Keep the car running. Go back to the house and lock yourself in if anything happens." Brian said. He stepped out of the car with his gun drawn. He walked slowly towards the gates.

"Larry, Steve where are you?" he called to the two officers. There was no response. He walked slowly forward until he broached the property line. Once on the opposite side of the metal gates, he saw what was holding them open: two lifeless bodies of his fellow officers.

"Call 911, Miss Godfrey. Tell the operator I have two officers down," He yelled back over his shoulder.

"My phone's not working. I'll go back to the house," Dani yelled back then she gunned the engine before speeding off.

Brian raced to his men. The light emanating from lanterns at the top of the gate allowed him to see a wide swath of the immediate area. It assured him he was alone, at least for the moment. He bent down over the first body. The officer was lying face down. He looked up and noted that the second man was slumped over in a sitting position with his back against the metal gate. Brian could hear the gate straining to close.

Brian rolled the first officer over. He could see no bruises or marks indicating the man had been hit by a fleeing car. In fact, there were no marks indicating any kind of trauma. He put his hand on the man's neck and pressed.

"Great, no pulse," he felt defeated. A breeze touched him and with it came a familiar smell. Brian reacted quickly. He turned in the direction of the wind and raised his revolver. "I know you're here. Show yourself, you bastard."

Beyond the circle of light was an opaque darkness. He strained to see into it. "I know you're here. Every murder case I've been on since I came to Temple Falls has left its mark or rather its smell on me. You can't help it if you stink," he said taunting the unknown. "Come on, show yourself." He pulled his revolver out from under his jacket.

"What makes you think your gun will kill me, Officer Smith?" A voice answered.

"Oh, I don't know, maybe it's because you're made up of flesh and blood and guns have a way of doing that."

R.P. stepped into the light. He was still dressed in rags like before, but his hair was almost completely gone. Brian thought about the baggie of hair in his pocket. The flesh on R.P.'s face was torn and bleeding. He stood twisted and hunched like before. It was an effort for him to walk. Brian's stomach churned at the sight of him.

"What the hell happened to you?"

R. P. seemed taken aback by the question. "Me? There's nothing wrong with me?"

"Nothing wrong with you? Have you looked in a mirror lately? Who tore up your face? Stay where you are." Brian commanded when R. P. took a step forward. The sound of car coming towards the gates reassured him. "I have backup on the way."

"You mean my niece, Dani?" R.P. laughed uncontrollably. "She can't help you. You forget she's a Godfrey. Her loyalties are with the family." He took another menacing step forward.

"Somehow I don't get the same feeling about her," Brian said.

A car door shut. From where he was standing, Brian could hear but could not see anything on the opposite side of the gates. The sound of the car door baffled him. It sounded heavier than a door for a small, compact vehicle. His first impression told him it was a truck. Brian glanced nervously towards the entrance. "Miss Godfrey, Dani is that you?"

"Miss Godfrey, Dani is that you," R. P. mocked. "I thought police officers were hard core, tough. You seem nervous. Do I make you nervous, Officer?" R. P. inched forward.

"I told you to stop," Brian pointed his gun at the center of R.P.'s chest.

R. P. stopped. With an exaggerated motion, he looked up the driveway towards the mansion. He nodded his head in acknowledgement of someone in the shadows.

Brian still couldn't see who it was. He glanced towards the entrance then quickly looked back.

R. P.'s eyes were locked on the young detective. It was an evil, menacing stare. He made a sweeping gesture towards the yellow police tape behind him.

"I see your officers found my young friend. I believe her name was Celia, no Susan. Yes, I do believe it was Susan. Lovely girl. Quite the fighter."

"You sick bastard. Why? Why did you kill her?" Brian asked. He wished he had a better view of the driveway. The sense that someone else might be nearby worried him.

R. P. closed his eyes. He ignored Brian's question. "Oh, I do love it when they struggle." He took a deep breath then let it out. "Please don't hurt me." He said in a high falsetto. "Then they let me do anything I want. Think of it Detective, a submissive woman willing to do anything to survive. Stupid girls. They think I'll let them go when I done. Can't do that."

"So, you screw them before you kill them?" Brian asked. "How many, how many have you killed?"

Again R. P. ignored the question. "Sometimes I *screw* them as you so aptly put it. It all depends on their fear. Yes, their fear," He mused. "He taught me to love the smell of fear. Ahhhh....yes...., I do so love the smell of fear. It's an amazing turn on." A visible shiver racked his body. Then he stopped and stared at the detective. Again in an exaggerated motion, he sniffed the air around him. "It's all around me tonight."

Brian glanced to either side. "What is?"

"The smell of fear," R. P. lunged at the detective.

Brian fired directly into the deformed man's chest. The first bullet stopped him. Several more made him topple over backwards. R. P. hit the ground with a thud.

Out of the corner of his right eye, Brian saw something move. He whirled towards the gates and the entrance to the Godfrey property.

"Come out now." He screamed tightening his grip on his revolver. R. P. had been right. He was afraid.

"It's me, Detective Smith, Dani," a woman's voice called.

"Show yourself Miss Godfrey. Slowly," Brian said. "I can't see you."

"Drop the gun, Brian," It was Cody's voice this time.

Brian took a step backwards. "Cody?"

"Cody's not here. He can't help you."

Brian looked down at the voice coming from the base of the gate. The officer against the gate was standing up. His eyes were open but vacant.

"What...how? No this isn't real. You're dead," Brian stammered.

"Am I?" A voice to his left answered.

Brian felt his heart skip. He slowly turned towards the sound of the voice. The twisted form of the man he thought he killed moments ago was also standing. Blood oozed from the front of R.P.'s chest. He was no longer hunched over as before. Instead, he was standing completely upright with his head bent slightly forward. His arms hung limply by his side.

Brian fired again. The bullet struck R. P.'s body ripping another hole in the rags that covered him. The bullets had little effect. R. P. refused to fall.

Brian pulled the trigger until the clicking gun alerted him to its empty barrel. He reached under his jacket and pulled out a new clip and shoved it into his gun. He pointed it once more at the approaching R. P. "What the fuck are you?"

R. P smirked. He stared at the detective with his eyes half closed. He didn't answer.

"NO!" Dani's screamed. She emerged from the other side of the gate running towards her uncle.

"Stop! Don't go near him," Brian warned.

Dani screamed again. She stopped and pointed to her left. The first police officer was sitting up. The second was staggering forward in stiff controlled steps.

R. P. stopped his forward movement. He put his arms out towards his niece "Dani, my love. Come to your favorite Uncle."

Dani looked at her uncle and took one step. Brian lowered his gun. "Don't do it, Dani. He's not real. Run Dani. Run to your car. We have to get out of here, now!"

He fired several more rounds into R.P. as he ran towards the frightened girl. When he reached her, he grabbed her arm. "Where's your car?"

"It's just beyond the gate. What about him?" Dani pointed at her Uncle.

"You can't help him," he pulled her up the driveway. "Give me the keys."

"They're in the ignition," Dani yelled scrambling into the passenger seat.

Brian threw himself into the car. He turned the key immediately.

As he put the car in gear he looked up. Three figures stood in a line across the entrance.

A blast of wind rocked the car. "Shit! Hold on," he yelled gunning the engine before finally releasing his foot from the brake. The small car lurched forward.

Diane screamed, "They're not moving. You're going to kill them" She closed her eyes anticipating the impact.

"Yeah, that's the point. Die again, you sons-of-a-bitches," Brian pressed the accelerator to the floor taking aim at R. P. in the middle. The car flew over the threshold. It reached the main road so quickly, Brian barely had enough time to negotiate the turn. He wrenched the wheel. The car tipped dangerously. He fought for control before speeding away from the estate. Several miles elapsed before either of them spoke.

"Did we hit them? I didn't feel an impact did you?" he asked glancing at his passenger. His knuckles were white from his death grip on the steering wheel.

Dani shook her head. "No, I didn't feel anything. Is Uncle R. P. dead? Did you kill him?"

"I thought I did the first time. Then he stood up. They all stood up. I don't understand any of this? " Brian voice was strained.

"What are we going to do now?" Dani asked.

"I have to think." Brian paused for a moment. He flexed his hands trying to bring the blood back into them. "The Cabin. I think we need to go there. Can you take me there?"

"Yes, why?"

"Just a hunch. What's that?" Brian asked nodding towards her lap.

"Something my grandmother told me to protect. I...I heard her tell me to get it when I went back to the house." Dani fingered Reynard's journal. "Turn after the next bend in the road."

Brian followed Dani's instructions. He didn't comment on her last statement of hearing from her dead grandmother. The whole night had been one of firsts. What was one more? A distinct numbness encompassed his brain. His thoughts were muddled.

Dani's instructions lead them to the entrance gate leading to the cabin. Under Brian's watchful eye, she got out of the car and opened it. When she returned to her seat, Brian tossed his phone to her. He felt like he was running out of time. It was an eerie, uncomfortable feeling.

"See if it works."

Perspiration dotted his face in spite of the cold.

It's a nightmare. This has to be a nightmare, he thought. He would have dialed the phone himself but his hands were shaking too badly. He didn't want Dani to see his fear. He recited the number for the police station to her. When the call went through, he allowed himself to relax a little.

"Great, tell the dispatcher where we are going. I think we are going to need help." He leaned back in his seat feeling in control for the first time that evening. "Yeah, definitely going to need some help."

Darkness surrounded the car. The headlights illuminated only a few feet of the dirt road ahead at a time. Brian didn't know if he felt more claustrophobic or vulnerable as he drove blindly down the road. Then there was this tingling sense of foreboding coursing through him. It was so strong Brian couldn't stop himself from looking anxiously into the trees for some unknown terror.

"Look out," Dani cautioned.

A particularly sharp bend came up suddenly. Surprised, Brian focused his attention on the road.

Slow down. Concentrate, He told himself. The tingling sensation dissipated the farther the car traveled away from the bend. Brian swiped his brow with the back of his hand.

Deep within the woods not far from that sharp bend sat a man in an old, white pick-up truck. His eyes followed the small car's bright headlights as it wove through the trees. He waited until the lights disappeared into the darkness. Once assured it and the occupants were gone, he turned the key. With great care, he slowly pulled out onto the road. There was no hurry. He had all the time in the world.

Chapter 32

"It's uncanny." Cody said handing the miniature back to Bennett. "Why didn't I notice the resemblance when I was a young boy?" Bennett shook his head.

"This demon has had years of practicing its deception. If it can live this long, it most certainly can deceive a young child. What I want to know is why your Grandmother chose to show the miniature to you in the first place? What if you had noticed the resemblance between Reynard and Ronald then? Would you be alive today? " Connie queried.

"Maybe in a way she was protecting me. It wasn't long after that I began fantasizing about living somewhere else," Bennett said. "Makes me wonder if those thoughts were my own."

Sami took the miniature from Bennett. "I believe your Grandmother knew you were not a true Godfrey. She managed to keep your parentage a secret which means she somehow fooled this demon."

"Maybe she had help," Katy offered.

"Help?" Bennett asked.

"Malsumis is not an evil God. He plays tricks but he is not evil. Not like the demon," Katy said.

"She's right. There are no evil Gods according to the Abenaki legends. Malsumis is a trickster," Sami reiterated. "He may have been helping your family all along just waiting for the right moment."

"The right moment to do what?" Bennett asked. Sami was interrupted before she could answer.

"I hear a car," Elodie said. She raced to the front window. "It's Dani and a man."

Everyone crowded around Elodie.

"That's my partner, Brian. I hope he called for backup," Cody said. He swung the front door open.

"Stop," Cody demanded as Dani and Brian came up the walkway. "Before you come in, you should know you might not be able to get out."

"What?" Brian was taken aback. "You're kidding, right?"

"He's telling the truth. We can't leave this house," Sami said coming up from behind Cody.

"Daddy? What's going on?" Dani asked her father who stood behind Sami.

"Darling, I wish I understood any of this, but something is holding us captive in this house. Why are you here?" Bennett asked.

"Daddy, Grandmother is dead and Uncle R. P...." before she could finish her statement a frigid blast of air knocked her and Detective Smith off the sidewalk. Reynard's journal fell out of her hands. Dani quickly retrieved it. She hugged it close to her body. A second blast of air quickly followed the first pushing the two of them farther from the entrance of the house. The wind howled in its pleasure.

"It doesn't want them inside," Sami yelled above the din.

Bennett locked eyes with his daughter. "You have to fight it, Dani," He stretched his arm out as far as he was allowed. "Come on, Dani."

Cody followed Bennett's lead and extended his arm as well. "Come on, Brian."

The cold wind escalated its assault. Brian struggled against its fury. He stood up only to have the wind punch him off his feet again. He fell off the walkway and when he did, he looked over at Dani. She was lying face down in a curled position on the lawn.

"Dani," he screamed against the wind's roar. When she didn't respond he crawled towards her. The wind fought his movement. He struggled against its ferocity. Finally, Brian reached her and put his arm around her waist. "Stay low. Crawl with me. Come on."

Dani nodded in agreement. She clutched the journal in her left hand up against her chest. With her right hand, she clawed at the ground while simultaneously pushing with her feet. Brian pulled her along as best he could until they once more touched the walkway. Now it was only a short distance to the front door.

"Come on," Bennett urged. "You're so close."

Brian nodded. The wind retaliated with another gust. When it subsided slightly, Brian shoved Dani ahead of him..

"Crawl, Dani, crawl," he commanded.

Still gripping the journal to her chest, Dani used her elbows to pull herself forward. The wind blew in one direction, shifted, then blew in another. Dani persisted. Every so often she would lift her eyes. Her father shouted his encouragement.

"Come on, darling. Not much further," Bennett yelled.

Then the wind changed. It began swirling and gaining momentum.

"It's a tornado," Sami yelled pointing to the emerging vortex.

Brian saw the approaching danger. He pushed himself forward. There was only one step up to the landing. It was the last obstacle to the front door. Dani was half a body length in front of him. Brian looked at Bennett, nodded, then grabbed the young woman around the waist. He pushed her with all his strength across the doorway into her father's awaiting arms.

"Got her," Bennett yelled pulling Dani into the house.

"Brian, grab my hand," Cody reached out to his partner. Brian strained against the powerful wind. Every time he lengthened his arm, the wind slapped it away. Brian refused to quit. The wind returned the favor.

"Come on, buddy." Cody urged. The tips of their fingers touched. Both men strained against the unseen force. They were about to lock hands, when the wind snatched Brian away. His body flew upwards with a sharp jerk. Cody watched in horror as the wind tossed him around like a rag doll.

"No," Cody screamed. There was nothing he could do.

The wind howled in its conceit.

"Brian!" Cody screamed again at the sight of the young man's body being thrown violently about. He couldn't tell if his partner was conscious. He silently hoped he was alive. Angry, Cody turned his shoulder like a battering ram and charged the doorway. His effort was rebuffed by a single burst of wind. It tossed him backwards into the foyer. Cody scrambled to his feet for another try. The wind anticipated his move. It slammed the front door closed.

"Did you hear that?" He said turning to Bennett.

"Hear what?" Bennett said.

"Someone laughed," Cody responded.

Chapter 33

Sami surveyed the assembled group. *Bennett, his children, my sister, Caroline's brother, Katy, the detective, his wife and me.* "I guess he has everyone who knows anything in one spot."

"What do we do now?" Connie asked.

"We wait. They souls of the dead are talking again. They're unified, too. They say he's coming," Sami said grimly.

Cody looked at the front door. He willed it to open. When it didn't, he shook his head in dismay.

"There was nothing you could have done. There's nothing you can do now, Detective," Sami said then she paused. A concerned look crossed her face.

"Adam has a message for you. I can't hear him clearly. The souls of the dead are all talking at once," Sami smiled wryly. "At least some things have returned to normal."

Cody looked at Sami. His face wore a pained expression. He wished he could hear Adam's voice. Seeing her husband's pain, Bess put her hand on his shoulder. She gave it a slight squeeze. Cody felt the softness of her touch.

"Thanks Bess, I love...," A loud banging coming from the garage interrupted his conversation. Cody bolted out of his chair drawing his gun at the same time. "Here we go again. Why won't the bastard just stay dead?"

"I don't think that will help you," Dani pointed at the revolver in his hand. Then she gasped. The sight of gun triggered her memory.

"Oh my God. How could I have forgotten? Daddy, Uncle R. P. is…is…" She wept. "Detective Smith shot him right in the heart but he didn't die."

The banging in the garage turned into a barrage.

"Make it stop," she screamed covering her ears.

Cody charged down the hallway towards the noise. Bennett planted a quick kiss on his daughters' cheeks before following Cody. Harry got in step behind Bennett.

"Do you think it's… it's Paul?" Harry asked in a trembling voice.

Bennett shrugged his response. "Cody, wait." He caught up with the detective before he could put his hand on the door knob. The banging in the garage stopped. An eerie silence followed. The three men exchanged frightened glances.

A slight clicking noise riveted Cody's eyes to the door. Someone was turning the knob back and forth. A tingling sensation shot up his spine. He stepped back bumping into Bennett and Harry as he did. The knob kept turning. Then it stopped. The three men froze. Everyone was fixated on doorknob. Cody lifted his eyes.

Click…click…click…

Adam, help me, Cody silently pleaded.

Click…click…click…

Bennett nudged the detective. He nodded in the direction of the door. "Should we open it first?"

Cody shrugged. "What do you think?"

"It's your call," Bennett said.

Cody rubbed his free hand against his pants. It was wet and clammy. He inhaled deeply. He clenched and unclenched the opposite hand holding the revolver.

"This might be the stupidest thing I've ever done," he said stretching his free hand towards the knob. He was about to touch it, when he hesitated.

Click…click…click…crack.

The three men stepped away from the door.

"Look at it!" Harry pointed.

The wooden door bowed inwards.

"It's like it's taking a breath," Bennett said in awe.

"Damn. Sure hope it holds," Cody added.

The door relaxed then bowed again. The loud cracking sound of splintering wood echoed down the hallway.

"What should we do? Run?" Bennett asked.

Cody put his hands on the door. "I don't know."

Rapid pounding broke the stalemate. The three men recoiled at the noise. It went on for several moments, then quit. A second brief silence ensued. Voices filled the hallway behind him. Cody could hear someone crying in the living room.

Bess? He wondered.

He wiped the sweat off his forehead. His heart was thumping out of control mimicking the rapid beating on the door. His clothes felt damp and weighed heavily on his body. He had to do something. Reluctantly, he stretched his hand towards the knob again. Before he could touch it, a cold draught of air blew down the hallway. Its strength and sharp bitterness surprised him. It reminded him of the whirlwind that carried Brian away.

"Shit," cried Harry who wrapped his arms around his torso in response to the sudden cold.

The door moved before Cody could comment. It bowed slowly towards him. Cody stepped back in fear. The force pushing from the other side of the door had to be enormous.

"What the hell," Harry cried. The color drained from his face leaving his skin a strange ashen hue. The sight of the door moving again was too much for him. He fled down the hallway leaving Bennett and Cody alone.

"It can't take much more," Cody said. He pulled Bennett towards the middle of the hall in anticipation of the door's destruction.

"Cody, look," Bennett nudged the detective. He pointed to the spot where they had just stood. A dim circle of light appeared. It wavered then disappeared.

"He can't break through," Katy said softly.

Her voice startled Cody. He didn't know she was in the hallway.

"Who?" He asked without looking in her direction.

"Adam, he's trying to reach you."

Cody felt his emotions overwhelm him. "Adam," he whispered reaching out towards the light.

The glow reappeared. It was stronger this time, brighter. An image of the young boy formed. He was moving his mouth and frantically waving his arms at the same time.

"I think he's warning us," Bennett said.

Cody stood riveted by the sight of his brother.

"Cody, maybe he wants us to run," Bennett reiterated more forcefully.

Adam disappeared.

"No," Cody screamed. "Don't leave". He took a step forward.

Bennett grabbed Cody's arm just as the door to the garage burst open. It hit the wall driving the knob into the sheetrock. Cody reacted quickly. He lifted his revolver firing several times into the blackness in front of him. Then he shrieked in horror. His brother stepped out of the darkness. A small red spot in the center of his chest was visible. It grew larger.

"It's a trick, Cody. Look away," Bennett pushed the detective. Cody fell against the wall. His revolver flew out of his hand. It landed on the floor in front of him. Before he could grab it up, the gun slid towards the open door. The men heard it clatter down the steps. The detective froze then rose to his full height.

"This isn't good. Maybe we better get our asses back to the living room," he whispered.

"Leaving so soon, gentlemen? Why? The party has just started," A voice called out from the other side of the doorway.

Bennett grabbed Cody's arm making the detective flinch. He pointed towards the door.

"What the…" Cody stopped. The sight of Bennett's stricken face startled him.

"R. P.," Bennett said.

Chapter 34

A man's hand holding the dropped revolver emerged from the darkness. Bennett still with a death grip on the detective's arm stepped backwards. Cody had no choice but to move with him.

"It's R. P.," Bennett repeated.

The hand moved towards the sound of his voice.

"Duck!" Cody shoved Bennett. The revolver discharged towards the motion. The bullet hit the wall behind him.

"Move, move, move," Cody demanded. The hand swung in his direction. Before it could fire another shot, Cody dropped to his knees. He yanked the door out of the wall and slammed it shut as the second shot rang out. The bullet splintered the middle of the door.

"Go, go, go," he scrambled to his feet. The two men bolted down the hallway. They were almost at its end, when Sami came around the corner carrying a small wooden chair. She ran past them without a word forcing the two men up against the wall.

"Sami, the door…," Bennett warned. He could see the knob moving again.

The small woman didn't stop. Running full tilt, she pulled the chair back slightly behind her then with a forceful thrust, wedged it under the knob thereby stopping the door's forward motion. She stood back and admired her work.

"That ought to hold 'em," she brushed her hands together. "Let's adjourn to the living room. We're running out of time."

Bennett and Cody remained pinned up against the wall. They were speechless. Sami walked between them with an air of confidence. The men were impressed.

"I guess we better do as she says," A bemused Cody chuckled. He noticed how white Bennett's face had become.

"You okay?" he asked.

"Yeah, sure," Bennett answered. "Let's go."

The men rejoined the group huddled in the living room.

"Now what do we do?" Bennett asked.

Sami took up a position in front of the fireplace. Her mood was somber. "Since your trip down the hall, the souls of the dead have been talking in fits and starts. I've only managed to glean a little bit of information."

"Can they tell us how to get out of here?" Cody asked.

"What about Uncle R. P.? Is he really dead?" Dani added.

Sami put her hands up. She stopped the conversation. "I said I only gleaned a little bit of information. Nothing more than that."

"Well, what's the information they can tell?" Harry asked.

His sarcastic tone of voice was not lost on Sami. She ignored him by turning away. She knelt down and placed several logs in the fireplace. With mechanical efficiency, she stuffed newspaper under them then lit it all with a match. The group watched her in silence. No one dared to interrupt. The dry logs caught fire quickly. Sami stood back and watched the flames grow. Finally, she spoke. "This entity is cunning. More devious than I gave it credit. Like all of us in this room, it has a strong will to live. Survival means everything." She faced the group. "The dead told us there were certain things we needed to do to defeat it. I believe we have solved the first task with the picture in the clock. We know that Reynard or Ronald as we know him has been the family butler for generations. This is one of the human forms this entity uses most often. This is his deception."

"Are you telling me the butler did it?" Harry smirked.

Sami glared at the young man. "This is not the time for joking, Mr. Cooper. I am sure Reynard would love to see you die laughing."

Harry dropped his gaze.

"So, if this demon has been taking the form of the butler and others for generations, how come no one noticed?" Cody asked.

"Malsumis," Katy said.

"Your trickster God?" Cody shook his head. "Why would he do that?"

"Ronald stayed in the background. By doing so, he attracted little attention. Now that I think about it, this gave him the perfect opportunity to spy on the family," Bennett stepped forward. "It had been that way for so long, no one challenged it. Did Malsumis prevent my family from seeing the truth?"

Katy nodded knowingly. "Malsumis."

"Something else," Bennett stared into the fire. "You believe my grandmother knew I wasn't a true Godfrey. You said you thought Malsumis was hiding this secret until the right moment. What makes this the right moment?

"Yeah. Adam told me the demon knows, remember? If he was talking about Bennett, how come the demon didn't know a long time ago that he was a...was a...?" Cody stumbled.

"Bastard?" Bennett said what Cody couldn't.

"Yeah, guess that's the best way to say it," Cody looked up at Bennett.

"I don't have all the answers. Neither do the souls of the dead," Sami said quietly.

"Do you think Malsumis tricked everyone all these years about the butler? I knew the Godfreys had a butler. I bet every police officer in Temple Falls for the last hundred years knew the Godfreys had a butler. He's probably been interviewed more than a dozen times considering the Godfreys have been implicated in every murder that has happened." Cody was flabbergasted.

"Cody, think about it. Haven't you read some of those old reports on past investigations?" Sami asked.

"Yeah, I think I've read them all."

"Do you remember any lengthy discussions about the servants, particularly the butler?"

Cody paused. "I remember...I remember...no, I can't recall anything being said about the butler."

"Malsumis," Katy said again.

"What about my sister?" Harry jumped into the conversation. "Why was my sister killed?"

"I don't have the answer for everything, yet. She might have found something out. She might have provoked this entity." Sami said.

"My sister was killed by a demon? I think you're all crazy," he turned away in disgust.

"So, moving on, we've exposed the demon's deception. The second part of this is that we have to kill it to be free, then we have to make it follow her into the Mekwi nebi, red water which we all believe to be Bloody Creek." Sami moved in front of Katy. "We know the young Abenaki woman leapt from a cliff into Lake Champlain. Lake Champlain isn't called Mekwi nebi. However, we believe Bloody Creek empties into the lake at some point. Possibly near here."

"Yes," Katy concurred.

Sami moved in front of Bennett. "And you said, Bennett that your great grandfather built this cabin on the site of Reynard's original home near a cliff. Am I correct?"

"Yes," Bennett said. "Do you think this is the cliff? The cliff where the young woman died?"

"It could be," Sami said.

"So, all we have to do is kill the demon then get him to follow her over the cliff. But we don't know if this is the right cliff." Cody said adding sarcastically. "This ought to be a piece of cake."

"Can you enlighten me about the countryside, Bennett? Is there a stream of water close?"

"There is a creek nearby. It might be an extension of Bloody Creek. I don't know."

"I guess we need to find a way out of this house. I suspect if we can locate where Bloody Creek intersects with the lake, we can find the cliff where this all started. Then we have to somehow get the demon to jump."

"It almost sounds backwards to me," Elodie said. "If we kill the demon, how can he follow her over the cliff?"

Sami sighed loudly. "We will have to hope the dead can help us or the Trickster. There is one more part of this I'm trying to figure out. Your Grandmother's note, Bennett."

"Here, I have it in my pocket."

Sami opened the tattered paper. She read it several times before she spoke. "The end is contained in his memories. Cryptic words, I must say."

Dani rose from her seat. In her hands she held a small brown book. "Before Grandmother died she gave me Reynard's journal. She told me to guard it with my life. Uncle R. P. wanted it in the worst way. He even threatened me." She extended the book to Sami. "Here, someone's diary is nothing more than memories, isn't it?"

Sami took the journal. The leather cover was worn and frail. The binding was so decrepit it barely held the book together. Sami opened it gingerly. It was several moments before she closed the journal. "It's in French. Can anyone here read French?"

"I can," A voice called from the now open front door.

Chapter 35

"Brian?" Cody was surprised by the sight of his young partner. "Stop!" Sami put her arm out preventing Cody from walking towards the door. Instead, she raced forward and slammed it shut.

"What's wrong? Why did you slam the door on him?" Cody asked.

"He wasn't your partner." She said flatly.

"What…?" Cody shook his head. "Sure looked like him."

"It wasn't him," Sami answered.

"How do you know? I agree with Cody. It looked like him." Bennett said.

"Yes, it looked like him but it wasn't," Sami said.

"Wait a minute. Is he dead? Is he talking to you?" Cody looked worried.

"No, he isn't dead. At least, I haven't heard him, yet," Sami gave Cody a reassuring smile.

"Malsumis is protecting us," Katy said.

"Again with the Trickster," Harry snorted.

"You are some kind of asshole, you know that, Harry. After everything that has happened tonight, you still think we're playing some kind of joke on you. How about explaining to all of us why we can't leave this house. Come on, big mouth. Explain it," Elodie stood inches from Harry's face poking him in the chest with her index finger.

"Enough!" Sami shouted. "We don't have time for this. Does anyone else know how to read French?" Sami reiterated.

"I might be able to decipher some of it. I took French in high school. It was a long time ago," Bess offered.

Sami handed the book to Bess. "Anything is better than nothing. Take a look. Do the best you can. There must be something inside this book that will help us."

"What do we do now?" Connie whispered.

"We wait," Sami sat down on the couch. Everyone followed Sami's lead and found a chair with the exception of Cody. He stood at the living room window staring out into the darkness.

"It sure looked like him," he said shaking his head in disbelief.

It was more than an hour before Bess looked up from the journal. She closed the book and pushed it away from her on the table.

"Did you discover anything?" Sami sat down next to her.

"I really didn't believe I would be able to understand any of it, but I did. The more I read, the easier it became. Kind of scary and strange." Bess was amazed. She looked over at Katy. "I think I was getting help."

Katy nodded in agreement.

"What did you learn?" Sami asked.

The group gathered around the table. Harry stood back from the rest but remained close enough to hear.

"Reynard spent more than a year living and trading with the Abenaki tribe he ultimately helped to destroy. In the first half of the journal, he wrote quite a bit about how they lived day to day. How much they helped him with his fur trading business. He actually had a great deal of respect for them. It made me wonder why he betrayed them." Bess pulled the book towards her and opened it. She turned the pages until she was in the middle.

"But something changed after that first year. The Abenaki let Reynard stay at their main encampment many times. Winters could be brutal in Vermont. Shelter was critical. Reynard would repay their kindness with gifts of fresh meat. When he wasn't with them, he was out setting up traps and hunting alone. During one of these hunting trips, he mentions discovering a strange place several miles from the tribe's main encampment. He writes that he stopped for a drink in the running water of a large creek. As he was drinking, he noticed something odd--the forest was abnormally quiet. There were no birds in the trees. No fish swimming in the creek. When he joined the tribe several days later, he mentioned what he had experienced to his Abenaki friends.

His story was met with silence. The Chief told him there was only one man who could explain. An elder who lived on the fringe of the encampment. The man, although taken care of by the tribe, lived alone. Reynard writes that he sought the old man out. When he arrive, the old man was standing outside waiting. Reynard said he was surprised the man knew he was coming. Anyway, he invited Reynard into his home. He proceeded to tell him a story. Bess ran her finger under the sentence as she read the entry.

"When I was a young boy, my father told me about a sacred place. A place where the world of the dead and the world of the living come together. A place where the dead can talk to the living. But you must not talk to them. If you do, they will try to bargain with you for your soul, your life. I was a curious and foolish boy. I had to see this place so I defied my father. I spent days searching the forest. Like you, I was thirsty and took a drink from mekwi nebi. When I finished, I realized the woods were silent. I thought Malsumis was playing tricks. Made the animals run away. Then I saw the spirit of my mother. She called my name. I remembered my father's words, but again I defied him.

It was my mother. I wanted to see her, hear her voice. So, I talked to her. She was so beautiful." The old man stopped in his narration. He closed his eyes. A single tear fell down his cheek. "It was a trick. She lied. She wanted my soul. I ran away." The elder went no further in his story, but he warned the Frenchman to stay away." Bess looked up from the journal briefly. Everyone was staring at her. She dropped her head and resumed.

"Reynard was a religious man. He dismissed the old man's tale as an Abanaki myth, nothing more. He was like most white men at that time, he thought the Indians were heathens. So, he ignored the old man's warning and returned to that beautiful spot anyway." Bess turned several pages. "He described the location of his camp along the banks of Bloody Creek at the bottom of a ravine near a series of large rocks."

"I know the place," Cody's eyes widened.

Bess nodded. She continued moving her finger across the page as she spoke. "Like before, there were no animals only an eerie quietness. He said the place was "mort" "dead". He didn't leave. He set up camp. Nothing out of the ordinary happened the first night, but on the second night, he wrote about a stranger entering his camp--another old man. Who surprisingly was also French." Bess's finger moved more quickly. "The old man was dressed entirely in furs like Reynard. His hair was unruly and snow white. His face had deep craggy wrinkles. His back was bent and he shuffled. Reynard says the visitor never offered his name. He only demanded food. All Reynard had was some dried meat which he gave him. The man sat near him by the fire. While he ate, Reynard studied him carefully. There was something odd about him that worried Reynard. It was his eyes. Reynard thought he saw a red glint in his eyes. He dismissed this as a reflection from the fire. When the old man finished eating, he asked Reynard questions about his life. All kinds of questions which Reynard willingly answered. Time passed quickly. The man thanked him for the food, got up and disappeared into the woods." Bess shut the book.

"And that's it. The rest of the pages are blank."

"Blank?" Bennett asked.

"Yes, with the exception of some red spots."

"Red spots? Blood?" Cody stood up and bent over Bess. She pointed at the spots on the page. "Sure looks like blood."

"Reynard didn't say anything more about the stranger?" Sami asked.

"No, there is nothing more about the stranger but..." Bess hesitated.

"But?" Connie said.

"There actually was one more entry." Bess opened the back of the book to the last page. "It could have been written many days even weeks later. The handwriting is definitely different. Whoever wrote this probably wasn't Reynard."

"What does this person say?" Connie asked.

"He says and I quote, "I'm free"." Sami and Bess spoke simultaneously.

Chapter 36

"I'm free," Cody repeated the words softly. "I don't think I like that statement."

"He said his visitor was a man dressed in furs. An old man with a bent back and white hair." Bennett was staring out the picture window. "Replace the furs with black pants and a white jacket and shirt and you have an old man just like Ronald."

Elodie and Dani joined their father at the window. Dani gasped and pointed. "It's him!"

"What do we do now?" Elodie looked at Sami. Her eyes were wide with fear. "Ronald is standing in the driveway."

The rest of the group rushed the window. Not far from the front of the house, barely illuminated by the light of the moon stood a bent figure of a man with luminous snow white hair. Next to him stood another man. A much younger man.

"Is that Brian," Cody said.

"Sister, what *are* we going to do?" Connie looked at Sami.

Sami was standing apart from the group. Her eyes were closed.

"Sister?" Connie asked again. Sami put her hand up stopping her from speaking any further.

Cody whispered into Connie's ear. "The souls of the dead must be giving her an earful."

Connie nodded in agreement. She pressed her finger against her lips.

Minutes ticked by until finally Sami opened her eyes. "We need a distraction."

"Why do we need a distraction?" Cody asked.

"We must go to Bloody Creek. We have to get to the place Reynard describes in his journal."

"That could be miles from here. How do you suggest we do that? We can't even get out of this house," Bennett was incredulous.

"Malsumis," Katy offered.

"You're right, Katy. You need to call upon Malsumis to help us. Dani, give your car keys to Cody." Sami instructed.

"Sure, let me give 'ole Malsumis a ring," Harry pulled his cell phone out of his pocket.

"Shut up, Harry. God, you're such an ass," Elodie glared at him.

"Both of you stop. We must work together to do what needs to be done." Sami turned towards Katy. "Your grandfather tells me he taught you a chant when you were a little girl. He says must recite it now."

"Okay," There was hesitancy in Katy's voice.

"He says he'll help you," Sami's voice softened. "Everyone into the foyer. Let Katy have the living room."

Katy separated herself from the group. She sat cross legged in front of the window. After a deep breath, she began a slow, rhythmic chant.

Everyone else huddled in the foyer. Cody strained to hear Katy's words, but she spoke too softly.

When Sami had passed the table on her way out of the living room, she picked up Reynard's journal and quietly passed the book to Dani then whispered. "Keep it safe."

"We should be prepared for any eventuality. Put your coats on, folks," Sami instructed.

"Do you think this will work?" Dani asked as she pulled on her jacket.

Sami looked over at Katy. "With any luck."

As Katy's chanting continued, coldness infiltrated the house.

"Man, it's getting cold in here," Cody turned towards the thermostat.

"Don't touch anything," Sami commanded. "We still have the fire."

"It's almost out. Can I throw on a log?" Bennett asked.

"No, wait. She's almost done," Sami said.

Something began pummeling the front door. Connie reacted badly to the familiar sound. Her entire body trembled in fear

"Oh God, it's here," She moved quickly away from the noise with her hands over her ears.

A whirlwind much like the one that carried Brian away could be heard howling outside. Katy stopped chanting. Rising from her position on the floor, she joined Sami near the front door.

"Listen to me, everyone," Sami putting Katy's coat around the young girl's shoulders. She raised her voice in order to be heard above the prevailing din.

"When I tell you to run. I want everyone to head for the cars. We won't have much time, so don't dawdle. Cody, you drive Dani's car. Bennett, will drive mine. Cody, you know the way. Bennett you must follow him closely. Whatever happens, don't get separated." She paused briefly making eye contact with each of them. "I'm going to open the front door now." Sami walked forward. "Once I open this door, I don't know exactly what will happen. Just remember, when I tell you to run...run!"

No one spoke. All eyes were on Sami as she walked towards the door.

"Oh, Sami," Connie could tell her sister was truly frightened. She reached out and touched her sleeve when she passed.

"It's all right," Sami patted her hand. "We'll be all right."

Sami passed the rest of the group summoning all her courage. At the front door, she paused and took a deep breath. Then she grabbed the door knob and turned. A burst of wind wrenched the door out of her hand. It banged against the wall taking Sami with it. She fell into Cody's arms.

Connie and Bess screamed simultaneously. They both pointed at the entry way.

A man stood in the doorway silent and unmoving. The wind whirled around him. He was impervious to the cold howling.

"Brian!" Cody exclaimed.

The young man didn't respond. His eyes stared straight ahead. They were vacant and uncomprehending.

"Brian, can you hear me?" Cody stepped towards him. "What's wrong with him?" He waved his hand in front of his eyes. "Is he alive?"

"The souls of the dead are telling me to follow my instincts. Cody, follow your instincts." Sami .

Those words had barely left her mouth, when Sami inhaled sharply. She reached out to her sister with one hand and grabbed at her throat with the other.

"What's wrong, Sister? Oh my god, she can't breathe!" Connie caught Sami as she stumbled.

Unseen hands wrapped around her throat in a viselike grip.

No one knew what to do.

It was Bennett who broke the impasse. He bolted towards the back of the room grabbing the journal out of Dani's hands.

"Daddy, no!" Dani watched in horror as her father rushed to the fireplace. He threw the book on the dying embers without hesitation.

The wind ceased. Sami gulped in a huge draught of air.

Brian blinked. The look of comprehension returned to his face.

"Cody?" he said

"Everyone run!" Sami yelled pointing to the empty doorway.

Bennett bolted past the group. He pulled Dani along with him. He met no resistance when he crossed the threshold. The invisible barrier was gone. Seeing his success, Cody pushed everyone to follow. He made sure Brian was in front of him when he, the last one out, slammed the front door.

Freedom never felt so good. Fear of what was awaiting them tempered their euphoria. Cody sprinted for the car. The wind was angry, he could hear it trashing the inside of the house.

"Whatever it is, it's pissed," he said.

"Where am I? What's going on?" Brian stopped short. Cody ran into him.

"I'll catch you up in the car. Move!" He yanked Brian forward.

Cody threw open the car door and shoved Brian into the back seat next to Katy, and Bess. Sami was already riding shotgun. He raced around to the driver's side. He looked at Bennett before jumping in. He gave him a wave. Connie was in the front seat of the second car with Elodie, Dani and Harry in the back. Bennett returned Cody's wave with a thumbs up.

The detective slid into the driver's seat and rammed the key into the ignition. The car roared to life.

"Everyone accounted for?" Cody hoped there were no stragglers.

"Everyone but him," Bess pointed at a lone man caught in the glare of the headlights.

It was Paul.

"How the.... It can't be," Cody froze.

"Go!" Sami put the car in gear then threw her leg over the console. She stepped on Cody's foot hovering over the accelerator. The car pitched forward.

Cody instinctively crimped the wheel to avoid hitting Paul. The car jerked to the left. Bess screamed when the car rocked.

"Don't stop," Sami pushed his foot harder.

The car careened down the drive while Cody struggled for control.

"What's he doing?" Bennett watched Cody's car swerve.

"Looks like he's trying not to hit something," Connie said. "But I don't see anything. Hurry! Don't let him get out of sight."

Bennett stomped on the accelerator.

"Okay, I got it." Cody felt Sami's foot leave his. "I didn't hit him. He wasn't there, was he?"

He looked in his rearview mirror. He could see the headlights of the other car.

"I didn't hear a thud or anything. He wasn't there, was he?" Cody asked again. His voice cracked.

"No, Cody. He wasn't there." Sami's calm voice soothed him.

Hunched over the wheel, he concentrated on the road ahead. Bennett's car followed closely behind.

"What happened? Where am I?" Brian looked around dazed.

Sami turned around. "More importantly, where were you?"

Brian looked at her with the most confused expression. "I don't know. I remember being on the ground, crawling towards the house then...then nothing."

"That's all you remember?" Sami asked.

Something in the tone of her question aroused suspicion in Cody. He glanced at her then looked away.

She doesn't believe him, he thought.

"Yes...no....there was this horrible smell. Like something dead," Brian looked out the car window. "What time is it? Where are we going?"

"We are on our way to Bloody Creek," Sami said.

"Bloody Creek? What the hell are we going to do at Bloody Creek in the dark?" The thought horrified Brian.

"Yeah, well first we have to get there," Cody nodded at the road ahead. He hit the brakes. "I think we have a problem."

The small creek not far from the driveway was now a raging torrent. Several of the old wooden planks straddling the water were gone. Those remaining were dangerously askew.

"What are we going to do? We can't cross that," Bess leaned over the car seat when Cody sat back. He dropped his hands off the steering wheel in resignation. "Now what?"

"We walk," Sami announced.

Cody looked at her as if she had grown another head. "What?"

"We have no choice. We walk." She pulled the handle on the door.

"Sami, we are miles from Bloody Creek. There is no way. And what about whatever it is that's behind us. It's pissed as hell and I get the impression it doesn't need a car to get around."

"Well, we can't sit here. We have no choice." Sami repeated. She stepped out of the car.

Bennett pulled up behind them. He called out the window.

"Hey, why did you stop?"

"The bridge is almost gone. Sami says we're walking. Is there another way around?" Cody hoped Bennett had a solution.

Bennett got out of his car, motioned for everyone to follow. Soon he was standing by Cody's window. "Walk? Through these woods? In the dark?" Bennett expressed all of the worries Cody was thinking. "There are some trails around here, but not for cars and none that go over this creek for at least a mile." Bennett pointed into the darkness. "We can try using the remaining planks to get to the other side or follow the creek downstream until we can find a way across. From the looks of it, we've got a long walk ahead of us no matter what we do."

"Okay, so how many flashlights do we have?" Cody did a quick inventory. "Just three?"

He took one after handing one to Sami and Bennett.

"Cody, I'm cold," Bess shivered.

"I think we can expect it to get a lot colder before this is over." Connie patted Bess's arm.

"Come on, everyone. Let's move," Sami walked up to the edge of the swollen creek. Her flashlight danced back and forth over the rushing water. "There are two planks left. You men help me push them together. Hurry."

It took the four men several minutes to move the first piece of wood but when they attempted to rearrange the second, the plank refused.

"I think there is some debris in the way." Bennett peered into the darkness.

"Never mind. We will have to make do," Sami stepped on the wide plank. With her arms extended like a tight rope walker, she raised her left foot and carefully placed it ahead of the other.

"Daddy, stop her," Elodie pleaded.

"Sami, no. Elodie's right. It's too dangerous," Bennett was horrified at the sight of the elderly woman balancing on the wooden plank.

"What's dangerous, Bennett, is staying here." Sami pointed her flashlight slightly ahead of her feet. The narrow ribbon of light exposed her path. Sami inched along slowly. She crossed the creek more quickly than anyone expected.

"I didn't think she could do it," Bennett whispered to Cody.

"I'm not sure I can," Cody replied. "Here, take my flashlight, Brian. I don't think I can hold it and walk across that thing at the same time."

Now on the other side, Sami yelled for the next person to go. She pointed her light downwards onto the plank.

Katy, Connie, Bess, Elodie, Brian, Dani and Bennett complied leaving only Cody and Harry on the other side.

"I'll bring up the rear," Cody announced.

"I can't," Harry said.

"Come on, Gentlemen. We can't waste any more time." Sami urged.

"Go, Harry," Cody demanded.

"I can't swim. What if I fall in?" Harry eyed the turbulent creek with despair. He took a step back.

"Don't think about that. Just go," Cody grabbed his arm.

Harry pushed him away.

"Okay, suit yourself." Cody took a step forward then stopped. A tingling sensation rushed up his spine. He turned away from the creek straining to see beyond the car he left behind. "Harry, something is coming. We're not alone."

A faint nasty odor warned him their time may have run out.

"Go, now, Harry," Cody shoved the man towards the plank.

Harry lurched forward. He looked over his shoulder. He could smell it, too. More terrified of what might be behind him rather than the water below, Harry rushed onto the wet plank. He took small mincing steps until he reached its middle. Then he stopped.

"Keep going, Harry. Don't stop," Connie yelled her support.

"I can't." His arms flailing, Harry teetered dangerously.

"Don't look at the water," Sami cautioned.

He tipped back and forth unable to maintain his balance. Finally, he took one more step at the same time a tree branch slammed into the plank rocking it violently. It was too much for Harry. He fell forward landing face first on the waterlogged wood. He wrapped his arms around the rocking board while his legs fell on either side into the water. His frightened scream echoed through the forest.

"Grab him," Bess screamed.

Bennett and Brian raced to the man's rescue. Together they steadied the board, then Brian reached for Harry.

"Let go and give me your hand," Brian said.

Harry hugged the plank. "No!"

The tree branch continued pushing Harry until the plank was in danger of tipping into the water.

Brian dropped down on his hands and knees at the end of the piece of wood. He inched his way forward until he could grab the arm of Harry's coat. At the same time, Cody stepped onto the board from the other side. His weight temporarily kept the wood from moving further.

"You gotta move Harry, now," Brian pulled his jacket with all his strength. "I got you."

"No!" The man was terrified.

"Do it, Harry. We can't leave Cody alone on the other side," Sami said.

Harry relented. Brian held onto the arm of Harry's jacket while he slinked the rest of the way to dry ground. Before he was off the board completely, Cody began his journey.

Bess followed her husband's progress intently. "Be careful, darling," she called. "That board isn't very wide."

"Thanks for reminding me," Cody quipped.

Brian and Harry reached the end of the plank. Thrilled to be safe, Harry scrambled to his feet forgetting that Cody was only half way across. Without his weight to hold the board in place, the force of the current plus the huge tree branch tipped the plank again. Cody fell sideways into the rushing water.

The coldness shocked him. He opened his mouth in surprise and immediately gagged on the cold water. The chaotic current pushed him downward away from the bridge. He heard Bess scream right before he went under, then he somersaulted in rapid succession. Slippery rocks prevented him from putting his feet down.

I'm going to die, he thought when he couldn't stop his forward motion.

"He's drowning," Bess screamed in horror when her husband disappeared into the torrent of water. "Cody!"

"Quick, Bennett. Is there a path next to the creek somewhere?" Sami scanned the side of the road with her flashlight. "Here, it's over here!"

Bess bolted towards Sami. "Cody!" she screamed in desperation. As she ran passed Sami, she grabbed her flashlight.

"Wait," Bennett yelled but Bess wasn't listening. She ran down the narrow path quickly disappearing into the opaque darkness.

"Come on. Everyone hurry." Bennett bolted after her. "Stay together as best you can."

"I'll go last," Brian called.

The dirt path followed the slope of the mountain downwards through the dense trees. Dim starlight barely penetrated the leafy canopy above. Bennett sprinted down the rocky path with the rest of the group close behind. Every now and then he would aim his light forward hoping to catch a glimpse of Beth, but the dark and serpentine course of the path hid her.

"Bess!" Bennett stumbled. He fell forward.

"Are you okay," Dani helped him recover.

"Yeah, I'm fine." He brushed his pant leg, then turned towards the group. "I can't keep up with her. Anyone see anything?"

"It's too dark. Not yet." was the general reply.

Bennett flashed his light into the trees. "I know the path follows the creek. We must be close. I hear the water. Bess, can you hear me?"

"Keep going, Bennett. She can't be that far ahead." Sami urged.

I'm not so sure, Bennett thought. A childhood memory tweaked his brain. He was chasing R. P. on a path very similar to this one. With every turn, he thought he would catch up with his brother, but R. P. eluded him. He kept running not paying any attention to which direction or how far from the cabin he had traveled until he realized he was hopelessly lost. It was hours before his father found him. Hours filled with thoughts of being mauled by a wandering bear all courtesy of his brother's constant barrage of horror stories about the woods. He never chased his brother into the forest ever again.

Bennett shook the memory from his head and concentrated on

the sound of the water. He jogged a few more feet, then stopped. The path diverged in two directions.

"Should we split up?" Elodie asked her father when she sensed his hesitancy.

"No," Bennett shown his light to the path running to the left. "the creek is on the left. She would have gone this way."

"Anything wrong?" Brian called from the back of the line.

"No, we're okay. Come on," Bennett followed his instinct and veered left.

He hadn't gone fifty feet when he entered a large clearing. He continued following the path until he was at the edge of the creek. Beyond the water, a steep incline strewn with rocks and trees pitched upwards. No available path going forward was visible. Bennett let his light travel upwards. He couldn't see to the top.

"The water seems a little calmer now, doesn't it?" Dani hoped.

One by one, the group gathered behind Bennett.

"Where are we?" Brian asked.

"I don't know. I don't remember this place," Bennett was genuinely perplexed. He moved his light up and down the edge of the creek. He stopped when it illuminated several huge boulders. The rocks were situated on one side of the creek forcing the current to go between them and the hill in a tight narrow curve. "It can't be. These rocks shouldn't be here."

Bennett cautiously touched the cool, grey stone with tips of his fingers. "They're real." He was surprised. The sound of violent splashing on the other side of the boulder made him retract his hand in fright.

"Pull your gun, Brian." An image of a black bear crossed Bennett's mind.

"Got it," Brian drew his revolver and leveled it towards the sound. "Point your flashlight over there, Sami." He pointed to the right side of the boulder.

Sami complied. The splashing noise came closer. However, it wasn't the bear they all expected.

"Cody!" Brian lowered his gun in relief.

His partner stepped into the light. The detective's clothing was soaking wet. His right arm was draped around Bess' shoulder for support. He was limping badly.

"I'm not ever swimming in that creek again," Cody joked. The group raced forward. Brian embraced his partner. "Man, am I glad to see you. Are you okay?"

"My ankle hurts but other than that, I'm fine." Cody squeezed Bess. "I'm glad my girl found me."

"Darling, sit down. Let Brian take a look at your ankle." Bess steered her husband to an available rock.

Brian knelt in front of his partner. He gingerly lifted the detective's pant leg. "Damn, Cody, how can you even stand on this ankle. You've got to be in a lot of pain."

"What? No, it's only a sprain," Cody lifted the pant leg a little higher. "It doesn't hurt that bad."

"Are you kidding me?" Brian looked at him with astonishment. "You ankle is mangled. I can see the busted bones."

"You're nuts. I'm telling you, it's fine. I'll be walking on it tomorrow. Why are you looking at me like that?" Cody looked at Brian then at Bess. "Why is he looking at me like that?"

Bess glanced down at Cody's ankle. "Brian, it doesn't look that bad."

"Yes, Brian, his ankle doesn't look that bad," Bennett offered.

"Okay, what's going on? Is this some kind of joke?" Brian stood up. "Am I the only one who sees the bones sticking out?"

"The trickster," Katy whispered.

"Did you say bones sticking out?" Cody grabbed the flashlight out of Bess' hand. He pointed down at this ankle. Then he directed the light at the boulders. "Hey, where are we?" Cody stood up. "How can we be here? This is impossible."

"How can you stand?" Brian shown his light on Cody's ankle. He let out an audible gasp. "There was blood...I swear..."

"Shhhh, listen," Cody demanded.

"I don't hear anything," Harry offered.

"Exactly. We're here folks," Cody's voice was tight.

"Here?" Brian responded.

"Yeah, we're in that dead zone."

"Sister, what do the souls of the dead say about this?" Connie said.

Before Sami could answer, Elodie screamed. She pushed through the group until she was able to grab onto her father. She was pointing towards the woods. "It's Uncle R. P."

"No, it can't be Uncle R. P. He's dead," Dani grabbed her father as well.

"Everyone stay calm," Sami stood in front of the group. She took Bennett's flashlight and switched it off. "We will be able to figure this out better in the light of day."

"What? It's still dark out," Cody said.

"Turn off your light, Cody." Bess instructed.

Cody complied, followed by Brian, then Bennett. Once all the flashlights were off, the darkness lifted. Daylight inundated the clearing.

"What time is it?" Harry queried.

"My watch says 7 a.m." Connie glanced at her wrist.

"Now this is more like it," Bennett studied his surroundings. It was the clearing he remembered. The boulders and steep incline were gone. The creek flowed gently past. No longer the dangerous torrent just moments earlier. "Where's Cody and Bess?"

The couple had disappeared.

"Someone help me," A woman's voice called through the trees.

Brian ran towards the sound of the voice. He froze when he came upon Bess kneeling beside her husband. Cody was sprawled half in, half out of the running water. "What's the matter with you? Aren't you going to help me?"

"It's all right, Mr. Smith. This isn't an illusion," Sami walked past the stunned detective. "Bennett, help me get Cody out of the water. Poor man is soaked to the bone."

Brian flopped down in a heap. Harry sat next to him.

"I don't understand," Brian said weakly.

Cody coughed. He waved everyone away. "I'm okay, I'm okay."

With the exception of a substantial bruise on his head, he was in remarkable shape. Bess gave him a huge hug.

"I was so worried," she said.

"Me, too. Where are we?" Cody asked.

"Well, if this is the clearing I know, we can't be too far from the road." Bennett walked up stream a few feet.

"Daddy, where's Katy?" Elodie was looking backwards.

"She was behind me," Dani turned around. "Where did she go?"

"Brian, did she leave the path?" Bennett looked at the weary detective.

"No, she didn't pass me," Brian stood up. "Sami?"

The elderly woman was standing alone. She had distanced herself from the group. Her face wore a grim expression.

"Sister, what's wrong?" Connie's voice registered alarm.

Sami shook her head sadly. "An illusion and an elaborate one at that with only one exception."

"What was the exception?" Bennett didn't like where the conversation was headed.

"R.P.," Sami's voice dropped.

"That's impossible. I shot him more than once," Brian ran his hands through his hair in nervousness.

"That's true, Sami. I saw him do it," Dani looked at her father in disbelief.

"He took her, didn't he?" Bennett said quietly.

"I'm afraid so," Sami's shoulders slumped.

"Oh, Sister no," Connie's hands covered her mouth in shock.

"That twisted son-of-a-bitch took Katy?" Cody was flabbergasted.

"What do we do now?" Connie asked.

Sami straightened her shoulders. Her demeanor changed. "We must go back to the cabin."

"Oh hell, no. I'm not going back." Harry shook his head violently.

"Fine, you stay here. If there aren't any more objections, lead us home, Bennett," Sami waved her hand towards the path.

Bennett quickly took the lead. When he passed Harry he whispered, "Lots of bears in these woods."

The return trip to the bridge was uneventful and quick. Harry rejoined the group shortly after Bennett passed him. He kept checking over his shoulder for any lurking wildlife.

"Well, look at that. I got wet for nothing," Cody pointed at the creek flowing lazily under a pristine bridge. There wasn't a single plank out of place.

One by one, they crossed the small span in silence.

The automobiles were as they left them parked one behind the other. Without a word, everyone returned to their designated seats.

"All an illusion," Brian shook his head in wonder as the group headed back to the cabin.

Chapter 37

"Home sweet home," Cody said sarcastically at the sight of the cabin. Daylight did little to improve its appearance.

Sami was the first one out of the car. Cody remained in his seat and watched the elderly woman step up onto the stoop, hesitate, then walk into the house leaving the front door open.

"I don't know if I'm ready for this," Bess quietly expressed everyone's feelings.

"I know what you mean, but we owe it to Katy. We got her into this mess," Cody swung the car door open. "Let's go."

He stood in front of the car waiting for Bess. When she did, he put his arm around her waist and gave her a squeeze. They walked towards the front door together, but stopped before entering the house.

"Safety in numbers." he whispered in her ear then turned and waited for the others.

"What do you think?" Bennett asked.

Cody sighed. "I don't know what to think. I almost burned up in my car. I nearly drowned. People who are dead keep coming back to life. I think I'm through with thinking."

"It's a nightmare," Brian added. "And I can't wake up."

"What about Katy? What is that monster going to do to her?" Bess again voiced everyone's concern.

"I have a feeling we're about to find out," Cody and Bess crossed over the threshold.

Sami stood in the living room with her head bowed, her back to the group. She was weeping softly.

Alarmed, Connie rushed to her side. "Sister, what have you learned?"

Sami turned around. She held the tattered journal in her hands. "He discovered my ruse."

"The journal. How did you...I burned it," Bennett was stunned.

"No, you thought you burned it. I had it the whole time," Sami dropped her head. "He killed her in revenge."

"Oh, no. Not Katy," Connie put her arm around her sister. "Are you sure?"

"It was Katy's soul who told me to return to the cabin."

Bess threw her arms around Cody's neck. Sobs racked her body. Cody wrapped his arms around her and held her close.

A sorrowful pall fell over the group. During the ensuing silence, the mantel clock bonged. Then bonged again in succession. It continued, prompting Bennett to glance at his watch.

"Strange. The clock shouldn't be..." Puzzled, he walked over to the fireplace. The hands on the face of the clock were spinning out of control.

He opened the glass door and put his finger in front of the moving minute hand. "Ouch," he quickly retracted his now bloody finger. The hands continued their spinning.

"Not again," Harry exclaimed. He ran from the room into the kitchen.

Bennett stopped Brian from following him. "Let him go. Sami, look at this clock. It's going nuts." He put his wounded finger in his mouth. He stepped aside for Sami.

"Katy says we missed something important," Sami said. "Take the clock down, will you, Bennett."

Before he could comply, Harry rushed out of the kitchen brandishing a big butcher knife. He held it inches from Bennett's chest. "Give me the car keys or so help me, I'll kill you," he threatened.

"Harry, please," Elodie pleaded.

"No, I'm done with this shit. I want out now," He poked Bennett.

"Think twice about that, man," Brian had drawn his gun. He pointed it at Harry.

"No, it's okay." Bennett pulled Dani's car keys out of his pocket. "Let him go."

Harry snatched them out of his hands.

"Think about what you're doing, Harry. None of us are in control. Can't you see that?" Cody hoped he could calm the young man down.

"Well, I'm taking control." He swung the knife forcing everyone to give him a wide berth. Then he bolted out of the house.

No one moved until Cody yelled. "Stop him!"

Then the three men ran after him.

"Let him go," Sami reiterated.

The men ignored her. Cody, Bennett and Brian continued in their pursuit. Harry jumped into the first car. He quickly locked the door before detective Davis could open it. Cody pounded on the window when the door refused.

"Leave me alone," Harry screamed. He started the car.

"Stop, you chicken shit," Cody looked for a rock to break the window.

Harry raised his middle finger. "Fuck you and the rest of your friends. I'm outta here." The car jerked forward sending Cody flying off the side.

"Son-of-a-bitch," Cody hurled a rock at the retreating car.

"Do you think he will make it out of here?" Bennett asked.

"I have no...," Cody stopped short of finishing his sentence. He watched as the speeding car veered sharply to the right then snapped back to center. Cody could see Harry struggling with the wheel.

"Hey, what's going on?" Brian watched the car swing to the left.

"Something's wrong," Cody said. "Let's go."

The small compact continued its erratic movement. Just as it reached the end of the drive, it again pitched violently to the right slamming into the nearest tree. A small flame appeared under the belly of the car.

The force of the impact turned the vehicle allowing the approaching men to see Harry behind the wheel. He was frantically struggling with the car door.

"Harry, hang on," Cody yelled. "We've got to bust the window."

"Cody, there's no time. The car's going to blow," Brian pointed at the escalating flames.

Bennett tugged Cody's arm. "He's right."

"No, we can't leave him there," Cody wrestled his arm free. Memories of his own recent accident propelled him.

Smoke was rapidly filling the cab of the vehicle.

"Help me," Harry screamed between gasps.

Brian joined Bennett in pulling Cody away. "You can't help him without dying yourself."

"No, no..." Cody fought the two men while they dragged him up the driveway. "It's not too..."

The car exploded with a vengeance.

"...late," Cody stopped resisting. He watched the flames consume the car.

"Here, I found this under the sink," Elodie handed her father a small fire extinguisher. "Oh God." She watched the flames in horror.

"Yeah, this won't do much now," Bennett let it drop to the ground.

Cody reached down and picked it up.

"Cody...," Bennett tried to stop him.

"Leave me alone." Cody pushed his extended hand away. He ran towards the burning car. He stopped a few feet away and sprayed the flames until the canister ran dry. Then his arm dropped to his side. Harry's charred remains were visible in the wreckage. Cody lifted the canister over his head.

"Fuck you!" He screamed. With all his strength, he threw it at the smoldering ruins.

"Cody," Brian reached out to this partner.

"Leave me alone. Go back to the house." Then as an afterthought he added. "I gotta think."

"Cody," Brian repeated.

"No, I mean it. Leave me alone." Cody turned away. He headed for the end of the driveway.

Bess joined the group. She saw her husband headed in the opposite direction. "Cody where are you going?"

Cody turned around. He waved at this wife. "I'm okay. I need a moment."

She didn't stop him. After many years of marriage, she knew when her husband wanted his space.

"Cody, it's not safe," Bennett called after him.

Cody waved him away. "I don't care."

"Do something, Bess," Bennett tried to enlist her support.

"I can't stop him anymore than I can stop the rain," Bess shook her head. "Why don't we follow him at a discreet distance?"

"I'm on it," Brian took the lead with Bennett and Bess close behind.

The morning sun shone brightly through the trees. It did little to alleviate Cody's foul mood. The dampness of his clothing was a constant reminder of the recent night's events. The death of Katy and now, Harry shook him to the core. The world was spiraling out of control and he didn't like the feeling one bit. The image of Harry burning kept replaying in his brain.

Stop it!, his brain wouldn't quit.

"Serves me right," he said out loud. With his head down, he

furiously marched forward. Fear had been replaced by rage. Walking allowed him to vent his frustration somewhat.

The wooden span came into view. He stopped several feet from it. Intermittent sunlight gave the cascading water a sparkling effect. If this had been another time, another day, he would have reveled in its beauty. But not today. Today it all looked evil.

"You're not going to beat me," He screamed at the silent woods. The image of Harry beating on the car window entered his brain. "I'm sorry, Harry."

"It's not your fault, Cody," a voice startled him.

"I told you to leave me alone." Cody whirled around expecting to see Bess. Instead, he saw Adam.

His brother was as he remembered right down to his wounded ankle.

"Adam?" Cody's feelings were mixed. He was thrilled, but he was wary.

"Adam," he repeated. He marveled at the vision before him. His brother looked so real. Nothing seemed ghostly about him.

"I...I know it wasn't my fault." He stared at his brother. "I just wished I could have stopped him."

Adam shrugged. It was what his brother always did when he didn't have an answer.

"Why are you here?" A strange sense of foreboding envelope Cody. He took a step back. "Why are you here?" He now regretted walking to the bridge alone.

Adam shoved his hands into his pants pockets. He shrugged again.

Cody took another step back. His brother took a step forward in response.

"You're not Adam, are you?"

A slight smile creased his brother's lips, then disappeared.

"I am Adam," The vision said.

"How come I don't believe you?" Cody eyed the apparition with suspicion.

Adam shrugged. He stepped forward.

Cody stepped back. "Tell me, what was your kindergarten teacher's name?"

Adam stopped. He shrugged.

"Oh come on, Adam. You had the biggest crush on her. Surely you haven't forgotten her name?" Cody's voice dripped sarcasm.

Adam lowered his head until his chin rested on his chest. His eyes became black as coal. They rolled upwards until they met his eyebrows. Slowly, Adam grinned.

A chill raced up Cody's spine. He wasn't looking at his big brother anymore. He was looking at evil incarnate.

Cody took another step back and felt the planks of the wooden bridge under his feet. The apparition followed his movement without stopping this time.

"What do you want?" Cody glanced at the running water. If he had to, he would escape into the water. He returned his gaze to the entity.

"What do you want?" he repeated.

Adam threw his head back. He laughed. A long, bone chilling laugh. He lowered his head and extended his arms towards Cody. "You."

Cody felt the center of his chest tighten. A sharp, excruciating pain exploded within him. He doubled over before falling onto the bridge.

I'm dying, he thought. *Adam, help me brother.*

A darkness descended. Cody lifted his head and watched as the world around him disappeared.

"Bess, I love you." He took what he thought was his last breath, when inexplicably the darkness lifted. As it did, so did the pain in his chest. Cody watched in amazement as his surroundings morphed into a different place. A place he knew all too well. The place where Adam died. The dead zone.

"Oh no, not here," Cody uncurled his body. He sat up. He searched for the demon. "Come on you, son-of-a-bitch. Only you could have brought me here. Or is this another illusion?"

"Akwi sagezo."

Cody scrambled to his feet. "Don't be afraid. You, you brought me here?" Her voice was unmistakable.

"Akwi sagezo."

"I know, I know, don't be afraid. Why did you bring me here?" Cody whirled in place hoping the Abenaki maiden would show herself.

"Akwi sagezo."

Cody could barely hear her words this time. She was leaving him.

"No, no, don't go," he cried. Beyond the edge of the creek he could see the familiar path up the ravine. He raced towards it. He stopped a few feet from his goal. The path was within reach, yet something was holding him back. He put his hand up and reached forward. His palm met with resistance. Undaunted, Cody turned on his heels and quickly crossed the creek passing the familiar boulders as he ran. At the other side of the clearing hemmed by trees, he stopped and put his hand up again. He felt the same resistance as before.

"No!" Anger and frustration welled up inside of him. He tested the boundaries of the clearing until every inch had been explored. He could find no way out. Exhausted, he leaned up against the big rocks. He was imprisoned.

Chapter 38

"Why are you keeping me here?" He hated this place. The clearing was exactly like he remembered it. Bright, cheerful completely innocent like he and his brother had been that day.

I wonder? A peculiar thought crossed his mind. He looked up at the biggest boulder. Every crack, every crevasse was eerily familiar.

"Here goes nothing," he climbed up and stood in the spot Adam had chosen years ago. An audible gasp escaped him. There, strewn across the surface was Adam's tackle box, his book and his fishing pole. Cody stared at the assortment.

"What do you want?" He turned slowly in a full circle drinking in every inch of the clearing. "I know you're here. You can't fool me twice. Come on you bastard. Grow some balls and show yourself," Cody continued turning.

He glanced down at the rock. Adam's paraphernalia was gone.

"Thought so." The familiar scene around him changed. Daylight disappeared replaced by a deep, impenetrable darkness.

"Now where are you taking me?" It wasn't the Abenaki maiden at the helm this time.

Disoriented in the opaque darkness, Cody sat down. When he did, he touched the surface beneath him.

Feels like wood, he thought.

A force pushed him backwards. He tried fighting back. The force was too strong. In a matter of minutes, he was lying on his back with his arms pinned to his sides. Any attempt to move was met with resistance .

What's going on? Where am I? He wondered.

A sound reached his ears. It was Bess. She was crying.

"Bess, I'm here. Don't cry," he called. Then he saw her. She was standing over him along with Brian and Bennett. The two men were comforting her.

They had followed Cody keeping slightly out of his sight. When he stopped at the wooden crossing, he began gesturing towards something unseen.

"Is he talking to someone?" Brian said.

"Looks that way doesn't it?" Bennett concurred.

"Do you think the Trickster is at it again?" Bess was worried. "Maybe we should let him know he's not alone."

Before they could act on Bess' suggestion, Cody clutched his chest. He fell backwards onto the bridge. Bess rushed forward to her stricken husband.

Brian reached him first. He knelt down and put his head to Cody's chest. Unable to hear a heartbeat, he felt the artery in his neck. He shook his head.

"Looks like he had a heart attack, Bess."

Bess gasped before dropping to her knees next to Cody. She wrapped her arms around his chest and sobbed. "He looks like he's sleeping."

What do you mean, I had a heart attack? Sleeping? I can see you. Cody couldn't believe his ears. He was looking right at Bess at least he thought he was. He could see the leafy canopy above him. He could hear water rushing underneath him. He felt the weight of Bess' head on his chest. He could hear her cry.

I'm on the bridge. I'm alive, he thought.

"Can you hear him, Sami?" Connie hurriedly approached followed by Sami.

"No, not yet." Sami looked so old.

"Is this another illusion?" Bennett asked Sami.

They think I'm dead. Hey, what are you talking about? I'm alive. Cody screamed. *Why can't you hear me? Why can't I move?*

"I'm not sure," Sami shrugged her shoulders in answer to Brian's question.

"I never should have let him walk away," Bess said dismally. Tears streaked down her face.

"I should have known better," Bennett said quietly.

"We all knew, including Cody, the risks of being alone out here. Now we have to deal with it." Sami said.

"We can't leave his body on the bridge. Let's get him back to the cabin," Bennett lifted Cody by the shoulders. Brian took his feet.

"You ladies lift him in the middle."

Cody felt himself rise upwards.

Only the sound of Bess weeping could be heard during the walk back to the cabin.

I'm alive. I'm alive, Cody couldn't break through his invisible barrier. He felt like his body was wrapped in a tightly bound shroud. He couldn't move at all. He could see the sky, the clouds and Brian's back as they walked. When he felt his partner take a step up and saw the sky disappear, he knew they had reached the cabin.

I'm back. The warmth of the house surrounded him.

Bess knelt down next to Cody's body. She lowered her head onto his shoulder.

I'm alive, Bess. Please don't cry. He wanted so desperately to hold her, to tell her he was all right but his body wouldn't respond. In the distance, he could hear the others talking, but couldn't decipher what was being said.

If only I could move, Cody struggled against his imprisonment.

"We can't leave him here too long, Sami." Brian glanced over at Cody.

"Yes, I'm well aware what the body does after death, Mr. Smith," Sami followed his stare. "But have you noticed anything different about your partner."

Brian walked over to the couch. He looked Cody over carefully.

Check my pulse, check my pulse, Cody prodded him silently.

As if on cue, Brian reached over Bess and touched Cody's neck.

"Nothing, no pulse." Brian announced.

Impossible! I'm alive. I'm looking right at you. Cody felt anger overwhelm him.

"What are you thinking, Sami?" Bennett wondered.

"How many dead bodies have you seen in your career, Mr. Smith?" She asked.

"More than a few," Brian said.

"Would you say Detective Davis looks like all those other dead bodies?"

"Yeah," He was irritated by her question.

Sami studied Detective Davis again. .

"Well, I've only seen one dead person in my life and I don't think his cheeks were as rosy red as Detective Davis's." Sami smiled broadly. "You know what I think, Detective Smith?"

Bess looked up at Sami, then down at Cody. She let out a shriek.

"That he's not dead." Sami pointed at Cody's face.

A small tear emerged from Cody's eye and trickled down his face.

Bess hugged Cody. "Oh, Cody, Cody, say something."

Brian scratched his head. "But there was no...I could have sworn..."

"Why can't he move?" Bess asked the question everyone was thinking.

I'm not dead, Cody felt relief even though he still couldn't move.

"Did he have a stroke?" Dani asked.

"No, I don't believe so," Sami walked away from couch.

Bess hovered over her husband. "What do we do now?"

"Sister, do the souls of the dead have anything to say about this?" Connie followed Sami.

Sami ignored her question. Instead, she walked to the fireplace and studied the clock on the mantel.

"You mentioned a problem with the clock some time ago, Mr. Godfrey. Would you mind taking it down for me?" Sami pointed upwards.

"Certainly." Bennett lifted the clock off the mantel and placed it on a small table in front of her.

"Be careful, Sami. It bit me the last time," he glanced at the small cut on his finger.

Sami smiled slightly at his comment, then returned her attention to the clock.

Its pendulum swung erratically during the move. It returned to its normal cadence once it was on the table.

"Maybe I should move that clock more often," Bennett listened to its steady tick, tock, tick, tock.

"Why is that, Mr. Godfrey?" Sami asked.

"Well, it usually takes a bit of finagling to get the pendulum to keep swinging." He pointed at a small stack of pennies on the mantel. "I have to rebalance the clock every time I move it. It took three pennies last time to make it swing right."

The pendulum continued.

"It'll probably start slowing down," he watched the clock. "Anytime now..."

Instead, the pendulum picked up speed. The minute hand ticked forward. Then it ticked forward again.

"It's moving faster like before." Bennett pointed at the face of the clock. "Look!"

The pendulum was swinging wildly. The hands on the clock were spinning out of control.

Sami reached for the clock.

"Sami, be careful. You can't stop..." before Bennett could finish his sentence, the clock flew away from Sami's outstretched hands. It hit the far wall then shatter into so many pieces.

No one moved. No one spoke.

"Daddy?" Dani timid voice broke the silence. She grabbed her father's arm.

"Sami, what's going on?" Brian eyed the room suspiciously.

"Cody! He's turning blue," Bess was shaking her husband's shoulders. "Help me!"

Bennett and Brian turned towards the couch.

"I'll start CPR," Brian announced.

"No. Ignore him," Sami demanded. To emphasize her point, she put her hand up stopping the men.

"What?" Bennett was surprised.

"Cody needs us," Brian sidestepped Sami.

She jumped in front of him. "No, it's a ruse. We've missed something in the clock. We have to find it now!"

"Oh God, Cody." Bess was hysterical.

Brian looked in anguish at Bess, then Bennett.

Bennett nodded towards the broken clock. "Let's do what she says. Elodie, Dani and Connie help Bess."

The two men hurried over to the remains of the clock. Glass was strewn over much of the surrounding floor. The brass encasement was twisted. The pendulum lay next to it. Mercury oozed from a crack in its glass. The face of the clock was missing.

"It couldn't have gone far," Bennett said when he noticed the discrepancy.

"Here, it's over here," Sami reached down and lifted the white piece of porcelain from under a chair. It too, was cracked in half. It fell apart when she touched it. She picked the two pieces up. She fit them together with great care.

"I've found what I was looking for," She nodded her head happily.

Everyone crowded around her with the exception of Bess.

"What did you find, Sister?" Connie wondered.

"Something Katy told me was important. She said I'd find it in the clock. And here it is." Sami read aloud:

"*A good man will cross over the abyss on the backs of his dogs. A bad man will fall into the abyss.*"

"I know that saying," Bennett said. "My father would recite it to me when I was a boy. He told me the Abenaki people believed this. The abyss was their version of hell."

"On the back of his dogs. I guess dogs must have been an important part of Abenaki life," Elodie mused. "Grandmother hated them. Wouldn't let them in the house."

"Has anyone in the Godfrey family ever owned a dog?" Connie asked Bennett.

"As far as I know, there has never been a dog on the place. Ever." Bennett emphasized his last word. He reached towards Sami. "May I?"

"Certainly," Sami let him have the two pieces. She turned towards the opposite end of the room where Cody remained on the couch. "He's breathing now, isn't he?"

Bess nodded. She looked forlornly at Sami. "But why can't he move?"

"Who said I can't move?" Cody touched his wife gently on the shoulder.

Chapter 39

Bess was overjoyed at Cody's recovery. "It's so good to hear your voice. What happened to you?"

"Yes, detective, can you enlighten us?" Sami added.

Cody held Bess in his arms for a long moment. "I'm so glad I can hold you," he squeezed his wife a little tighter.

"We are all glad you're back. What can you tell us?" Sami repeated.

Cody reluctantly let his wife go. "I don't know if I am adding anything new to all of this. First of all, I never should have gone off alone. That's for sure. When I got to the bridge, Adam appeared. At least, I thought it was Adam. This being said it wanted me. Then the next thing I knew, I was being held prisoner next to those boulders by Bloody Creek. I climbed up the biggest rock and found Adam's fishing pole, book everything we took that day. Just where we left it. I remember feeling like someone was there with me. Then I was back on the bridge. Well you know the rest."

"What do we do now," Bennett asked Sami.

"We go to Bloody Creek," with that pronouncement Sami walked towards the front door.

No one followed.

"Daddy, she can't be serious," Elodie shook her head.

"Oh, I'm very serious. We have to get to Bloody Creek, if we want to win," Sami's voice was calm but determined.

Cody rose slowly from the couch. He declined Bess's help. "Sami, we've tried to get there. You saw what happened. We've lost Harry and Katy in the attempt. How many more have to die?"

"Exactly, Mr. Davis. How many more have to die? Harry and Katy are but a few of the people who have lost their lives to this demon over the centuries. We've been given clues about how and where to kill it. Yes, Detective Davis, we have to get to Bloody Creek."

Cody shook his head. "Wish I hadn't thought of that blasted creek. No, this has gone too far. I won't go."

Bess touched her husband's arm. "Darling, I believe Sami's right. We must. Katy would want us to do this."

After a long pause, Cody nodded in agreement. "But I don't like this."

Bess smiled. The group gathered behind Sami.

"Luckily, we have not lost all our cars." Sami looked towards the garage.

"Connie's car and..." Cody followed Sami's look down the hall. "Aw no, I'm not going through that dead man's clothes looking for keys."

"I will," said Sami. "I've been assured Paul is quite dead. He said so himself." She smiled. "Come with me."

Cody hoped someone in the group would stop him. No one offered. He sighed in exasperation. "Lead on, McDuff," he said wryly.

Once they arrived at the end of the hall, Cody touched Sami's arm. He nodded towards the chair wedged under the door knob.

"Are you really sure about this?"

"Quite sure, Detective Davis." Sami pulled the chair away. "Paul Godfrey won't be bothering us."

The smell of a decomposing body greeted them when the door opened.

The odor didn't deter Sami. She stepped briskly into the garage.

"Seriously?" Cody reluctantly followed her.

The body was lying exactly where it was originally placed. The garage was amazingly undisturbed considering all that had gone on before. With the exception of the bullet holes in the door, no one would have ever known.

"Help me, Cody," Sami tugged at the rug surrounding Paul.

It only took a few moments to unwrap the body and several more to find the car keys.

"Can't imagine what a beautiful woman like Caroline would see in a man like him," Cody covered Paul with the rug again. "She could have had anyone..." He stopped before finishing his sentence. An odd thought came to him. He looked at Sami.

"Yes, you're right, Cody. She could have had anyone," Sami concurred.

"You know who she was seeing, don't you? And you didn't tell me?" Cody's astonished look didn't surprise her.

"Yes," Sami nodded.

"Who?" Cody probed

"He didn't kill her," Sami said.

"That's for the law to determine. Why can't you..." Cody stopped. "Brian? My young partner, Brian. He was having an affair with Caroline? How do I know this? I'm going to arrest that son-of-a-bitch."

Sami grabbed him. "No, you mustn't. It's not that simple," Sami stepped between the detective and the door.

Cody glowered at the petite woman.

"Think about it, detective. Have you ever had this thought before?"

"No, but..." Cody felt his anger rising.

"This entity will do anything to survive. Why has it chosen this moment to give you this tidbit of information? Because it wants to get Brian out of the way. One by one, it is trying to get rid of us."

"So what do we do?"

"Right now, Detective Davis, we must get to Bloody Creek. All our lives are at stake. I realize your distress at his misconduct, however, I believe he was used by the demon."

"Yeah, he was used all right," Cody stepped forward.

"Beating him to a pulp won't help either," Sami countered his move.

"Quit reading my mind," Cody moved again.

"Then put all those thoughts away. He didn't kill Caroline. You must believe me when I tell you this. If it weren't for the souls of the dead guiding me and Malsumis creating illusions, we would all be dead. This demon is growing weaker. We have to take advantage of its diminishing power now."

"It's growing weaker?"

Sami sighed. "It meant to kill you, Detective, but it couldn't."

Cody's mouth opened then closed. He shook his head in disbelief. "If its power is going away as you say, then why can't we just wait it out. Why do we have to go to Bloody Creek at all?"

"We must make sure this being can never live again. The only way to do that is to end its life where it began." She gently touched his arm. "Trust me."

Cody patted her hand. "I guess I have so far."

She held onto his arm. "Do not confront Detective Smith about Mrs. Godfrey just yet. We must all be unified in our purpose."

When Cody didn't respond, she squeezed his arm. "Promise me."

"All right, all right." Cody jingled the car keys. "Let's go."

Chapter 40

Detective Davis could barely control his anger when he ushered everyone out of the house. He wouldn't look Brian in the eyes.

Sami stood next to him to prevent any outbursts. She waited until the last person was seated before getting into Connie's car. Bennett was chosen to drive Paul's Mercedes.

Cody hesitated. He looked back at the house, then at the two cars. "This is insane," he whispered.

Resigned to his unknown fate, he pulled open the car door and took his position at the wheel. He rolled down the driver's side window and waved at Bennett. "This better work, Sami. We've run out of transportation."

Sami said nothing. Instead, she waved Cody onward.

"Heaven help us," Connie whispered the moment Cody put the car in gear and pulled away from the house.

"Here goes nothing," Bennett said to his girls as Cody moved forward.

"Do you think we will get away this time?" Elodie took her sister's hand.

"I hope so," Bennett put Paul's car in drive. He drove a few feet away from the bumper of the first car.

"Me, too. I don't want to go inside that cabin again," Brian added.

The small caravan worked its way slowly to the end of the drive.

"So far, so good," Cody's voice betrayed his nervousness. "At least this time, we're not driving in the dark."

He turned out of the driveway. Bennett remained close behind. The familiar bridge came into view.

"Looks okay. Think it's safe to cross?" Cody slowed the car down to a crawl.

"Only one way to find out, " Sami nodded towards the bridge.

"What if the bridge is really broken? Maybe we're seeing a normal bridge as an illusion. Maybe you should get out and check first," Connie leaned as far forward as she could to get a better view.

"Maybe we should just drive. Go Cody," Sami was losing her patience.

"You know, Connie has a point..."

"I said go," Sami's left foot came over the console. She pushed the accelerator to the floor. The car flew forward.

"Hey!" By the time Cody dislodged her foot, they were well past the small bridge. He slammed on the brakes and turned towards Sami. "Never, ever, do that again."

"Don't have to. There are no more bridges to cross," Sami folded her arms in triumph.

Cody swept his hand through his hair. "I think I just aged 20 years."

"Sister, are you trying to kill us all?" Connie admonished Sami.

"We must get to Bloody Creek. No more questions. Trust me." She directed her last statement to the passengers in the back.

"At least Bennett is still with us," Cody looked in the rearview mirror. He could see Bennett at the wheel with Elodie right next to him. "It's because of him this demon is growing weaker, isn't it?"

"Yes," Sami didn't elaborate.

"Any ideas who Bennett's real father is?"

"I haven't given it much thought," Sami said.

Cody paused. "You know…"

Sami put her hand up and stopped him before he could say anymore. "It won't do us any good discussing this right now."

Cody looked over at Sami. "Right."

The reluctant caravan continued forward. Every now and then, Cody would look to the right then the left in anticipation. The world seemed completely normal.

It wasn't long before the entrance gate heralding the end of the road came into view. A collective sigh arose from within Cody's car with the exception of one person, Sami.

"This isn't right," She declared.

"What?" Cody looked at her in disbelief.

Sami sat with her arms folded. She stared at the road ahead shaking her head. "Nope, the souls of the dead are telling me not to leave. They want us to turn around. And I'm not crazy, thank you very much." She gave Cody a withering look.

Cody slumped back. "Yeah, you are if you want me to turn this car around and head back to hell. What are the souls of the dead telling you?"

Sami pressed her fingers against the side of her head. She closed her eyes and fell silent.

Bennett rapped against the driver's side window. "Hey, what's the hold up? Aren't we going through the gate?"

Cody got out of the car. "The souls of the dead said we shouldn't leave."

"Have they given a reason why?"

"I think they are now," He looked back into the car at Sami.

Brian joined the two men. "Something wrong?"

Cody gestured towards Sami. "She's communicating."

Elodie joined the group, followed by her sister. She stood close to her father.

"If I was a smoker, I would really like a cigarette right about now," Cody shoved his hands in his pants pocket.

Elodie pulled out a pack, tapped it on her hand and offered one.

Cody shook his head in refusal. "I said, if I was a smoker."

Bess and Connie got out of the car leaving Sami alone.

"They must be giving her an earful," Connie looked back at her sister in dismay. "They must really be upset."

"I wonder why?" Bess said.

"Probably because they want us to go back," Cody offered.

"Go back?" Dani's voice registered alarm.

A heated debate ensued. The group was so involved in their conversation, they didn't notice Sami had left the car.

"Hey, where's Sami?" Cody was shocked at the sight of the empty seat.

"Look, over there," Brian pointed at the far end of the fence line.

In the distance, at the juncture where the fence disappeared into the forest, stood the small woman.

"Come on," Bennett broke into a jog.

In a matter of moments, everyone was gathered around Sami.

She put her hand up to silence Cody before he had a chance to speak. "I'm sorry I worried you. Something important came up." She clapped her hands then followed with a whistle.

"What are you doing?" Cody leaned down and whispered in her ear.

"A good man will cross over the abyss on the backs of his dogs. A bad man will fall into the abyss, Detective Davis." She smiled knowingly. Once again, she clapped her hands and whistled.

"A dog? You're calling a dog?" Bennett peered into the trees.

"Not a dog, Mr. Godfrey, dogs," Sami whistled one more time then waited.

It wasn't long after the last whistle, before a single dog emerged from the row of trees. A large dog of no particular breed walked slowly forward. It's short coat was deep, shiny black. It's ears were small and raised in a listening position. It walked over to Sami and sat down in front of her. Another dog, about the same size as the first followed. It sat next to the first. Soon five dogs surrounded Sami.

"I'll be damned," The sight of so many dogs quietly waiting at Sami's feet astonished Detective Davis.

"No, Detective Davis, hopefully Reynard will be damned," Sami countered.

"How are we going to get all those dogs into one car?" Connie asked.

"We're not, Sister," Sami turned away from the dogs and confronted the group.

"Was anyone surprised by our recent trip away from the cabin?" Sami asked.

"Not particularly," said Bennett.

"I was," Sami continued. "The demon fought so hard to keep us contained in that cabin, then all of a sudden, it let us go. Why?"

"It wanted us to go to Bloody Creek?" Cody answered.

"Yes, detective, it wanted us to go to Bloody Creek. The wrong part of Bloody Creek."

"What do you mean, the wrong part?"

"I'm going to show you," Sami turned back to the pack and addressed the large black dog. "Show me." She commanded.

The lead dog sprang into action. It sniffed the ground in either direction. Finally, it stopped in front of a large bush and pawed at the dirt

"Gentlemen, remove that bush," Sami waved the men forward.

Without a word, the three men approached the bush. Bennett reached into the center of the foliage. He gave it a tug. The bush held. Cody approached the bush from the other side. He grabbed it close to the ground.

"On three. One, two, three," Cody braced himself as both men pulled. The bush came out of the ground easily.

A path was revealed. The black dog barked its approval. With the pack close at its heels, the lead dog followed the narrow, dirt path into the trees and disappeared.

"Go!" Sami yelled.

With Bennett in the lead, the group fell in line and followed the dogs. The narrow path wound its way through the rough terrain. After several moments, Bennett turned to Sami "Where are the dogs? I don't see them anymore".

"You won't for now". Sami pointed up ahead.

In the distance, Bennett saw the cabin. "What? Have we been going in circles?"

"What…how did the cars?" Cody pointed at the cars parked in front of the cabin.

"Well, as Katy would say, Malsumis," Sami put her hands on her hips.

"Bennett, I asked you questions about the first cabin that was built on this sight," Sami walked towards the front door.

"Yes, I believe I told you Reynard built it close to the cliff where the young woman jumped."

"Back in that time, cabins were usually built near a source of water, correct?" Sami continued.

"I'm not a historian but that makes sense to me." Bennett concurred.

"The dead told me something interesting a moment ago. Bloody creek where Reynard betrayed the Abenaki and the cliff that ultimately claimed the life of the young Abenaki woman are right here, near the cabin." Sami opened the front door and waved everyone inside.

"Seriously, you want us back inside?" Cody looked at Sami in horror.

"Yes, I will explain." She motioned again for everyone to enter.

Reluctantly, the group re-entered the cabin.

"Now what?" Brian looked at Sami.

"Follow me," Sami turned towards the back of the house. The group did as she requested and followed her through the hallway and kitchen. She stopped at a door leading to the outside. With great flourish, she threw it open.

"Do you hear it?" She asked.

Elodie looked at her father, then her sister. "Does anyone know what she is talking about?"

It was Bess who stepped forward with an answer. "I think understand. I hear water. Bloody Creek must run not far from the backside of the cabin, right?"

"Yes, by keeping us imprisoned as the demon did, we never realized we were so close," Sami pulled the door shut.

The sound of a man screaming echoed through the house.

"Come on. That came from the front yard," Cody turned towards the sound. When he reached the living room, he ran to the picture window

"Oh my, God," he whispered. Out in the driveway stood the old butler. He was dressed in his usual attire of a white shirt and jacket with black pants. His clothing was torn and dirty. His slight stoop was more pronounced and his face was distorted in rage.

"That's Ronald…and…" Bennett couldn't complete his sentence.

"Is that Katy?" Bess said in wonder.

Cody felt a touch on his arm. He looked down and saw Sami nodding towards the window. He let her move in front of him.

Sami nodded. "Yes, Katy has returned for a brief moment.

"Why sister?" Connie took her place next to Sami.

"Wait and see," came Sami's cryptic answer.

Cody pointed at the old man. "Look at his face."

The deep crags in the butler's face grew deeper.

"It looks like he's drying up."

"A part of his soul lived in that journal. He's dying," Sami said.

Ronald pointed at Bennett. "You! Everything will end because of you." He grabbed his head in pain and fell backwards onto the gravel.

Sami smiled. "I think it's your turn, my dear." She whispered.

Katy smiled and raised her arms to the sky. A bright glow surrounded her forcing those watching from the windows to close their eyes. When they were able to see again, a young woman stood where Katy had been.

"Wha...?" Cody looked down at Sami.

"I think our trickster, Malsumis has been playing us," Sami smiled broadly.

"Is that...?" Elodie was mesmerized by the sight.

A pretty Abenaki woman stood before them. Cody guessed her age to be about sixteen.

"Malsumis wasn't protecting us. He was protecting the dead. He was protecting her," Sami's smile broadened even more.

"What?" Cody was completely lost.

"I think when you see what I think is going to happen, you'll understand," Sami nodded at the young girl. "Go, it's time to end this."

The young woman smiled in return. She walked towards the writhing man on the ground. As she approached him, the pack of dogs Sami had called earlier appeared out of the woods. They stood behind the young woman growling in unison at the old man.

"Come on, everyone." Sami stepped away from the window and hurried to the front door. Once outside, the confrontation between Reynard and the young woman grew.

With the pack still at her heels, the young woman ran past Ronald.

"The Trickster" Cody said softly.

Ronald screamed and grabbed at her ankles as she ran past. He angrily pushed away from the ground and staggered to his feet. He turned and glowered at the group standing on the stoop. His pristine white jacket was smeared with blood and dirt

"Wow. Grandmother would not like all those spots," Elodie whispered.

"He looks really pissed," Dani's voice quivered.

A bright aura enveloped, Ronald. It pulsed then grew brighter.

"What's happening to Ronald?" Elodie shielded her eyes from the brightness.

"I don't know." The light forced Bennett to close his eyes.

When the light dimmed, Ronald was gone, and in his place stood a man dressed in leather with animal pelts hanging from his waist. His face was covered with a thick bushy beard and his hair fell below his shoulders. His eyes were a fiery red.

"Reynard," Bennett whispered. "Has Malsumis been protecting him, too? Is this another trick?"

"Yes, Bennett. It is the ultimate trick. One, not even this ancient demon saw coming," Sami folded her arms in satisfaction.

Reynard raised his fists and shook them at the sky then he screamed again. He turned and ran in the same direction as the young woman.

"Quick! Everyone, follow him," Sami pointed after Reynard.

With Bennett in the lead, Cody, Dani, Brian, Elodie, Sami and Connie ran towards the cliff.

"I see her," Cody exclaimed.

In the distance, the young Abenaki woman was standing at the edge of the cliff with her back to the lake. Her arms were raised upwards towards the heavens. The five black dogs stood in front of her in a defensive posture. Their eyes were focused on the path in front of them.

A cold, frigid blast of air pushed through the group. Unable to stand against its force, the twins fell over. Bess felt herself pushed into Dani and Elodie. The three women collapsed in a heap. Brian grabbed the trunk of a tree before the blast could knock him over.

Cody tried to turn around to help, but he, too was no match for the powerful force.

"What's happening?" he screamed. He felt like he was fighting a hurricane.

Sami forced her head up. She pointed towards the bluff. "Look".

Reynard was now standing several feet in front of the young woman. He stood with his feet spread apart and his arms outstretched. His fingers were bent into claws. He was screaming unintelligible words in French. When he took a step towards her, the wind punched him from behind forcing him to fall into the pack of dogs. They responded with a fury. The sound of screaming, growling and the tearing of clothes and flesh could be heard over the wailing wind.

"Oh, God," Bess closed her eyes against the massacre.

Soon, Reynard's screams could be heard no more.

"Look," Sami cried. She pointed towards the cliff.

The young Abenaki woman, now forever free, turned from her tormentor and stepped off the edge of the cliff. She hovered briefly before disappearing. The dogs each holding onto Reynard's lifeless body dragged him after her. They let him fall into the abyss before they, too, disappeared. A calmness descended.

"Bess, are you okay?" Cody looked up to see his wife getting up. "Brian? How are you doing, man?" Cody reached out to his partner.

"I'm okay, I guess," Brian sat down on a nearby rock.

"I want to go home," Dani whimpered.

"I second that one," Elodie put her arm around her sister.

"Hey, take a look," Bennett motioned everyone forward. He held something in his hand.

When the group reached him, Sami took a fur hat from him. She felt a warm breeze caress her.

"First, he has to die, then he must follow her over the cliff." Sami took another look at the hat then tossed it against the wind. The breeze shifted catching the hat in a small whirlwind. It dropped it into the water below.

"Bennett?" A voice called out.

Bennett looked towards the sound of the voice.

"R.P.?"

His brother walked forward. He was no longer stooped with his arm dangling forward. His clothing was filthy and ragged but other than that, he appeared quite normal.

"Bennett!" R.P. rushed to him and grabbed his brother in a big bear hug.

"How did I get here?" R. P. asked.

"You don't remember?" Bennett responded.

"I shot him," Brian's voice quivered as he looked at Cody in confusion.

"I don't remember anything," R. P. frowned.

"Maybe it's best," Connie touched his arm. "The Trickster." She said knowingly.

"What about Paul? Did he really die or was that a trick, too?" Cody asked.

"No, Malsumis won't protect a murderer," Sami said.

"So, he did kill Caroline," Brian said.

"Oh yes, Caroline told me so a long time ago," Sami said

"Why didn't you tell me?" Brian was stunned by her reply.

"Or me?" Cody added.

"Well, for one, what proof did I have. Information from the souls of the dead? You wouldn't have believed me, Cody and I'm sure your Captain would have laughed you out of the precinct. No, I had to let things take their natural or unnatural course as it were. Paul's death was an accident. Unfortunately, so was Harry's and Katy's."

"How am I going to explain all of this?" Cody asked.

"Caroline tells me that Paul kept a diary. It's hidden in a fake bottom drawer of his bureau. That should help you close the case," Sami patted Cody on the shoulder.

"I'll make sure you get it, Cody," Bennett also patted Cody on the back.

"I guess that ties up all the loose ends but one," Cody walked towards the edge of the cliff. He looked down at the swirling water below. A feeling of sadness enveloped him.

"Is this the end, big brother?" He whispered. "Adam?"

An image of his older brother appeared near the bluff. It waivered slightly.

"Hey big brother. I was hoping I'd see you again," Cody's elation was short lived.

"Can't stay. Gotta go, lil' brother but I'll be watching."

Cody nodded forlornly, "Kinda figured this would happen. Can't come back, uh?"

"Dunno? Maybe," Adam shrugged.

"Don't worry, Cody. I'm sure I'll hear from him," Sami patted his arm.

"It's like losing him all over again," He reached out to the fading image.

Adam waved. "Later." Then he was gone.

"Is it over?" Bess put her arms around Cody and gave him a squeeze.

Cody shrugged and wiped a tear from his cheek.

"Malsumis is happy," Sami smiled.

"I hear the souls of the dead. They're happy, too," Connie said with glee.

"Shhhh, listen," Sami put her finger to her lips.

The sound of a dove cooed in the distance. The Reservation was alive.

"Yes, I do believe it's over."

www.ingramcontent.com/pod-product-compliance
Lightning Source LLC
Chambersburg PA
CBHW020100310726
48970CB00002B/415